Hooked on the Heart

Hooked on the Heart

MADDIE EVANS

Philangelus Press
Boston, MA

ISBN: 978-1-942133-56-8
Cover design by Once Upon a Cover
Editing by Charity Horniek
Section art by HailMarii Art

CHAPTER ONE

Colin awoke on an air mattress with a song from the second floor echoing through his empty apartment.

Good morning, sweetie.

Good morning, sweetie.

Wake up and eat breakfast.

Sweetie, wake up.

Above his head came creaking that his brain decoded as footsteps. That meant Colin had just "met" his upstairs neighbor, and he already knew three important things about her: she woke up as early as he did, she didn't live alone, and she was a soprano.

By contrast, she must not know two important things about Colin. Namely, that someone had moved in downstairs, and also that he could hear every single thing she did in her apartment.

This apartment was a dump. Colin would have to drag his twin out to the trash bin behind the restaurant and collar him for suggesting the place was fit to live in. "Yeah," Austin had assured him, "the restaurant's landlord also owns a couple of apartments in Brighthead, and he'll cut you a break on the rent."

Colin stared at the ceiling, wondering if anyone else would have rented this place at all, at any price. The trouble was, after he'd sunk all his capital into buying a restaurant, he couldn't be picky about where he lived.

Colin only had to stay for a month, anyway. Then a second apartment would open up, and he could move into the landlord's other building—the better one. If Colin's past exploits had taught him anything, it was that he could deal with anything for a month.

Once his belongings arrived, it wouldn't be so bad. He'd slunk in last night with one duffel bag, one lamp, and an air mattress. The apartment came with a couple of furnishings that were neither good enough for the previous tenants to take nor bad enough to schedule a bonfire and invite the neighbors for s'mores. "Partially furnished," Colin's brother had called it.

Colin chuckled. Yeah, he ought to drag Austin out into the parking lot later today. His twin was probably in stitches.

Overhead, the singing stopped. She must have a kid, but although Colin braced himself for the inevitable thumping of a child leaping out of bed and racing for the kitchen table, that never came. Maybe she knew about the sound issues and had trained her kid not to make noise? Momentarily he heard a door shut, and the shower went on.

Good idea. Colin rolled off the air mattress and took a deep breath. Fruits de Mer opened at eleven-thirty, and today was his first day as its owner.

Dale met Colin at Fruits de Mer's back door with a handshake followed by a hug, and even though he wasn't even thirty, Colin struggled to keep up with this exuberant guy in his sixties. "I was up half the night worried you'd back out of buying my restaurant." Dale had a thunderous laugh to match his electric personality. "Land alive, you're a dead ringer for Austin. You'd better not be Austin pulling my leg."

"I'm me, I promise. He's the humorous twin." Colin tugged his well-worn black chef's coat with its stand-up collar. "Lead on."

Dale led him through the kitchen entrance, flipping on the lights as he passed. "First thing I always do is inventory."

"Same," said Colin, so Dale took a clipboard and stepped Colin through the process he'd developed over the past ten years. Colin mentally noted changes he'd like to make, every so often stopping Dale with questions. "Why aren't we checking dates at the same time?" "What made you stock the walk-in this way?"

Dale had a story for every decision, but they were on a time crunch, so he promised all that after. "I'll stick around long enough to talk your ear off, I promise." They compared the inventory list to the spreadsheet anticipating the restaurant's daily demand, and Dale took notes. "Oh, and we're getting a linen delivery today. Every few months I ask for a bag of ragged-out towels, so I set that up as well, but you'll need to make a reminder for yourself."

Austin walked in wearing a white chef's coat. "I've got that handled. Don't worry."

Dale exclaimed, "Whoa, double vision."

Austin rubbed his hands together. "Double the fun. Except I'm the organized twin."

Dale pulled out a second checklist. "Next we run through the whole building and make sure everything is in place, nothing's broken, everything's turned on that needs to be—"

With each step through the front of house, Colin fought a grin. His own restaurant. He'd sleep on an apartment floor for a year if it meant he could finally put his stamp on a place—really his own. No other owners to coordinate with, no one pushing back on every single suggestion and then making new demands that needed to be pushed back on. *His own.* The window treatments that needed to be cleaned, or the table that wobbled just a bit—all Colin's. The server stand that needed a new dry erase marker? Colin's. For that matter, the dry erase marker that Dale pulled out of his pocket and left at the station? Also Colin's.

Austin caught his grin and smiled right back. It was real. It was finally happening.

Wedged into Dale's postage-stamp-sized office (Colin's office) they called three suppliers to arrange deliveries, and then Dale exclaimed, "Road trip!"

They hit the terminal markets and scouted out anything that might make great specials for the rest of the week. Dale said, "This is all you, my friend." Dale introduced Colin to his favorite sellers, and Austin added, "Yes, you're having double vision," so often that Colin couldn't keep count. Every time Austin said it, he got more energized, and Colin got less—but that was fine because Colin wasn't here for the interactions.

He was here for the food. What was plentiful? What was on sale? What just seemed amazing? How much were lobsters this week? Why did the mushrooms look like even their own mother wouldn't love them? Why was no one buying this cheese just because it was a little pale—and how much of it could they reasonably move in a week?

Dale gave input on amounts, plus a suggestion to avoid calamari. ("We never do well with that," he said, and that was a shame because Colin liked cooking it.) Regardless, Colin left the depot with plans for an entire week's specials, and then he and Austin loaded up the restaurant's truck.

Back at the restaurant, the back of house staff began arriving, all of them in black chef coats like Colin's. His new employees.

His own restaurant. He was actually doing this.

"This is Bill, your sous chef, who knows everything there is to know about grilling anything." Dale couldn't help bragging on everyone, of course, but Austin was at his side making wiseacre remarks to bolster everything Dale said. "Alex knows all the vagaries of the broiler. If you don't want steaks sent back, Alex is your man."

The front of house staff began arriving, all of them outfitted in black pants and white shirts. Danielle was the server who walked in and glared at the stack of linen napkins and the bin of silverware that needed to be rolled into those napkins. She exclaimed, "Who closed last night?" and then rolled silverware the whole time Colin was being introduced to the new arrivals. A second server, Ally, showed up and joined Danielle with rolling silverware. "I figured I'd do it for opening because last night was a deep clean," she objected, but Danielle only side-eyed her.

Austin said, "Danielle and Ally are our veteran servers, and they're magic at keeping customers coming back for more. They know how to warn the kitchen when they've got an eight-top seated right after a six-top, and they know how to space out the tickets so the kitchen doesn't end up in the weeds for twenty minutes with thirty orders at the same time."

Bill said, "Also, they split the long tickets."

Danielle said, "Because we do our jobs."

Austin said, "That's the point. And the kitchen does their job, too, by looking out for the servers."

Colin knew that game, where the cooks would just happen to make mistakes that meant the servers got a hot meal. Sometimes you grabbed a ticket off the kitchen printer and someone had ordered your server's favorite food, only you accidentally made two. Well, someone had to eat the second one, right?

A woman banged through the back door, short but built like a refrigerator. She snarled, "Quit having a party in my kitchen."

Dale gestured. "May I present to you, the Dish Dame."

The Dish Dame glared at Colin. "Are you the new owner? Because I have rules for my dish pit. No sharps in the bottom of the sink. Don't you dare dump your pans in my clean area. Leave me alone to do my work."

Colin raised his hands. "Your domain is yours."

She said, "And I get steak once a week."

Colin said, "That may have to change. We should be giving you steak every night."

She snorted at him. "I don't need your pity. Once a week does me good."

Austin was biting his lip trying not to laugh, and Colin inclined his head as he stepped out of her way.

The cooks were prepping by now, and Danielle had rolled all the silverware. Ally was vacuuming the front of house. "Colin," yelled the broiler guy, "how do you want us to *mise* the butter? This joker's doing it all wrong!"

Colin called back, "Do you actually want a style guide for how to *mise* your butter? Or do you want to do what you know best?" and the line cooks high-fived one another.

That looked like success. Colin checked the prep list, then opened his knife roll and dumped out a bag of onions to start chopping.

Everything about this restaurant could become what Colin wanted it to be—a thought simultaneously thrilling and terrifying. If he got a bad review today, he could believe it was still Dale's place they were panning. A year from now, when people hated it, they would be hating Colin.

That combination of "vulnerable" and "amazing" was the reason Colin had wanted to buy his own restaurant. He just hadn't counted on the vulnerability feeling so...well, vulnerable.

Finally, he called everyone together for the pre-shift meeting. "We're going to have some rough spots as we change gears, but the most important things are going to stay the same. The teamwork, the drive, the importance of keeping our guests happy, the love of good food and a good presentation, and a genuine commitment to excellence. I'll be right here with you all the way, answering questions and manning the fry stations and dealing with irritated customers. You can count on it."

He had a good team, and he was willing to work hard. Fruits de Mer would be a reflection of everything Colin loved about cooking, and he'd be able to entice others to love it, too.

Chapter Two

While stacking yarn in the sales cubes, Natalie paused to inhale the scent of the twisted hank.

Eyes closed, she imagined what this hank of yarn wanted to become. One hundred grams of washable wool in fingering weight meant it was intended for socks, but once a knitter or a crocheter got her hands on the skein, it could turn into anything at all. Socks for sure, but what about a shawlette (or even a shawl)? A hat? An infinity scarf, long and drapey enough to wrap double around the neck for protection against these brutal Maine winters?

Anything could happen to this tight galaxy-colored skein of yarn once you put a hook or needles to it, and that was the joy. Or at least, it should become something. It would be a shame if someone bought it and then tucked it down in their cedar chest along with the rest of their stash, intended for "someday" but getting used never.

Which, unfortunately, was how most of Natalie's yarn stash was spending its time these days.

Natalie checked the clock, then hurried to finish stocking. She ought to get the coffee maker set up and make sure the new calendar was posted.

Someone banged at the front door. That had to be Lilah, forgetting her keys again—except it wasn't the shop's lone employee. It was one of the customers.

Natalie glanced again at the clock. The customer pointed to her watch and then back at the door. Translated from Retail to English, that meant, "I know you're not open yet, but I want something anyhow."

Natalie unlocked to the sound of jangling bells. "The register isn't even up."

"I'm so sorry. I'm running late, but I was hoping to nip in for a set of replacement needles before I headed out of town." The woman rubbed her gloved hands together. "Dark wooden double pointed needles, dark couch, not enough light, not paying enough attention—"

Natalie winced. "Sounds like a disaster. Did you get hurt?"

"Fortunately, no. The needle snapped when I sat on it, but it didn't puncture my jeans." Metal needles did sometimes get embedded in an arm or a leg, occasionally resulting in a tetanus shot or stitches. Wooden ones preferred to give their lives to save their owners. The customer added, "But you can't knit socks on three DPNs, so here I am. Do you have any size twos?"

"You can knit socks on two DPNs." Natalie's hand went right for the slot to where the twos were hanging. "It's just difficult."

The woman took the packet and handed Natalie a twenty. "Thank you so much. You're a lifesaver."

Natalie went to the register. "Hang on while I get your change."

"That's the emergency opening fee," the woman called over her shoulder as she dashed out the door. "Keep the change."

Natalie froze, unsure if she should accept. Didn't matter. The customer hadn't given her a choice.

Lilah entered the store as the woman exited, then grinned at Natalie. "Well, aren't you just chronologically challenged?" She beamed as she shifted a gigantic duffel bag on her shoulder. "Or is my phone running ten minutes early?"

Natalie mustered a smile. "Just saving the world, one set of replacement needles at a time."

Lilah unzipped her jacket. Her fingernails were green today. "I don't suppose it's ever occurred to you that maybe the whole world doesn't need saving? Or that you're not the one who has to save it?"

Natalie hurried to get the calendar posted on the bulletin board, then readied the coffee maker. The morning Sit and Stitch would begin at ten-thirty, and everyone who showed up seemed to drink gallons of the stuff. In the back, Lilah opened the duffel bag and revealed more yarn.

"I have to see that," Natalie sing-songed.

Lilah replied in the same key, "You already have a thousand pounds of yarn in your apartment."

"With room for a thousand more." Natalie grinned. "I love the colors you dye."

Lilah spread the skeins out on the table. (Oh, and she had a yellow accent nail, too—clever.) When Natalie reached for one, though, Lilah snatched it back. "When was the last time you actually sat down and crocheted something for yourself?"

Natalie opened her hands. "Hello? We're in a yarn store. I crocheted ten different samples last week."

"Other than swatches." Standing akimbo, Lilah tilted her head. "And other than shawls or hats to display in the windows. When was the last time you made something for yourself?"

"I don't need anything for myself." Natalie didn't reach again for the yarn. "I made two hats back in September."

"Which you donated to the homeless coalition."

Natalie said, "And a blanket."

"Which you donated to the family shelter."

Natalie folded her arms. "They needed donations, and why shouldn't they have a beautiful handmade baby blanket?"

Lilah waved her down. "Then add in all the test-crocheting you do for Brooke. My point is, you keep buying beautiful yarn for yourself and then you don't make yourself anything. I want you to enjoy the yarn the way you used to when you loved it. So—" She held the yarn at arm's length. "If you want one of these, you can take it, but you have to promise to make something with it. For you, not for anyone else."

Lilah was offering a sweet skein of silky merino fingering weight in a tonal green. It even had sparkles in it. Something like that... Natalie could pair it with a steely grey skein she'd bought last month to make a triangular scarf, soft and sweet, perfect for wrapping point-down under the V-neck of her coat to remind her that even in the darkness of winter, spring would eventually return.

Natalie didn't take it.

Lilah's smile ebbed. "Come on. You have to stop doing everything for everyone else. It's not your job to protect everyone from the discomforts of normal everyday living."

"Oh, I'm going to make someone uncomfortable all right." Natalie turned away from the pretty, squishy yarn and returned to prepping the store. "I seem to have gotten a new downstairs neighbor, and he wrecked my shower this morning by turning on his. He turned on the water, and that turned off mine."

Lilah grimaced. "The landlord still hasn't fixed that?"

"The house is old."

"If it's that old, it should be condemned."

Natalie waved her off. "I'll just tell the new tenant how the house works, but if I'm in a mood, that's why."

The clock hands hit ten, and a jangle of the door bells announced the second customer of the day. Natalie pivoted because customers came first, and always would.

This one was a man with a specific look about himself—a mix of confusion and concern that Natalie had come to translate as, "I have never worked with yarn and therefore have no idea what I'm doing."

"Welcome!" Natalie went to stand alongside the register.

"May I help you?"

"I certainly hope so." The man had copper-black eyes and kept glancing around like a master spy behind enemy lines. "I needed to get here before my wife, and maybe you can work a miracle for me."

From the rack where she was stacking her yarn, Lilah turned to watch. Natalie said, "Miracles are our specialty."

He shook his head. "My wife's best friend just got engaged, and my wife will be her maid of honor. The bride is a knitter, so my wife wants to buy the yarn she'll use to make a shawl to go with her wedding gown."

Natalie nodded. "I can help you pick it out."

"The catch is," the man said, "my wife seems to think we're on the verge of bankruptcy, as if one nice ball of yarn is going to put us over the edge. We all agree high-quality yarn is supposed to be expensive, but she's stressing about it." He paused for effect. "Therefore, I came up with a plan. Can I leave cash behind the counter, and then you can tell my wife that whatever yarn she ought to buy is on an unexpected discount—as in, it would only have been discounted for her—and use that money to create the discount?"

Natalie could see Lilah past the man's shoulder, staring with her mouth open.

The best Natalie could manage was, "I can give you five reasons why that's not going to work, and that's without even thinking about it."

The man deflated. "I was afraid you'd say that."

"For one thing," Natalie said, "without knowing what the bride wants to make, I can't hazard a guess as to how much it should cost, let alone whether your wife's budget would cover it. Also, what happens if I write a receipt for the lower amount and then the bride wants to exchange it?"

The man folded his arms. "My wife would love to give her friend something she'd get excited about, and the bride goes bonkers for amazing yarn."

Natalie said, "I could estimate the yardage for a shawl,

but what style of shawl does she want to make? What yarn weight? What size?"

Eyebrows raised, the man opened his hands.

Natalie added, "Does she want to make a triangular shawl, or a wedding ring shawl—or the entire wedding dress?"

The man's shoulders dropped. "You're right. This isn't going to work."

Natalie cocked her head. "Why can't you just tell your wife to double how much you think she should spend?"

"Oh, you've saved us! I never once thought of communicating with my best beloved." The man's eyes sparked. "My wife is... Well, let's just say, we're an even match. I wanted to intercept you and make an end run around her protests. She'd think she spent fifty dollars on yarn, when in reality she'd have spent a hundred or a hundred fifty. She's an extraordinary person. She deserves to splurge every once in a while."

Lilah still hadn't returned to hanging yarn on the display board, as if beholding a unicorn.

There had to be a way around this. Didn't Lilah say Natalie was the problem-solver? And was this not a problem?

Natalie narrowed her eyes and gave a wicked grin. "Okay. I have a plan."

She pulled a gift card out from the desk and flashed it between two fingers. "I will run your credit card to create a gift card for however much you think your wife should spend on the bride. When your wife comes into the shop, I will give her the gift card." Natalie pointed to the sign over the counter that said gift cards were non-refundable. "She will think the money's been spent, but what she won't know is that *your* gift card comes with a very special amendment in that afterward, you can get the remainder back in cash."

The man's eyes shot up. "You are brilliant. Not as brilliant as my wife, but substantially brilliant." He handed over his credit card. "Load that thing with enough to pay for a handknit wedding ring shawl or whatever you just called it, and we'll see what happens next."

From across the room, Lilah said, "Would the bride happen to be Shelly Novick?"

The man's head picked up as he laughed. "This is such a small town. Yes."

Natalie grinned. "Oh, she's going to adore this."

While Natalie was running the card, the man opened his computer bag and wrote in a tiny notebook. He flipped open the cardboard holder for the gift card and attached three sticky notes inside, then wrote his wife's name on the outside. "My wife is going to give you flack about this. Just peel off the notes one at a time. Then she'll target the flack at me. Also, this is my phone number. Warn me while she's en route to lop my head off."

Natalie chuckled as she took the gift card back across the counter. "She sounds amazing."

The man looked momentarily baffled. "She really is. She deserves something nice for once."

After he left, Natalie tucked the card under the ledge at the checkout desk, along with a note about who and what it was for. "Call me if I'm not here," she printed, underlining it. If Lilah intercepted this man's wife, Lilah would know what to do, but Natalie's cousin Brooke might not, and Brooke minded the store in the evenings.

Lilah sighed. "Could you imagine being married to a man who walks into a yarn store all bothered that his wife might not spend *enough* money?"

Natalie said, "Remember the guy who came in and said he couldn't afford to pay what his girlfriend's skill was worth?"

Lilah beamed. "Is he single again? Because that sounds like another catch."

Natalie shrugged. "I wasn't even in the store when it happened. My mother called me up special to tell me about him."

Lilah hung the last of her skeins on the display board. "We need to get you set up with a man who values creativity, and then when it's time for you to get married, he can drop a hundred fifty on my hand-dyed yarns, and we'll both be in heaven." She raised her eyebrows. "Well? How about we find a man who can make you fall in love with crocheting all over again?"

Natalie shook her head. "Not necessary. Remember those thousand pounds of yarn you said I don't need?"

Lilah laughed. "You haven't found the right yarn yet. Or the right guy."

CHAPTER THREE

It was eight o'clock, and dinner service winding down when Austin called across the kitchen, "I need an owner over here."

Since there was only one owner, Colin shut his laptop and headed to Austin. He called, "Behind!" as he passed Bill at the sauté station.

Austin thrust a stapled takeout bag into his hands. "It's a delivery."

Colin tilted his head. "Have you scouted out an awesome woman for me, and you're dispatching me even now to her house with impressive food?"

Austin rolled his eyes. "Deliver it back to your apartment, numbskull, and eat it. Then get to sleep, because you're destroyed." Austin waved him off. "It's not busy, and there aren't any hot women here tonight for you to drop by their table and flash your smile as the new owner before comping their meal and asking them on a date."

Colin's eyebrows shot up. "I would not!"

Austin smirked. "You mean, not *today*. It does work."

"I know it works." Colin glanced aside. "You taught me

that trick back in Kennebunkport."

Women always liked the idea of "restaurant owner" a lot more than they liked the idea of "Colin Young." Austin never lacked for a girlfriend, and after Austin taught him the comp trick, all Colin had to do was act the part. He'd have company for the next few weeks, sometimes even a couple of months.

"I've blitzed you all over the local papers, so everyone in Brighthead should know your name and your face." Austin grinned. "Then, when we have our grand change in ownership celebration this weekend, I'm going to pull the same scam without the hassle of being the owner. Tonight, though? Get out of here."

Today had been peppered by calls to various outlets as well as some of the local papers that were running business spotlights. This weekend should be busy. By contrast, Tuesday night wasn't a draw for anything. A good day to learn the ropes, but a bad day for receipts. Austin was right. Colin might as well leave.

Colin glanced at the takeout bag. "Is this an apology for that apartment?"

Austin laughed. "You've lived in worse."

"The thing is," Colin protested to himself ten minutes later as he glanced around the apartment kitchen, "living in a dump is part of the college mystique. There's no mystique in Brighthead."

And hopefully no mice or roaches. That hadn't even occurred to him before he'd walked into the place. At least the fridge stayed cold.

Alone for the first time in fourteen hours, Colin had questions. Questions such as, "If I set my takeout on the table, will the entire table list to the side and crash my dinner to the floor?"

That settled one thing. If he met any women here, the thing to do was bring them to the movies or maybe another town entirely—but not to his apartment. Even the arrival of his furniture wasn't going to salvage this. "Restaurant owner" had appeal, but "Colin Young, who lives in a hole" was steadily losing its cachet.

Colin sipped sparkling water out of a quart-sized takeout container, limes and ice rattling around the straw he'd jammed through a hole in the lid. The best drink service: always ready to hand, and no clean up afterward. Considering how many pans he'd scrubbed in his time, disposability wasn't a small consideration.

First things first. He stripped out of his non-skid shoes, black chef coat, and black pants, and changed into "civilian garb." Then, carrying the clothing that smelled like grease and smoke and garlic, he went into the cellar. There he found a washing machine, alongside a dryer that was rumbling like an earthquake with what Colin assumed were the other tenant's clothes.

He dropped his clothing into the washer, added the soap, hit the button to start—and then stood in darkness and silence because the circuit had blown.

Wasn't this exciting? Colin set his phone to flashlight mode, then began scanning the basement for a breaker box.

Above him came footsteps, and momentarily he was joined by a second flashlight beam. "Nice to meet you," said the woman holding the other light. "I assume you're the new tenant, and Denny didn't tell you the trick to running both the washer and the dryer?"

Colin said, "There's a trick?"

"This entire building is a trick. The first trick is not knocking it over." The other tenant crossed the cellar's dirt floor to the far wall. Colin focused his light on the breaker box while she threw first a smaller breaker and then the whole house breaker. The lights flared back on, and momentarily the boiler roared back into life. "Denny swears he's going to fix that someday."

The woman turned out to be a striking brunette, dressed in jeans and a flannel shirt and work boots. Colin glanced at her left hand to see if she was wearing a ring. She wasn't.

They headed back to the white laundry machines

standing together beneath a wooden shelf. "The trick is to get the washer going first, then the dryer." She hesitated. "Oh, and you have this on warm. You have to start it on cold, then after it's on, change it to warm."

Colin's eyebrows shot all the way up. "Does anything work in this building?"

"Most things, but you need to finesse them. The mailboxes may or may not lock the first time. Sometimes you need to give the front door a push, but that's more a problem in the summer when the humidity makes the wood swell." She was saying all this as though it were normal to have to trick your house into functioning. "The front door doesn't have a working lock, by the way. You'll have to keep your apartment locked all the time." She turned on the washer, starting at cold, and it banged and roared like a 1960 Chevy. After ten seconds, she flipped it to warm, then turned the dryer back on without starting it at "air fluff" and working her way up to the higher temps. The dryer made a sound like sand rolling around the drum before it began roaring again.

Natalie spoke louder so he could hear her. "If you want to start a load and I've got something in the dryer, you should turn off the dryer, start the washer, and then re-start the dryer."

Colin frowned. "The landlord didn't disclose any of this."

"He never does. Denny dumps the communication work on me." She turned to him. "I'm Natalie Prescott, by the way. Your upstairs neighbor."

Colin let her lead the way out of the cellar because he wanted to watch her walking in those jeans. On the landing, where they could talk without raising their voices, he said, "Well, I'm your downstairs neighbor, the infamous Colin Young."

"Infamy!" Natalie mock-gasped. "I haven't had one of those living here yet."

Colin said, "Don't get used to it. I'm only staying long enough for another apartment to open up."

He opened the door, and Natalie followed him. "May I come in?" She stepped inside as though he'd said yes, which Colin was sure he hadn't. "Even though you just moved in today and you're not staying long, I need to ask you a favor."

He looked her up and down, and, well, yes. He would do this woman a favor. Those rich brown eyes, the glossy hair to her waist, the flannel shirt over well-fitting jeans on legs that stretched all the way down to her boots—yes, favors could be made to happen. "What can I do for you?"

Natalie leaned against the counter, free of any fear that it would collapse at her back. Colin took that as a good sign. "This building is terrible. You've probably figured that out."

"Location, location," Colin said. He could still hear the washer and the dryer through the floor.

"Yeah, I can walk to work, and Denny also owns the mini-mall where I keep my yarn shop." Her eyes lit on the quart-sized take-out container serving as his drinkware. Her head swiveled as she looked around the kitchen. "Wait a minute. Don't you have anything in here?"

Colin shrugged. "I do own things. They're arriving on the weekend."

"Oh, okay." She brushed some hair from her forehead. "What you've figured out so far is that the washer and dryer trip the circuits on a regular basis. As you also heard, they're horribly noisy. I try not to start a load too close to when normal humans would want to sleep, or else the first-floor tenants will hear nothing but grinding and slamming for two hours."

His eyebrows shot up. "Good to know."

"Since we're both using the same machines," Natalie added, "please don't leave your clothes in the wash all day, and I won't either. I set an alarm on my phone."

Colin glanced her up and down again. She was maybe getting to be less of a do-a-favor-for-her person and more of a tolerable person.

She said, "The favor I want to ask is if you hear my

shower go on, please don't turn on your shower at the same time. It takes all the water."

Colin frowned. "Yours gets cold?"

She shook her head. "My shower literally turns off if you turn on yours."

He recoiled. "Why? There's only one set of pipes?"

"I have no idea. I asked a plumber once, and he couldn't imagine what was going on behind the drywall to divert all the water to the first floor. But I need to shower and get to work in the morning, and if you turn on the water while I'm in there, I'm left with soapy hair and no water."

Colin hummed. "Except I have to get to work too."

She nodded. "I figured a tenant as infamous as yourself had devised a nefarious scheme like working to keep the rent paid, so I was wondering if we could negotiate a schedule." She caught sight of the bag on the table and said, "Fruits de Mer? Why?"

Colin started. "Why not?"

With a slight roll of her eyes, she said, "It's an overpriced lunch for tourists."

Colin folded his arms. "Is that so?"

"Locals don't go there. It's pretentious stuff, starting with the French name. If you want a meal, you go to Sparrows." She snickered. "Well, no harm done. Once your stuff arrives, you don't have to resort to takeout."

Colin gestured to the rickety kitchen with its two electrical outlets, a humming fridge dating back to the Clinton administration, and an electric stove that had all four burners lined with silver foil. "Do you really think I can cook on *this*?"

She looked at the stove, then back at him. Her expression changed. "Are you serious?"

He snorted. "I'm not a miracle worker. There are limits to my skill set."

She fell silent.

It would be nice if he could impress her, maybe get her to back down. "I guess I could boil water." He huffed. "I'm hardly whipping up a five-star meal in this kitchen."

Natalie looked aside.

Okay, who was she? "Which store do you work at?"

Her expression changed to delight. "Bright Stitches, the local yarn store. I can teach you to crochet," she added. "My cousin Brooke co-owns it with me, and she's the knitter."

He cocked his head. "That's not in the same mini-mall as Fruits de Mer."

She shrugged. "Denny owns a few properties. We're the strip mall nearer the center of town. So what brings you here?"

Colin narrowed his eyes. "Fruits de Mer."

She backed up a step. "Oh. I'm sorry."

He arched his eyebrows. "Maybe I can do something about the pretentious tourist lunches."

"Or the pretentious name?" She shifted her weight. "You came here for that?"

Colin huffed. "I didn't move to Brighthead for the apartment."

Her laughter brightened her whole expression. "You'd have moved right back out again. How'd you even hear about Brighthead?"

"My brother worked at Fruits de Mer. When my last restaurant was being sold, he told me to get over here, so I did. My brother hooked me up with this apartment, though, so maybe I never realized he's my mortal enemy."

Natalie said, "And what do you do at Fruits de Mer?"

Irritated, Colin said, "What do you think I do? I do whatever needs to be done." Natalie made it seem like she was being friendly, but come on. "Is there anything else I should know about this building? Like not to slam the doors or else I'll scare the mice?"

"The landlord sends in a pest company on a regular basis, so there aren't vermin. He also sprays for moths on a regular basis because of all the wool in my apartment." She ran a hand through her hair. "We get plowed out pretty good in the wintertime. Summers, if you stay that long, you're going to bake."

Colin pointed to the dilapidated oven. "Well, at least something will be baking."

Again she looked momentarily worried. "It's not so bad if you keep the windows open, though. I've lived here two years, and I've survived."

Natalie either had no money or no standards.

She edged toward the door. "Well, just listen for my shower before you turn on yours, and I won't run the washing machine when you need to sleep."

Colin said, "Most nights I'm going to be working until close, so it's probably not an issue unless you do laundry at midnight."

"Second shift is the worst." She started to turn away, then pivoted back. "You know, I can teach you to cook."

Colin snapped, "Oh, can you?"

She nodded. "It's a lot cheaper than ordering in. Even if you're getting a discount, I know how it adds up. My kitchen setup isn't great, but I've made it work, and yours is larger than mine."

Colin fought annoyance. "So if I come upstairs with a bag of groceries, you'll teach me to make coq au vin?"

"Real food. You're a real person." With a roll of her eyes, she stepped into the hall. "If you want me, I'll be upstairs."

Colin rolled his eyes as he closed the door. Talk about deceptive packaging. That woman was something else.

Austin had put silverware into the bag, so Colin ate right out of the takeout containers. His dishes were still in Kennebunkport. Steak and potatoes, and a side salad. A roll with butter. Even a slice of chocolate cake. What a darling snub from Miss Natalie of the Upstairs Apartment. Real food? What was he eating, air?

Her opinion had better be the outlier, or Fruits de Mer was going to go down like the Hindenburg. Austin, though... He'd have known if the restaurant were limping along the road to bankruptcy.

He texted Austin, "My upstairs neighbor just informed me we serve overpriced lunches to tourists."

No reply. Austin was working. Colin added, "Thanks for

the dinner."

It was late now, but not late enough to go to sleep. Colin pulled out his tablet computer and looked at the restaurant's social media accounts, but then he heard a voice through the ceiling. Natalie's voice.

This was going to be annoying. Shouldn't an apartment be soundproof? At least a little?

She seemed okay other than hating his restaurant, although that felt a bit like saying, "Other than that, Mrs. Lincoln, how was the play?" Even if she loathed the food, saying a restaurant owner couldn't cook his own meals was rude.

Maybe she thought restaurant owners were like landlords and just cashed the checks. Some owners did treat their restaurants like an investment, hiring a general manager to do all the day-to-day stuff. Austin had that role right now. Natalie had asked what Colin did there, and truth be told, at his previous restaurant, he hadn't spent as much time cooking as he would have liked. Based on experience, a lot of his work was going to be in administration. He'd be out at six o'clock in the morning pricing specials at the terminal markets, or he'd be tinkering with the menus, rethinking their advertising campaigns, working out the budgets, handling staff issues, and on and on and on. He'd done all that in Kennebunkport, but there had been three other owners at the time whom he could split it with.

Selling CharCuties had been the right decision. It had left Colin with a nice chunk of change to put his own stamp on a restaurant.

From above, he heard Natalie say, "Did my maid of honor show up?" followed by, "Oh, good. I wanted to take care of her myself."

New information: Miss Natalie was engaged. Colin hoped she wouldn't bring over her fiancé during the hours Colin was home. Paper thin walls and ceilings would mean he'd hear anything they did together.

"Lilah was gushing over what a good husband he'd

make." More laughter. "Well, tell her she can't have him!"

Colin washed his silverware, then disposed of his takeout containers. Natalie was good looking, but given her engagement and the fact that she despised Colin the Restaurant Owner, there was nothing for him here.

CHAPTER FOUR

During the Thursday afternoon Sit and Stitch, the door jangled open. Natalie looked up from teaching a client how to do a popcorn stitch to find Shelly Novick, the bride—unaccompanied by a maid of honor.

"Hey!" Natalie called. "Come take a seat."

Shelly joined them at the table with her takeout coffee. "I've been on my feet since five o'clock in the morning."

It was two in the afternoon. Lilah danced over to her with a smile as brilliant as her handknit stranded colorwork sweater. "Show off your ring! I didn't get to see it last time you were here."

Shelly displayed her hand with so much joy that Natalie smiled. With any luck, Shelly's future husband would be similarly supportive of her yarn habit.

Lilah took the seat next to Shelly, talking a mile a minute. Natalie went back to the woman working the popcorn stitch.

The crocheter said, "I hate dropping the loop off the hook."

"It's unnerving," Natalie admitted. "But after you get used to it, you'll start trusting it more. Try one more time.

Five double crochets in the same stitch." That was easy enough. "Then drop the loop off the hook and put the hook back through the loops of the first stitch, then pick up your loop again and pull it through."

"Oh!" The crocheter chuckled as the stitch formed. "That was a lot easier than it sounded."

"Most stitches are." Natalie stood. "It's only yarn. If it fails, you can rip it back."

Lilah said, "Nat? Why don't you sit with us and work on your own project?"

Natalie said, "In a bit," which meant, "Never." Instead she tidied behind the counter, helped another client interpret a crochet chart, and then rang out someone who was buying a sweater quantity of worsted weight wool.

Natalie teased, "Beware the sweater curse."

"I'm trying to invoke the sweater curse," the customer muttered. "It's for my mother-in-law, and I want her to fly home."

Natalie forced a laugh, but the customer looked serious. Natalie said, "That's a lot of work for someone you don't like."

The woman gathered her package with a tight smile. "I'm proving I have the patience to stab something fifty thousand times."

Oh, dear. That didn't sound fun at all.

Natalie felt better today. Her downstairs neighbor had seemed nice enough, albeit completely helpless, and this morning, he'd gotten his shower before she'd even sat up out of bed.

On the downside, drinking soda out of a quart-sized takeout container was a level of poverty Natalie hadn't seen before. Compounded by the fact that he didn't know how to use his own stove...? That he *might* be able to figure out how to boil water...? That sounded awful.

She'd put her foot in her mouth by insulting the restaurant, but anyone poor enough to have to drink out of a plastic soup container couldn't afford takeout every day. Did he treat himself like a dog, eating kitchen scraps?

Wait, did restaurants actually do that? Maybe that wasn't a takeout bag as much as a garbage bag.

She stifled a shudder.

For all that, though, her downstairs neighbor looked pretty sharp, and he was well-spoken. Moving his shower time meant he wasn't holding her insult against her. He could have made her life miserable.

She could return the favor, but only if he swallowed his pride enough to take her up on the offer to show him how a stove worked.

Shelly and Lilah were still chatting, and Natalie made sure the gift card was in the right place. If the universe hated them, the maid of honor would walk into the shop right now, but instead the bell jangled, and in came a woman in her sixties, her mouth one tight line.

"Ms. Lavender Paul," Natalie exclaimed, mustering all her enthusiasm. "I have something for you."

Bright Stitches reserved a small section for gifts and other local crafts, and it was to those that Natalie headed now. "I saw this and immediately thought of you."

She opened a box before Lavender's unsmiling face. Inside was a metal dragonfly on a long stake, its purple wings quivering on springs, its back lined with solar panels.

Lavender took the lawn ornament from Natalie's hands and examined it.

"It lights up," Natalie said. "The distributor says that after a sunny day, it should shine for five hours."

Lavender kept pivoting it this way and that, studying the way it caught the light.

From the Sit and Stitch table, Natalie heard muttering. This she ignored.

Lavender said, "Any other colors?"

Natalie said, "Eight colors."

Lavender's lips pursed tightly. "Order the rest."

Fighting a smile, Natalie reached under the shelf and pulled out two shopping bags. "I already did."

Lavender wrapped the first dragonfly ornament back

into its box while Natalie handled the payment.

Lavender hefted her own bags out to the car because Natalie knew from experience that, first off, Lavender would take offense at any offer to help, and secondly, Lavender's car would be crammed full of junk, so Natalie wouldn't be able to easily get the bags into the car for her anyhow.

The instant the door jangled shut, one of the knitters said, "Why do you do that? Her property is already an eyesore."

"She loves lawn ornaments." Natalie forced a smile. "I knew on sight that she'd love those."

Another woman said, "Remember that inflatable rabbit she had on the lawn for Easter?"

"That finally blew away at Thanksgiving," added the grousing knitter.

Lilah bounced over to the table from the back of the store. "It makes her happy, and her happiness makes me happy when I see her lawn all decorated."

The grousing knitter muttered, "Her lawn is barely bigger than her station wagon. It looks terrible."

Lilah said, "Take it to the zoning board. There's no bylaw against decorating every square inch of a station-wagon-sized lawn."

The knitter side-eyed Natalie. "You don't need to encourage her."

The knitter might have a point, but what did it hurt anyone to look at several dozen lawn ornaments? Besides, the solar dragonflies were made locally, and local crafters needed the income. Stained glass mobiles, wind chimes, hand-turned wooden bowls, shell paintings—if Natalie could move products for those artisans, all the better.

It worked like that for yarn, too. Lilah was one of six local independent yarn dyers featured in the shop, and Natalie gave them prominent display space. Indies sold well during the summertime, when Natalie pushed their "local yarn" as "souvenir yarn." Lilah in particular tried to capitalize on that angle, giving her colorways names like

"Brighthead Pier," and matching the colorway to the location.

Profit margins were so thin to begin with that the local artisans needed every bit of help.

Meanwhile, Lilah had her phone out, directing the irritated knitter toward the Brighthead-dot-gov website where she could demand the Select Board discuss lawn ornaments at the next bi-annual town meeting. It would never get on the agenda, and that was fine. Making useless complaints to the Select Board was something of a hobby in Brighthead, and just like the yarn supply, the complaints never ran out.

Shelly approached the counter with four skeins of silvery-white yarn, and Natalie's stomach lurched. "Those are so pretty," Natalie said, hoping the prompt would hit home.

No knitter ever resisted the invitation to talk about a future project. Shelly beamed. "I've been thinking for a while that I need to make myself a wedding shawl. A pi shawl. Maybe with a few thousand beads on the border."

Natalie flipped over the yarn to read the label. Fingering weight yarn. Nice high twist. Local dyer. Perfect color.

It also fit neatly into that gift card waiting behind the counter. Natalie prompted, "Have you picked out a pattern yet?"

Shelly brought it up on her phone, and Natalie's brain whirled as she tried to figure out how to make this work, because she was not going to let down that man and his maid of honor wife.

The shawl on the screen was amazing, with a flower motif starting from the center and long peaks like stained glass windows raying toward a border that undulated like waves. "You're going to look amazing." Natalie paused. "You know, if you wait two days, I may have something else for you instead."

Shelly shook her head. "This yarn is perfect."

It was. It was completely perfect for that shawl, and for this bride. "I promise, if you wait two days, you will not be disappointed."

Shelly frowned. "These are only eight skeins of this colorway, though. I don't want to lose them."

Natalie opened her hands. "How about this? I'll set all eight skeins aside for you behind the counter, with your name on them. I'll even remove them from inventory as if they were sold. Just wait two days because I've got something coming in that I think you'll love even more."

This was true. Most knitters would love their best friend even more than eight skeins of silky high-twist silver-white fingering weight yarn.

Shelly leaned across the counter. "Give me a hint."

Natalie leaned back and whispered conspiratorially. "You deserve something amazing, and I have never steered you wrong."

Shelly's brow furrowed as she thought, but Natalie would have staked everything on never having gotten it wrong. She listened to people. She waited to make a recommendation until it was exactly the right thing, and then when she made a suggestion, it was on point. That's what you do, Natalie always told herself. When you care about people, you listen to what they're saying and hear what they're not saying. That way, when you make an offer, it goes right to the heart.

Shelly sighed. "Fine. I'll wait two days. It's not like I was going to cast on tonight."

Two thousand yards of yarn went into a bag, and Natalie sealed it with Shelly's name emblazoned across the front. "HOLD!" Shelly still looked reluctant to leave it. "I could buy it and exchange it later..." but Natalie reassured her until she finally stepped out the door.

Immediately, Natalie texted the maid of honor's husband. "Shelly chose yarn, and it's on hold behind the counter. Send in your wife today or tomorrow."

He texted back immediately. "Scathingly brilliant. Thank you."

Natalie warmed inside. She'd done it, and three separate people were going to be so happy.

CHAPTER FIVE

In her apartment, Natalie sang while she cooked. Every so often, Birdie Holly sang back from his perch, and the guinea pigs wheeted at her from their cage.

How long had it been since she'd crocheted something for herself? Lilah wasn't being fair about that—not entirely —because Bright Stitches did need display items, and Brooke always needed testers for her patterns before she could sell them. Natalie had been doing that for ages.

She didn't keep those, though. Invariably some customer would offer the cost of the yarn for the finished item, and Natalie would let it go.

Charities needed donations, as well. Preemie hats, blankets for sick children, chemo caps—it never ended. Maine was so cold. The homeless needed hats and scarves and mittens. Everyone needed something, so when it came time to choose her next project, Natalie never got past their needs to her wants.

A knock at the door made Birdie Holly shriek, and Natalie called, "Hang on a sec," then washed her hands and looked out the peephole. It was the new neighbor. Cole? No, wait, Colin.

He looked embarrassed as she let him in. "I'm sorry to bother you, but I was wondering if I could borrow your vacuum cleaner."

"No problem." She brought him inside. "It's such a pain, that first week after you move, trying to find everything."

Colin gave a nervous laugh as he followed her to the living room closet. "I know exactly where it is. It's on a truck between here and Kennebunkport."

It clicked suddenly. "Oh, so you're sleeping on the floor, and—let me guess—you don't trust how well the previous tenants cleaned before they left?"

"I can see exactly how well the place was cleaned, but I'm blaming the landlord because if they didn't even run a sweeper over the carpet before handing me the keys, that's what it looks like."

Natalie checked the vacuum bag. "I think it's good to go."

"I'll bring it right back, thanks." As he wheeled it through the kitchen, Colin looked over her shoulder toward the stove. "What are you making?"

"Chicken chili." She turned to him. "Do you want some? I make huge batches and freeze it for later, so there's plenty."

Colin chuckled. "Ah, the miracle meal, eating without cooking. How is that any different from takeout?"

She returned to the stove. "How can it not be more different from takeout?"

As she stirred it, he looked over her shoulder, then checked out everything else on the counter.

He frowned, and a pang struck Natalie's heart. He'd told her he couldn't cook. Now he must feel like she was rubbing it in his face. "I can show you how to make this if you want."

He sighed. "You're not going to let that go, are you?"

She tried to sound enthusiastic. "I offered."

He glanced at the counter. "Cream cheese? Not sour cream?"

She nodded. "Cream cheese makes it smooth. It's got

another ten minutes to simmer, but then it'll be ready. I'll show you."

He got a mischievous look in his eyes. "Okay, then. Show me."

Really? He was willing to learn? She stirred it again, then said, "Well, not much is going on now."

He said, "Your apartment is laid out differently than mine. Mind if I take a look?" *Taking a look* was two steps back into the living room he'd just left. "Whoa, yarn. Lots of yarn."

Now that he mentioned it, she did have a bunch of visible yarn. There was a pair of skeins on the bookshelf and a partial skein next to the TV. She'd left a half-done project on the couch. He couldn't even see into the sealed bin beneath the windows, bulging at the sides. She wouldn't factor in the cedar chest in her bedroom. "I thought I told you, I run a yarn shop."

"I didn't realize you ran it out of your living room." He grinned. "What are you knitting?"

"Crochet," Natalie corrected automatically, then caught herself. "Sorry. Crochet is the one with the hook. Knitting is a pair of needles."

"I stand corrected." He didn't look offended. "Also, unless I'm mistaken, you have a lot of animals."

Natalie shrugged. "Not that many. There's the guinea pigs, the parakeet, and a pair of anoles."

"And a fishtank." He glanced around. "What, no hamster? No cats?"

She'd nearly gotten a cat, but then Lilah had found a home for every one of the litter born in her barn. "I could, but I'd have to pay cat rent."

"Cat rent is ridiculous. It's not as though the cat is running up the utilities watching TV all day, and you already paid a damage deposit." Colin looked up at the ceiling. "You have nicer woodwork than I do. Only half my doors have the corner pieces. Also, your bedroom and living room aren't attached to one another. My bedroom is on the other side of the living room."

"The building wasn't designed to be apartments." Natalie paused. "It would have been pretty as a single-family home, wouldn't it?"

"They added this kitchen, didn't they?" He looked around. "Okay, and that makes sense, the way the entrance and the front stairs are designed. The front entrance must have been part of the original living room. My bedroom was probably an office."

"There's an attic, too, but it's not useful for anything." Natalie flinched. "At least, I hope not. I've never tried going in there, but I think the maintenance guys have gone in once or twice."

"Adding a second bathroom might explain why the showers turn one another off. Also why my kitchen is so much bigger than yours." Colin wandered back over to the chili where it was simmering. "Now I'm curious as to what this place looked like when it was all one home, like which walls they added."

She said, "Could you stir that?"

He looked at her, a little sad. "Don't you think I'll ruin it, given my inexperience with real food?"

Natalie glanced aside. "Don't be like that. We'll turn you into a real cook."

"Thanks so much." Colin huffed. "By the way, do you know the difference between a cook and a chef?" When Natalie shook her head, he said, "A chef turns his head when he sneezes." Ignoring Natalie's *eww* sounds, Colin took up the spoon. "I'm still a little mind-blown by the cream cheese. You just stick the whole block of cream cheese into your chili? And it's edible?"

"I promise you, it's delicious." Natalie pulled out a knife and started cutting the cream cheese into cubes.

He said, "Oh, so you do *mise* it."

Mise? "You cut it up so it melts faster," she explained. "Once it's softened up, we can stir it in evenly. Then we add half and half."

Colin frowned as he stirred. He used his left hand, and he did a weird wrist-twist as he did it, not going around the pot so much as lifting up and around in an elliptical motion. It looked awkward. "Not heavy cream? I was hoping to have a heart attack so I didn't have to sleep on the air mattress again."

Natalie laughed. "My mother's recipe calls for heavy cream, but I'm not buying it just for this."

"Yeah, that would be a pain." Colin turned to her. "And what do you serve this over? Real mashed potatoes?"

"Thanks for reminding me. I need to start the noodles." She dug out the pot, filled it with water, then went into the cabinet for the noodles. While she was doing that, Colin took the knife from the cutting board and stuck it in the sink, then started running water into the dishpan. As he squirted in some dish soap, she said, "You don't have to do that."

"Of course I do. Or does Denny show up to wash the dishes?" Colin rolled his eyes as he pushed up his sleeves. "I may be a food monster who eats fancy takeout, but I do know how to wash a cutting board." He waved idly behind him. "Don't mind me."

Natalie set the table while dishes made their way from the hot soapy water through the rinse water and into the rack. He said, "What else needs prepping?"

Waiting for direction? "What exactly do you do at Fruits de Mer?"

Colin shrugged. "Well, nothing right now, since I'm here and not there. But I have heard of chopping and shredding things. What toppings do you put on the chili?"

He and she exchanged looks, until finally he said, "Please tell me you don't eat it naked."

Rather than flinch, Natalie pointed to her shoulders which were, notably, covered in a flannel shirt.

"Very funny. You can reassure your boyfriend I'm not interested in taking off your clothes. May I go hunting?"

Two minutes later, he'd come up with a bag of tortilla chips, her cheddar cheese, and the container of sour cream. "What this needs is an avocado." He glanced at the pot of chili. "Okay, baby. Time to defile you with the cream cheese."

"You're such a skeptic. It's amazing." Natalie edged him aside and added the cream cheese cubes. "Give it a minute to soften up, and then stir again."

"I'm so glad my technique meets with your approval." Again he sounded touchy, but Natalie ignored it because she wasn't criticizing him. She wasn't even looking at him.

Her phone rang, and she glanced at the screen. "Hang on. It's my cousin." She left Colin in the kitchen and answered while she headed into the living room. "Brooke, what's up? Did my maid of honor show up?"

Brooke laughed. "No, but it's hilarious that you've gotten so attached to this outlandish situation."

Natalie said, "You have to admit it's adorable."

"I haven't been involved at all other than receiving your dire warnings." Brooke hesitated. "But there's been a development. Shelly, bless her overenthusiastic heart, has decided to knit her entire wedding dress."

Natalie exclaimed, "What?" loud enough that Colin turned in the kitchen.

"She left a voicemail telling me to guard all eight skeins of that yarn with my life."

"Easily done. They're all in the bag." This was a problem. Eight skeins of yarn were not four skeins. She couldn't remember the exact price, but the gift card wouldn't cover it all.

Brooke went on, "Also, we got a box of ceramic yarn bowls from Craig over at Bar Harbor. I set them up on the shelf, but I'm not sure that's the best place. They look fragile, and the floor looks unforgiving."

"I'll take care of that. Oh, and guess who bought all eight light-up dragonflies?"

Brooke laughed. "You're terrible. I hope she doesn't tell anyone where she got them, or else we're going to have lawn ornaments of the threatening variety left in front of the shop."

"It was at Sit and Stitch. All of Brighthead knows by now."

"Thanks. I'll wear my suit of armor to work. Actually, Lilah and I are switching shifts tomorrow because she's got the economic planning board tonight and wants to come in late."

"Good for you! When the maid of honor comes in, you'll get to meet the heroes of the day." Colin was still in the kitchen, so Natalie added, "Dinner's nearly ready. I'll talk to you tomorrow."

In the kitchen, Colin looked up from the chili, seeming concerned. "Your water's boiling. Also, I tasted the chili and it's a bit bland. Should I add anything?"

"You sneaked a taste? No fair." She grinned at him. "You can add seasoning to your own if you want, but not the whole batch."

"Fair enough." He turned off the heat and stirred in the half and half, and she dumped the noodles in the water.

She said, "You know more than you think you do."

He studied her. "How do you mean?"

"You shut off the burner before adding the dairy." She stirred the noodles in the hot water. "I think you can do this on your own."

"Turning off the stove: quite the challenge." He turned back to the sink and washed the measuring cup, the plate that used to have the cream cheese, and anything else he could find. This was so weird. She was going to finish dinner and have two bowls and some silverware to wash. Or maybe nothing, if Colin planned to wash those, too.

She pulled a can of peaches out of the pantry, and he gave a dry, "Canned peaches, how cute."

Why did he keep poking fun at everything she did? It wasn't like he could do better. She handed him the can opener.

Then Natalie felt bad because he fumbled the can opener. Like, really fumbled it. He couldn't get the wedge to clamp on the lip of the can, and once he did, he looked momentarily lost because at first he turned the crank the wrong way. He had dexterity to spare while he was doing everything else, but it embarrassed Natalie to watch. She occupied herself getting out the serving spoons, and when she was done, he had the peaches in individual bowls. He carried those to the table while she puzzled out what to do with the chili.

"I don't have a lot of serving dishes," she admitted.

Colin said, "Scoop it out of the pot. We'll survive. If worse comes to worst, I'll fetch some takeout containers, and we can serve the noodles from that."

"You're mean." She dished out noodles for herself. "Just for that, I'm not serving you. You'll have to decide your own proper proportion of noodles to chili."

"Wow, harsh. My heart breaks." Colin loaded up his bowl, and they ended up at the table.

She poured water for both of them. "Just like at a restaurant, except I'm not going to make you drink out of a soup container."

"I'm going to need to leave you a tip. If only I could remember where I left that little card with the ten, fifteen, and twenty percent calculations already done for me." He raised his glass. "*Bon appétit*, to the founder of the feast."

Raising her own glass, Natalie tilted her head. "To cream cheese and vacuum cleaners!"

Colin tried the chili. "Okay, I stand corrected. The cream cheese pairs well with the chicken and the white beans. I'm going to need this recipe."

Natalie sat up. "You will?"

"The flavor profile is muted, but that's easily adjusted. You've created a nice texture." He reached for the toppings. "Now, though, we load it up with fun and games and see what else happens. I'm not sure the cheese isn't going to overwhelm the whole thing after the first bite."

She tried the tortilla chips. "These are good with it."

"Something salty like that is a slam dunk." Colin smiled. "Next time, though—avocado."

Natalie wrinkled her nose. "I don't do much with avocados."

"We do everything with avocados. Overfunded lunch-bound tourists love them." Colin's eyes sparkled. "I'll show you how to cut them open, though, so you don't end up at urgent care making friends with a surgeon."

She brightened. "Oh, you probably know all those tricks, don't you?"

Colin looked irritated again. "My brother is the trickster twin. But this is very good. I'm sorry for doubting the magic of cream cheese."

CHAPTER SIX

Fuming, Colin vacuumed. Natalie was fully committed to mocking his restaurant, even to the point of feeding him a bland meal in order to drive home the "reality" of her food.

Cream cheese, though. That wouldn't have been his go-to idea for white bean chili, if he'd ever wanted to make it. He knew how to make chili, of course. It was one of those staples everyone kind of knew in the back of their minds, but CharCuties hadn't served it. Who goes to a restaurant for a staple food?

At least, not the kind of restaurant Colin wanted to run.

It had all happened so fast. He and his friends had done well with CharCuties, and then when they'd gotten an offer to buy the name, the menu, and the rights to both it and the second location they were about to open, it was too good a deal to pass up. Plus, the four of them had begun getting under one another's skin just a little too deep. It was time to head in four different directions.

But even so, as of last September, Colin was secure that he'd be staying in Kennebunkport for the next few years. Then, one crisp January morning, he'd awakened in

Brighthead.

He finished vacuuming the living room and the bedroom, rewound the electrical cord, and carried the vacuum cleaner back to his food nemesis. Natalie thanked him for returning it, meaning she must set the bar so low it was actually on the ground. Then she said, "Hang on," and she handed him a container with another meal's worth of chili.

Colin held the warm container in his hands. "Are you sure? You were making a huge batch so you could have leftovers."

She said, "Of course I'm sure. And if you come back tomorrow, I'll show you how to cook something else."

A fiery retort started in his brain, shot down to his gut to lock and load—but then he caught it in his throat as if he were dealing with a scammy customer. Colin had learned not to shout at the comp vultures. He just shut them down.

By contrast, Natalie looked so earnest as she insulted him. Earnest and cute.

He glared at her. "What's your game with this?"

Was she attempting to make a ham-handed reference to that joke about chefs—that they could cook for five thousand, but on their own would resort to a cheese sandwich eaten over the trash can?

She recoiled, faking a hurt expression. "I thought you'd like to cook with me, that's all. You had a good time tonight."

That was a long game, if that was what she was doing. It didn't make sense.

He'd better get out of here before he said something that made his next month's living situation intolerable. If he said what he was thinking, she'd be starting her laundry at three o'clock in the morning, followed by jumping jacks over his bedroom at four and pre-wrapped slices of American cheese in his mailbox at five. He needed a way never to talk to her again.

He said, "Give me your phone." Once he had it, he typed

into her contacts, "Colin Downstairs" and then his phone number. Save.

That done, he said, "Text me if you come up with anything else I need to know about the building, like how opening a window will cause the left side of the house to subside into the ocean."

He texted himself from her phone so he'd have her number, too. That should keep her off his doorstep.

As his phone buzzed in his pocket, Natalie said, "What do you want for lesson number two?"

Chest tense, Colin handed back her phone. "You're the one who knows all about real food. Whatever happens next, I'm sure you'll make it real."

Colin wasn't halfway down the stairs again before he was texting the landlord. "Denny, the upstairs tenant. What's her deal?"

Something had gone horribly wrong, and Colin needed to know the scope of the situation before he dealt with Natalie again. Either she was the nastiest woman on earth or else she was delusional, but somehow he'd gotten entangled with...this. With a bully who had a knife at his back and wanted to keep jabbing it. She said the landlord let her deal with incoming tenants. Did she have a key to his house? Could she get into his mailbox? Would she bang up his car?

Denny replied, "She's been around for a while, and I told her to expect a new tenant this week. Why?"

"I'm having issues with her."

Denny responded, "What kind of issues?"

Colin frowned. "Just general obnoxiousness. Did you tell her who I am?"

Denny said, "I figured you'd do that. I'm not up in your

business unless it affects the house."

"Actually, speaking of the house, an outlet is dead in the living room."

"Got it. Is it okay if my electrician comes into the apartment tomorrow? It's not 24 hours' notice."

Colin put the chili into the fridge. "Yeah, that's fine."

"My other tenants said Natalie was helpful, so I always let her break in the new renters."

A second later, Denny added, "I can tell her to back off if you need me to."

Colin dropped onto the kitchen chair and stared at the phone. Finally he replied, "I can deal with her for a month. She's just rude."

Denny texted, "That's a first. She's usually straightforward. Whatever she says, take it at face value."

Natalie had been here two years and seen multiple tenants already? Gee, how could any renter bear to leave such a wonderful apartment? A steal at half the price. Or was she driving them away?

Colin rubbed his temples and stared at the phone screen, but nothing further showed up.

All right, then. What if he tried to take everything at face value? Natalie said she hated Fruits de Mer, and that was clear. She said Colin didn't make real food, and tonight she'd fed Colin what she considered real food. She'd offered to teach him to cook when he could cook just fine. He couldn't whip up a five-star meal in the apartment's lousy kitchen, but—

Colin breathed, "Oh. Blast."

Last night, he'd gestured to the forty-year-old stove with its untrustworthy burners and said, "I can't cook on this."

What she'd heard was, "I can't cook."

She'd asked him what he did at Fruits de Mer, and he'd said, "A bit of everything." Not that he owned it. He'd never introduced himself as the owner. He said he'd gotten a job where his brother worked. She'd assumed he came here because he needed a job. He'd explicitly said his brother had found him a cheap apartment.

She'd watched him fumble her can opener because it was a right-handed can opener, and he was a lefty.

In Natalie's mind, he was an unemployed kitchen staffer who'd fled to his brother, and his brother had wrangled him a job.

"Oh, boy," he whispered, wondering if Natalie could hear the realization blooming in Colin's head right through the thin floors, or if she'd wonder why he was talking to himself at all. But then again, she'd been singing to herself.

Taken at face value, the way Denny said... Natalie must actually think she was teaching Colin to cook.

That wasn't mockery. That was sincerity. Natalie wanted Colin to explore the world of food—the joy of turning ingredients into a meal. She had joy and wanted him to share in it.

That was...

Refreshing.

Sometimes when Colin made chicken with a roasted garlic sauce, he squirted a few drops of lemon right at the end to brighten up the flavors. The lemon juice was tart, of course, and thinking Natalie was mocking him was tart—but all of a sudden, everything else was standing out in contrast.

She'd been friendly to him even though she had no idea who he was. To her, he was just Colin Downstairs who chopped things up, cleaned the tables, and listened to sous chefs discussing flavor profiles but without ever comprehending a single word. He was the dish dog, scrubbing pans on the outskirts of a world he didn't understand, but she liked him anyhow.

She'd seen what looked to her like abject poverty, and there was a simple thing she could do to boost Colin out of the hole.

That was kind of sweet. No wonder her in-absentia fiancé had locked her in so young.

Colin paced all three of his rooms, then returned to his phone.

What on earth should he do now? He could march

upstairs again. *Hey, I'm here for the third time this evening because you seem to have underestimated me. I do a whole lot more than wash plates and wipe down tables. I'm the person who designs these overpriced meals for flatlander tourists, and when you insult that restaurant, you're insulting me.*

She would apologize. She'd be so embarrassed that she'd been teaching an accredited chef how to dump cream cheese into white bean chili. She might try to defend herself with, "Well, your food is still overpriced frippery."

But on the other hand, she worked at a yarn shop selling overpriced yarn and decorative frippery. Colin knew better than to say, "You can buy a hat at Walmart." Handmade hats and blankets were luxury items, too. If his business depended on discretional spending, then so did hers. People needed to eat. People didn't need to knit.

A single text would clear it up. "I accepted your chili under false pretenses. I own Fruits de Mer. I know how to cook."

She would text back, "I'm sorry. I didn't realize. But keep the chili anyhow because food is food."

Over. Done. Except would she still be as friendly afterward?

He texted her, more than a little shaken. "Are you completely serious that you want to teach me to cook?"

She replied right away "Of course! Do you want to make something tomorrow?"

As of now, Colin had exactly two friends in this town: his twin brother, and his upstairs neighbor. One text would straighten out the miscommunication, but it also would halve the number of Brighthead residents who would talk to him.

She added, "Name it. We can get started."

Colin had an easy out here. Although Dale was closing tonight, it was the last time. "I'm working until close every night from now on. But thanks anyhow."

Problem solved. Now he'd just need to make sure she didn't leave little containers of chicken soup in front of his door.

She replied, "You said they don't open Mondays. I get out at four on Monday, so we'll do it then."

She remembered his schedule? How could she have paid attention to all the little details and missed the big one?

She texted again, "Just say what you want to make."

Colin's brain dial-toned. The floor creaked overhead. *No, please don't come downstairs.* He was having a hard enough time managing this conversation without her immediate presence.

She texted, "Hamburgers? Spaghetti? Tacos?"

The only thing that came to mind as a reply was, "I'll buy the groceries."

He needed to get out of this situation. She was blowing up his phone, pushing for him to agree to be helped. This was the opposite of all those women he comped chocolate cake for because they were looking for a good time. Natalie was looking to give him one.

She replied, "That's not necessary. You'd be my guest."

Yeah, no. "I may be confused about what's going on, but I do know food costs money. Students pay teachers, not the other way around. If you cook something for me, I'm buying."

That came out of him a bit more earnest than he'd intended. Chalk it up to trying to seize some little bit of control in an out-of-control situation.

Natalie texted, "I'll send you a list. But I need to know what you want."

Colin checked her three options. "Tacos."

She replied instantly. "Tacos are fun. Monday, then!"

"Sure. Monday. Thanks."

Colin clicked off the phone and left it on the charger. The misunderstanding could remain until Monday.

CHAPTER SEVEN

Natalie recognized the maid of honor the moment she stepped into the store. There wasn't a wide-eyed stare this time. Instead, she gave a commanding scan of the entire shop before alighting her eyes on the counter and immediately identifying who was in charge. The man had said his wife was an even match to him, and with her take-charge attitude, this had to be her.

Natalie got to the woman before Brooke even turned away from the shelves. "Welcome to Bright Stitches. May I help you?"

"I hope so." This was definitely Shelly's maid of honor. Shelly was a runner, and this woman had a similar confidence in the way she moved. "I'm told that Shelly Novick picked out yarn but left it behind the counter, and I'm here to buy it for her."

Natalie said, "Of course. I've been expecting you," and headed for the register.

For the first time, the woman seemed uncertain. "How?"

Natalie set the yarn on the counter, then handed over the gift card. "Because your husband got here first, and he left something behind the counter for you as well."

The woman opened the card and gasped. "Wait, stop. We can't afford this!"

Natalie pulled off the first of the husband's sticky notes and handed it to the wife. In his squarish handwriting, it said, "Yes, we can."

She looked up at Natalie. "What? Is he an idiot?"

Natalie handed her the second sticky note, which said, "Yes, probably."

The total came up on the register, and the woman took a step back from the register. "Why would he do this?"

Natalie handed over the last of the sticky notes, which said, "Because he loves you."

The woman didn't ask anything else. There were tears in her eyes.

Because he loved her. That was too sweet. Not only did he love her, but he'd gone far out of his way to look out for her happiness—and he knew her. He knew what she'd say. He knew how to disarm her with his words. He knew how to say what she needed to hear.

Lilah had been all over a perfect husband wanting to fund his wife's yarn habit, but the reason a man would want to buy her yarn was he wanted to bring her joy. A man like that would take the trouble to get to know what made a woman's heart glow, and then he'd breathe on that spark to encourage it to the point of flames. "Is that what makes you smile?" he'd say. "Then that makes me smile too."

Last night, Colin hadn't smiled. Ideally, he should have smiled when she fed him, but every time they interacted, he acted like he was assembling a thousand-piece jigsaw puzzle with no picture on the box. He must be in a tough spot, losing his job and relocating to a new town without anything and starting a new job all at the same time.

Natalie glanced at the yarn and the woman and the gift card, and here was the problem: yarn to make a dress quite definitely exceeded the total on the gift card.

Well, profit margins were pesky things, easily swatted aside. Natalie hit the button for a twenty percent discount, then took the gift card and handed the woman her receipt and a dollar fifty-eight in change.

The woman looked at the yarn, then at the receipt. Her face darkened. "Yeah, sorry, no. My husband may be an idiot, but I'm not a thief."

An even match, indeed.

A minute later, more money had crossed the counter, and the woman had Shelly's yarn in a bag on her arm.

Natalie said, "Please give it to her before tomorrow, otherwise I'm going to have a very upset customer on my hands."

The woman shook her head. "The whole world is backward and forward right now." She looked up. "Thank you. That was amazing of you to help us surprise Shelly. She's going to be so happy."

Natalie warmed to her toes. "That was the idea."

The bell jangled open, and Lilah sprang inside. "Oh! Are you the maid of honor?" She laughed as the woman shook her head. "Your husband had so much fun planning this. Shelly nearly made me jump out of my skin yesterday because I was trying to suss out how much yarn she needed and what kind, and then she decided to buy it all right then."

Natalie exclaimed, "Wait! So you're the one who got us into this mess?"

A smile spread over Lilah's heart-shaped face. "Totally! But you got us out of it, so I'm going to absolve myself." She nodded to the maid of honor. "It's a pleasure to meet you, considering you were the lynch pin of the entire operation."

Brooke was just leaning against the far wall with a grin plastered across her face. "Don't mind me. I had nothing to do with this."

The maid of honor laughed. "Well, whatever you all did, thank you. I'll let Shelly know you were part of the conspirators."

Lilah rubbed her gloved hands together. "I love it! The crafty conspirators! I think I'll name a crafting guild after us."

The second the door jangled to a close behind Shelly's maid of honor, Lilah turned to them both with her arms in the air. "There's going to be a crafting guild! And I'm going to start it!"

All three of them sat around the Sit and Stitch table, Brooke constructing a shawl pattern based on notes jotted on a sheet of graph paper, and Natalie putting the finishing touches on a hat for the homeless ministry.

"It was serendipity." Lilah had changed her nail polish to a sparkling purple ombre. "The economic planning board kept going back to the idea that it would be nice to do something for all the local artisans, but every time I made a suggestion, they kept saying it was beyond the scope of the economic planning board. They wanted it to be some other group doing this thing or that thing. I mean, the Board is good for putting up a sign on the rail trail saying Sparrows is a quarter mile on the right, or this way to the antique stores, but when I suggest programs that will drive business to the shops, the answer is always the same."

Brooke made another note on her graph paper. She was wearing fingerless gloves—her own design and her own knitting—something she did nearly year-round. "Which, if you'll recall, is exactly what I said when you wanted to run for the open seat on the economic planning board."

Lilah leaned back in her plastic chair. "What we need is a crafting collective, kind of like a union of crafters and artisans in this part of Maine. Then we can band together to help one another. We can offer one another our expertise. We can give each other room in our shops, and we can put together our marketing power to make for greater reach."

Natalie had the hat pattern memorized, and her hook was doing its own thing as she flew through a row of half-double crochets. "What would that look like?"

"Imagine something like the chamber of commerce, except only for artists, craftsmen, artisans, and other types who do that. We set it up, and then we can do things to bolster each other. We can put together a craft fair. We can have a demonstration day, or offer classes, or loan our skills to one another. We could swap space with one another in our newsletters. So for example, we sell Craig's yarn bowls in our shop, but we could talk about Craig's ceramics shop in our newsletter, and then Craig could talk about Bright Stitches the next time he emails his newsletter."

Brooke frowned as she thought. "We could signal-boost one another on social media, as well."

Lilah nodded. "That's the kind of thing I'd love to see. Artists helping artists! And then over time, we could have a lot of influence. We could offer scholarships, or we could get our work into galleries and museums, or we could even have a museum of our own!"

Brooke said, "All of which is very far outside the authority of the Brighthead economic planning board."

"Exactly. Someone has to start it. Therefore, it needs to be us."

Brooke tilted her head. "In our excess spare time?"

"Last night I got together the paperwork to become a nonprofit, and that looks like it shouldn't be too bad. We don't even need much money to get started. We could meet virtually, or we could meet in the store here. I'm sure some of the crafters have larger spaces, or we could meet at a restaurant like the running club does."

Natalie thought about Fruits de Mer, and how a large group of artists might appreciate the high-end food. It would keep Colin in a job, at least. "That might work."

"I know it would work! Artists are the nicest people when they aren't being petty about competing with each other. But a collaborative would eliminate all the competition because we'd all be working together for a world where the point is art for the sake of art, not being cut-throat and pushing one another out of a very slim market share. We'll be expanding the market for everyone." Lilah grinned. "Think how many flatlanders come to Maine, wanting to spend money on Maine things. Let's put the Maine artists front and center. We'll make sure tourists don't look at a mass market painting of a lighthouse when they can have a locally produced painting of the actual Brighthead lighthouse."

Brooke shook her head. "Slow down. The idea is great, but what would this entail? Because someone would have to organize all this, and if you haven't noticed, we have a shop to run."

Natalie said, "I can help."

"You're already helping everyone on earth do everything." Brooke sighed. "The point is, the three of us alone can't spearhead this. If you're going to set it up, Lilah, there's got to be a lot of people involved. We'll need a core group of volunteers."

Lilah nodded. "The first thing we do is start connecting on social media. I'm going to set up a group, and once we've got a group, we can start trading ideas and see if anyone wants to participate."

Brooke nodded. "Keeping in mind, at all times, that anyone who volunteers is only going to do about a quarter of what they say they will, Natalie aside. Natalie will do exactly everything she promised and then look around to pick up anyone else's slack. No offense."

Natalie frowned. "How is that offensive?"

What was it with people lately, acting like they were going to protect Natalie from herself? Even Colin last night kept trying to say she needed to eat her own food, as though she were about to starve to death because she gave one serving of chili to a guy who hadn't even finished moving into his apartment.

Lilah said, "We could establish an artists' colony where all the local artists can live in tiny houses, and we could collaborate, and we could even attract people from outside Maine to come live in the artist colony!"

Brooke gave a non-subtle roll of her eyes. "Yes, this is all eminently doable. Go on. Do we found a university next, or do we dig a moat around the property and declare sovereignty as our own island nation?"

"We could fund college scholarships." Lilah continued as if she hadn't heard. "We could fund artist in residence programs and give artists the freedom they need to explore deep into their artwork."

Brooke looked up. "Now that, I do like. But it's a long way down the road."

"It's not. You could run an artist in residence program right out of your house if you wanted to." Lilah grinned. "I looked it up last night after the economic planning board finished."

Natalie said, "How do we find funds for all that? Before you can have an artists' colony or an artist in residence program, you need property, and we don't have any. Are we going to recruit fifty thousand artists into our guild and ask each one of them for ten dollars? Because land and a house around here won't be cheap."

Lilah said, "What if we started with a small undeveloped property and put four tiny houses on it? The artists' colony doesn't all have to be contiguous property. And it's like Truro and Marfa. Once you get a bunch of artists living in one place, you'll start attracting others because people will start to think of your town as an artistic hub."

Brooke said, "And as we all know, New Englanders are famously open to people who don't quite fit the mold." Lilah flinched as Brooke met her eyes, then added, "They're especially open to change in northern Maine."

"Let's not talk about changing the character of the town just yet," Natalie said. "The first step would be getting the artists together in one place to talk. Set up a social media group, and then we won't even have to buy them a cup of coffee."

Brooke raised her eyebrows. "I can get onboard with

that."

Lilah said, "I'll do that tonight, and I'll put out the word. So, what do you think I should call it?"

Brooke said, "The Brighthead Crafting Guild."

Natalie whistled. "You just whipped that out of your head."

"I name patterns all the time," Brooke said. "And it's a working title anyhow, just something to call the group until we can make people vote on a real name."

A customer came into the shop. Brooke got up to say hi while Lilah searched things on her phone. Natalie went back to work on her hat. She could make another of these, or she could use the remaining yarn in a coordinating scarf. Anyone who got a hat from one of these charities was in a terrible place, so they deserved a little beauty. They needed to know someone cared enough not only to give them a means of warmth, but to care about the way they did it.

Like Colin: it wasn't about just putting calories into a human body. It was about putting in the thought to make the meal satisfying, as well. He could microwave a cup of instant soup, sure, or shovel potatoes into yet another a takeout container from his job, but shouldn't a meal be more about caring?

And about being together, too. He'd asked if they could make tacos. Natalie didn't like tacos because they were messy. Fruits de Mer wouldn't make tacos, though, so if Colin wanted them, she'd have to teach him to make them.

Plus, him drinking out of a takeout soup container made her sad.

Natalie texted Colin a list of what they'd need. Taco shells. Salsa. A packet of taco seasoning. Ground beef. Lettuce. She already had a tomato. Cheddar.

She added, "Some of this is more than one meal, so we'll split the bill."

He replied, "I'm not worried. Which grocery store do you recommend?"

She sent him directions (no, it wasn't in Brighthead) and

then crocheted the next round wondering how else to make the tacos fun for him. Olives? He'd been all over her about not having an avocado, so should she tell him to get guacamole? Or would he think having him buy all this stuff was taking advantage of him?

Brooke returned to the table. "You look worried. Has it finally occurred to you how much time an artists' collaborative is going to take?"

Natalie shrugged. "I'm thinking about tacos."

Brooke tilted her head. "You don't like tacos."

Natalie smiled as she started the next round. "I'm willing to learn."

CHAPTER EIGHT

Monday. Boxes.

Even though Colin didn't own much, his apartment was lousy with boxes and furniture. For a chef who believed in *mise en place*, it was agony to have nothing in its right place, and no right place for anything.

He rubbed his temples to summon the energy to start unpacking. It failed to appear.

Saturday had been an awesome re-launch of a Brighthead landmark, complete with photographs, a speech, a cocktail hour (with every single member of the waitstaff onboard the whole day) and all the stops pulled out. Lots of specials, lots of discounts.

Had he told Natalie he did a bit of everything? He'd done a lot of everything on Saturday, from kitchen prep to visiting all the tables to washing dishes. On the bright side, his staff seemed to respect him because he had no qualms about getting his hands soapy. On the less-bright side...? He'd had to do it all over again on Sunday.

Austin thrived in this atmosphere. He even joked that he'd swap his white coat for a black one and visit the tables as if he were the owner. *Thanks for visiting! Is everything delicious? We love feedback! Oh, your waitress is Danielle? She'll take good care of you.* Over and over and over, Austin could pull it off, but for Colin, socializing was work. Colin would rather peel a thousand pounds of potatoes than chat up a hundred tables.

A knock at the door. Colin didn't bother getting up. "Hello?"

From the other side, he heard, "It's Natalie, from upstairs."

As opposed to all the other Natalies he knew in Brighthead. "Hang on."

He'd gotten two steps toward the door when he realized what a mess the place was.

Three steps before he thought, *But at least it's all in boxes.*

Four steps and he was at the door thinking, *She'd better not offer to unpack this for me.*

He opened the door, and Natalie started. "You look exhausted."

"Really, really long weekend." He gestured behind himself. "Also, my life arrived."

She flinched. "I'd offer to help, but I suspect you'd rather forget about it. Do you still want to make tacos?"

What was it he'd just thought about chopping vegetables rather than talking to people? If he made tacos, he'd have to do both.

He must have unconsciously made the world's most exhausted facial expression, because she backed off. "It's okay if you're too tired."

He shook his head. "I didn't mean no.*"*

Colin accompanied Natalie upstairs with his grocery bag of taco fixings. She got out the frying pan first, then found a cutting board and a knife. A blunt knife. "So," he began, unpacking the paper grocery bag, trying to figure out how to ask without sounding critical, "do you have a knife sharpener?"

She said, "No."

Colin clenched his jaw. Most knife injuries came from

blunt knives that skittered away from the things they were supposed to be slicing, and Natalie worked with her hands. She needed a sharp edge.

She added, "I'm scared when they're too sharp."

Colin said, "They need to be able to split the atom. It's safer that way."

She shuddered. "We're not splitting atoms. We're cutting tomatoes."

He said, "And an onion. And garlic."

She turned to him, puzzled. "An onion? Wouldn't that be in the seasoning packet?"

Now would be the perfect time to clear things up, except Colin was already so tired from the day.

When he didn't answer, she said, "Well, I guess—"

"I'll just get all this chopped up, then," and Colin took her lousy knife. He chopped the onion, then the garlic. The first thing he was going to do after clearing things up with her—exactly the first thing—was get his honing steel out of his knife roll and do Natalie a massive favor. Meanwhile, Natalie was looking up what people do when they don't just dump a packet of seasoning into the ground beef.

She recovered well, though. She showed him how to fry up the onions (although she had the heat too high) and then added the garlic, and then she had him add the ground beef right on top of them rather than pulling them out of the pan. Colin did it all as directed, then spooned off some of the grease. Finally, in went that horrific abomination, the taco seasoning packet.

For all that this was abominable, though, Natalie wasn't. "I work with two other people," she said in response to his question, and out spun this long story about a life lived in the orbit of a yarn shop. "My mother owned it for twenty-five years," Natalie said. The shop had stayed in the same location, and Brighthead's economy had resurged around it at about the same time that knitting and crocheting had enjoyed a comeback. Meanwhile, Colin washed up anything he'd already used and stacked it in the drying rack. "It was my grandmother who taught me to knit, but my mother taught me crochet," Natalie said as she shredded cheese. "I used to watch her darting that hook in and out of a blanket while she watched her shows, and finally she taught me how to hold a hook and tension the yarn. At first she'd start me off and do the first couple of rows, but then I started doing my own, and I had all these big plans. I'd make blankets for my mother and my grandmother and my aunt for Christmas, and all my school friends." She laughed. "Except then I learned just how long it takes to crochet an afghan. And how much yarn."

Colin said, "So you need yarn, a hook, and time?"

"And a pattern," Natalie said. "Kind of like how cooking takes food, cooking equipment, and a recipe. But once you learn the basics, you're able to do everything you need to."

Colin side-eyed her. "That's it? Just a few techniques, and your work is in a museum?"

Natalie said, "There are skill levels, but once you have the basics, you can both feed yourself and make yourself a scarf. Like, sure, you can have a pattern full of bobbles and half double front post crochets and brioche—"

Colin said, "By which I assume you mean not the bread."

Natalie hesitated. "Brioche is a bread?"

Colin laughed.

"Well, you can pick up the other techniques later, like cables. I have this pattern I want to try where you're working with two colors, and the cables are the contrast color, so it stands out—" she stopped. "Sorry. I don't want to bore you with all that."

Colin waved a hand. "Never apologize for being excited about the thing you love. You're making me love it, too."

"Thanks." Natalie sounded uncertain. "Anyhow, Brooke is a year younger than me, and she prefers to knit. I can do both." After a hesitation, she added, "I'm bicraftual."

Colin was opening the taco shell package. "Is it that big of a divide?"

"You wouldn't believe it. Some people get into huge fights about knitting or crocheting, and there are all sorts of misconceptions about what's good for which purposes."

She chuckled. "But it's fine. It's all fine. Except for crocheted socks, which I made once but were uncomfortable. Too bumpy."

Colin found a baking pan to heat up the taco shells. "This is a whole world I never even knew about."

Natalie said, "First, I'll teach you to cook, and then, I'll teach you to crochet. After that, you'll be perfect."

Colin straightened. "Except for my massive ego, which will only get worse once I've achieved documented perfection."

"Oh, that's a conundrum." Her nose wrinkled. It was cute. "Because the more perfect you get, the more imperfect you become. I can't untangle that skein."

He started filling the taco shells.

Natalie said, "Wait, what are you doing?"

He stopped in place. "Aren't we going to heat them up in the oven?"

She said, "You heat the shells empty."

This was awkward. At CharCuties, they'd always heated the mini-tacos full. It made them less prone to shattering, which also made their youngest diners less prone to shattering. Colin said, "Sorry, I didn't realize." Again, kind of true. He kept going, though. "I guess we'll find out what happens."

She said, "I'm so sorry. I should have been clearer about what we were doing."

"I can't imagine this will destroy them." He shoved the pan into the oven and turned back to the sink.

She said, "You wash your hands after every single thing you do."

He shrugged. "It's a restaurant thing."

"Would the health department close you down if you didn't?" She didn't wait for an answer. "You must go through a gallon of hand lotion every week."

Colin laughed. "Yeah, it's rough on your skin after a while. Winters are worst."

"I can imagine." She bit her lip. "I'm sorry about the taco shells."

"It's not a big deal. I didn't even think to ask." She looked upset, and Colin just wanted to ease her anxiety. "You're doing me a favor, right?"

He felt better now than he had downstairs. It helped being in Natalie's kitchen with no expectations, just her leading him on a tour of her life. She wasn't about to demand her money back or stiff his server on the tip or complain about a food problem that didn't exist. She didn't expect anything from him at all, and for one blessed moment, he could hear someone taking genuine enjoyment in food—yes, even with that horrific taco seasoning packet that he should have lied through his teeth about and said no, they didn't have any.

"I wanted you to enjoy tacos," she said. "Oh, but that reminds me—" and she got out a clear plastic tub of guacamole. "Since you like avocados!"

Colin nearly exclaimed, "Avocados are my mortal enemy!" but he didn't because it was impossible to explain the supply and demand issues without adding, "Because I'm the one paying when they turn into compost." Instead he laughed and thanked her, and then he got the tacos out of the oven to plate them and deliver them to the table. "That dish is hot," he said by reflex, and she laughed again.

One bite, and her eyes widened. "The taco shells aren't falling apart!"

Colin said, "See? Heating them filled wasn't a disaster after all."

For a dazzling moment, the worry evaporated from Natalie's face, and she relaxed. They loaded up the tacos with lettuce and cheese and tomatoes (and yes, guacamole) and Colin enjoyed eating with her while she told him about other toppings they could have used.

He needed to cook for her. He could pull out all the stops and present her with a meal that would leave her satisfied and stunned, something she'd text her friends about and, unfortunately, her fiancé, too—although so far she hadn't even mentioned the guy. What kind of marriage

66

would that be? If Colin were ever to get married, he'd want it to be to a woman he couldn't stop thinking about. And if Colin thought about something all the time, he talked about it.

She said, "Enough about food. What about you? Where'd you grow up?"

"I grew up in Portland." He shrugged. "After I got out of school, I lived in Kennebunkport for a few years."

Natalie gestured that he should go on. "What did you do in Kennebunkport?"

"The restaurant I told you about," he said, although he hadn't exactly told her about it—just mentioned it existed. "The place was called CharCuties. It started out as three culinary graduates who wanted to pull in some quick cash over the summer before taking off to parts unknown. Add in guy number four, who owned a food truck." Colin rolled his eyes. "It already sounds like a brilliant business plan, right? Our intrepid heroes picked a tourist town out of a hat and decided on a charcuterie-themed gourmet food truck, because that makes sense, with the idea that they'd all crash in the same one-bedroom apartment and take turns working the truck and parking it outside any tourist trap or festival they could find. They even offered to hire out the truck for a whole day for people's weddings or family reunions."

Natalie laughed. "And...?"

"The most bizarre part of the story is that it worked." Colin joined her laughter. "A gourmet jack-in-the-box charcuterie food truck was a hit, so next thing you know, there was a storefront, too. Four owners, right? So the menu went in four different directions, but no one cared as long as it was charcuterie-themed. Not only that, but because a bunch of nibbles is infinitely customizable, the place ended up being a natural for families with small, picky children. Just like that, the menu ended up with options that were vegetarian, vegan, Kosher- and Halal-friendly, texture-sensitive-friendly, allergen-friendly—you name it, we could adapt to it."

Natalie said, "How'd you get in with them?"

How to finesse this? How about another true statement that in no way answered her question, but sounded like it might? "When the fearsome-foursome of founders opened the storefront, none of them had management experience, but Austin was already managing Fruits de Mer. He popped out to Kennebunkport for a couple weeks to advise. Fourteen days later, he went back to Brighthead, and I stayed."

Natalie said, "He knew one of the owners?" and Colin nodded because that was completely true.

Colin added, "A few years later, CharCuties was doing a land-office business with the truck and the storefront, and we were about to open a second restaurant in Freeport when two guys showed up with an offer that was too good to turn down. The truck and both locations got sold, and I moved up here with my brother."

She said, "How'd your brother end up here?"

This was less treacherous territory. "Austin landed a summer job at Fruits de Mer during college, and then Dale, the owner, asked him to come back after he graduated. The thing about the restaurant industry is the high turnover. You hire someone, and they're great for three months, but then they're gone." Colin shook his head. "You're constantly recruiting, but that's not entirely a bad thing. You don't want anyone to be manning a fry station for five years, right?"

Natalie said, "Servers, though?"

"Servers are different. At an upscale place like Fruits de Mer or CharCuties, servers could pull down forty dollars an hour in tips on a busy night, so they'd do just fine. There's no upward mobility, but there's cash, so they stay. The dishwasher, though? The bus boy? They need to move on and do something else. Dale pegged my brother as a long-hauler and told him if he stuck around, he'd be floor manager within six months. Austin came back after graduating, and that's what happened. Floor manager, and later general manager."

Natalie said, "And then he brought you here, so that's good."

Warm inside, Colin said, "Yeah, it is."

She said, "What does a general manager do?"

"Everything," Colin said. "You rely on your general managers when the owner's not around. They're the ones handling guest complaints, keeping an eye on the inventory, keeping the cooks from goofing off—everything. They're on their feet the whole shift, and they're basically 'you' if you're not there."

She said, "You're saying Austin should just open his own restaurant."

"After managing a restaurant for three years, Austin wants nothing to do with owning one." Austin could have been part-owner. He'd declined, saying he'd rather be free to walk away, and Colin didn't object because after years of negotiating with three other part-owners, he hungered to make all the decisions. "Anyhow, there's always job openings, and Austin gets those filled as well."

Natalie said, "Is it nepotism if Austin gets you into management?"

Colin said, "I hope not...?" and Natalie grinned.

"Well, I hope not, too. I co-own the yarn store with my cousin, remember?"

Austin and Colin were still working out the schedule, but there would always be at least one brown-haired, blue-eyed Young walking the floor at Fruits de Mer, one in a white coat and one in black. If Colin handled morning prep, then Austin could show up just before the pre-shift meeting in time to hear Colin going over the daily specials. In the lull between lunch and dinner, Colin could get out for a while, although maybe not. Fruits de Mer prepared "Family Meal" for the servers and back of house staff during the in-between time, sometimes cooked by Colin himself.

Colin might step out during Family Meal, otherwise he'd be in the building eighty hours a week, six in the morning to midnight, six days a week, with no reprieve. You don't get sick days, a professor had lectured everyone during culinary school. With four owners at CharCuties, they'd split it all up among themselves. No floor managers, just each other, and even at that, they'd all pulled fifty- to sixty-hour weeks.

No wonder after twenty years, Dale wanted to get out.

Colin said, "So it's you and your cousin, and one employee. And your boyfriend?"

She shook her head. "No boyfriend."

"Fiancé," he corrected. "Sorry."

She held up her left hand. "No fiancé."

He frowned. "Do you or do you not have a maid of honor you keep talking about? Or do I wake up every morning hearing you sing to your ladies in waiting?"

She met his eyes, puzzled, then laughed. "The maid of honor! I have to tell you this story!"

While they devoured taco after taco, she spun out a crazy tale about yarn purchased by well-meaning friends who were circumventing one another and had no idea what they were doing—but through it all there was love, and Natalie was delighted by it. Delighted that the bride had such good friends. Delighted that a man wanted to make his wife happy by pleasing her friend. Delighted for every one of them.

The light in Natalie's eyes made her beautiful. "Meanwhile, Lilah was gushing about wanting a husband who'd go that far out of his way to spend extra money on yarn."

Colin only heard, *this gorgeous woman is not attached.*

That opened the field right up.

He could have tacos with Natalie and not constrain himself to thinking about how pleasant it was to have a friend in Brighthead. He could laugh and maybe flirt. They could find a spare hour when his restaurant wasn't demanding his time so he could watch TV with her, or talk, or cuddle. That was way far ahead of where they were right now—but she wasn't dating anyone.

She could be dating him.

She already enjoyed herself with him. It wasn't that far of a leap to just keep showing up. Keep being here and cooking with her.

After dinner, he washed her dishes, tingling every time she reached around him to lift something off the dish rack. Facing into the sink, he enjoyed her voice and her movement, and he slowed the process because he didn't want it to end. After he fished the last fork out of the basin, he dumped out the water and laid the dishcloth across the faucet.

She made her own dishcloths. The dish towels were crocheted as well. Bright colors, intricate designs, and wow, they worked well. They could even scrub glass.

Natalie said, "Now that you're fed and rested, do you want help opening boxes?"

About to say, "Sure," Colin stopped with his throat closed tight and his eyes burning. Instead, he said, "I'm not going to look at the mess now."

The minute she opened a box, she'd figure him out. She'd look at the high-end cookware or get one glimpse at the books and say, "What's all this?" She'd wonder momentarily if this was Austin's gear. She'd hunt for the best interpretation and think maybe Austin had upgraded his own stuff and dumped his excess on Colin.

Then she'd figure out the truth, and hard on the heels of cooking tacos together, she'd be disgusted and say, "What a waste of time."

Colin didn't want to disgust her. He wanted to keep talking to her.

She gestured to the steps. "Just a couple of boxes. It'll go faster with two."

She was right, unfortunately. But without any way of keeping her from the boxes marked "kitchen" or "living room," he couldn't accept.

"I'm planning to move out of this building in a month," Colin said.

Natalie smiled brightly. "The cool thing about boxes is you can put things back in them. Living out of boxes for a whole month would be wicked depressing."

She had a point. And yet. "Tonight, I'm just going to figure out how to set up my TV so I can zone out."

She didn't say anything for a moment, then ventured, "Do you want to watch something up here? My TV's already set up."

Equally uncertain, Colin said, "What would you want to watch?"

Between the two of them, they had the regular assortment of streaming services. Colin suggested a sitcom called Corner Gas on the grounds that it was funny...and it wasn't a romance. Although it involved a restaurant owner, and that was getting a little too close for comfort. Natalie said, "I've never seen it," and Colin replied, "You're in for a treat!"

A sitcom wasn't going to send her into his arms, and right now, Colin needed to back right off. All the way off. He was new in town and missing his friends from Kennebunkport, overworked and overwhelmed. Natalie was sweet and helpful and innocent, and he had no right to make any moves on her. None. If he could predict which end of the couch she'd be sitting on, he'd go sit on the opposite side.

While she was setting up, Colin picked up a twisty thing of yarn. "What are you making with this?"

She turned. "I'm making nothing with that right now. I think it would make a nice pair of fingerless gloves, don't you?"

"Then why is it out? Oh, because you've got yarn all over the place." He meandered from furniture to furniture, picking up yarn twists. "Natalie, I don't know how to say this, but I think you have a problem."

"My problem is that it takes five minutes to buy a hank of yarn, and five hours to crochet it up." She pointed to the one in his hand. "Stroke that. It's soft and squishy. How can I say no to soft and squishy?"

He pointed to the guinea pig cage. "Is that how you ended up with those, too?"

"Their owner was getting rid of them because his kid had allergies."

Colin said, "And the anoles?"

"College kid was going back to school and couldn't take them with him."

Colin sat on the edge of the couch, stroking the yarn. "You collect unwanted things. Me included."

"The yarn is very much wanted. It's just that there's always something else to make."

Colin tossed her the yarn twist. "Make this next."

She laughed. "I'm making hats for the homeless, and this isn't the right type of yarn."

"Nat, I'm promising you this from the bottom of my heart. There will always be unfortunate people who need hats and scarves. You, on the other hand, deserve a nice pair of fingerless gloves made of squishy yarn, and there's only one of you. If you don't make them, you'll never have them."

She hesitated as if she couldn't speak, then looked away quickly. "Well, I feel like for me it's a luxury, but for other people it's a necessity."

Colin pointed to the yarn in her hands. "You bought it for yourself, right? Natalie in the past knew that Future Natalie deserved something luxurious. Go get your hook."

She set the yarn back on the shelf and got the show started. "I need to finish a scarf first, and anyhow, it's not that simple. I'd have to wind the yarn and pick out a pattern."

He said, "I'll wait."

She replied, "What else would you like to learn to cook?"

Colin shrank back into his seat. Maybe pushing her to make something for herself was some sort of fiber arts social error. He couldn't code-switch with her. She was uncomfortable with the subject, but he hadn't thought he was pushing her. Fumbling in his brain, he said, "Can we make pizza?"

Pizza would take time. They'd be working together. There were plenty of techniques for her to demonstrate to him, and he could watch her moving as she made it. He added, "I can figure out the ingredients for that. Dough and sauce and cheese. What day?"

"You're off Mondays, so how about next Monday?" and just like that, they had an appointment.

A cooking lesson. Not a date, as such.

The show started, and she sat on the far side of the couch, watching and hooking in and out of the fabric. And laughing. So much laughter. It erased the tension that had overtaken her when he asked her to crochet for herself.

Colin kept sneaking looks at Natalie.

She was gorgeous. She was single, and she lived right upstairs.

Also, she was the most honest person he knew, and he couldn't figure out how not to keep lying to her.

CHAPTER NINE

Wow, Colin.

Wow, wow, wow, Colin. Natalie kept thinking about Colin on Tuesday as she opened the store. He'd left his apartment at six-thirty in the morning, and it bugged her how the management at that restaurant was going to work him to death. Unless he was coming back mid-morning and heading out again before she got home, he was working very long days. Did restaurants have to pay overtime? The waitstaff didn't even get minimum wage.

Natalie straightened the shelves and repositioned the gifts in the local craft section. Lilah had brought in a group of tiny paintings on miniature easels, and they each carried a hefty price tag. They'd go in a heartbeat once tourism season started, but for now, they were taking up space because if you lived in Brighthead, you weren't looking for a miniature painting of the Brighthead lighthouse or the Brighthead statue, aka Myth Brightman. In fact, the people most likely to be able to afford these paintings would be the folks living on Skyline Drive, and they could see the lighthouse for real by looking out their picture windows.

Colin.

Stop. Not now. There were also beaded earrings for sale, plus pictures made from sand and seashells and sea glass. All of that glitz in the window would draw tourists into the shop come summer. For now, it would have to rest.

Lilah danced into the shop and first thing, exclaimed, "Oh, good!" before snatching three skeins of tonal green yarn from her own display. "An order came in last night, and they'll pay extra for rush shipping. I'm glad this didn't sell yet."

Natalie said, "I'll take it off the inventory."

"I'll handle it. Oh, sorry," Lilah said as the door jangled again. "I forgot to re-lock it. We're not open yet."

It was one of their regular customers, Gertie, an elderly woman who lived three blocks away with her daughter. "I know, but I was wondering if I could get you to finish this for me."

Natalie flinched. Finishing work was such a pain, but Gertie's eyesight was so bad that while she could knit, she couldn't do the final work of weaving in the yarn ends to make them disappear into the project.

Lilah said, "Natalie's busy today. She can't do it."

"Oh, there's no rush. I keep making these shawls for the folks over at the nursing home because they get cold, and they love having something handmade." With a muffled thump, she dumped a bag of knitted shawls onto the Sit and Stitch table. "I'll come back for them next week."

Natalie sighed. But still, it was for a customer. It was for a good cause. And Gertie couldn't do it herself.

Lilah ushered Gertie back outside and pointedly locked the door at her back. With the gift section dusted, Natalie went to look at the shawls, and she groaned. "Seriously?"

Every piece of yarn has two ends: that's a given with a yarn project. The crafter has to do something with the ends—also a given. If the project gets big enough, the project goes into a second skein, which means four ends, or six ends for three skeins. If the crafter changes colors, there are two ends for every color change.

Gertie had worked up four shawls in the zig-zaggy diamonds of entrelac knitting, with each row a different color.

Natalie noticed a dropped stitch, and she picked up the shawl to get a better look. She could repair a dropped stitch, sure, but that meant using some of the leftover yarn tail after weaving it in. And of course, Gertie had snipped the ends within two inches every time. That was barely long enough to get it woven in, and not enough to secure the dropped stitches.

Lilah came over to Natalie. "Give them back to her. Tell her you can't."

"It's for the nursing home."

"This is ridiculous. She knew she couldn't weave in all those ends. She has to know she's dropping stitches when entrelac requires turning the work every few stitches. She doesn't care because she made it your problem. Make it her problem again."

Natalie said, "And then who's going to do it for her?"

"Not your issue to solve." Lilah huffed. "You know what? No, I'm going to make it Brooke's issue. If you won't stand up for yourself, Brooke will do it."

Natalie said, "Don't be cruel to Gertie. She can't see."

"She can see well enough to knit. She needs to knit in a straight line and leave a long enough yarn tail for you to weave it in. I know she's been told that before because I'm one of the people who told her." Lilah sat down with an address label. "It's not cruel to tell people they need to clean up their own messes."

Colin cleaned up his own messes. That was so weird, but maybe it was a restaurant thing, like washing his hands all the time: he scrubbed dishes while in the act of cooking. He insisted on washing up afterward, too. Yet, he'd refused to let her go into his apartment to help him unpack.

Natalie looked through the shawls, each with more ends than a can of worms, and all those ends short. Plus, a few dropped stitches on every one.

Lilah added, "She doesn't even buy her yarn from us."

"She's on a fixed income."

Lilah snorted. "As opposed to you, who print money?"

Natalie set the shawls to the side because at work, her time belonged to the shop. She'd take care of these later.

Colin, though. Colin had wanted Natalie to make something for herself, and she'd balked because it felt selfish when there were so many people who needed things. Why, last night while watching three episodes of Corner Gas (and laughing a whole lot) she'd nearly finished the scarf to coordinate with the hat she'd made earlier. It was warm and wonderful, and someone down on her luck would smile to wear it.

Colin had said, "Yes, but won't you smile to wear those gloves you were talking about?"

To which Natalie had replied, "We should make a list of everything you'll want to cook."

Natalie hadn't had a man in her apartment in six months. Well, excluding Denny the landlord and Gus the insect assassin. She'd broken up with her last boyfriend because he never paid attention to her, whereas last night, Colin paid her lots of attention. Was that just his way? Or was he attracted to her?

Because gosh, that guy? She sure was attracted to him. His shoulders were broad and strong. Whatever he did in that kitchen, he did it a lot. Lifting sacks of potatoes or cases of wine must do wonders for the biceps and shoulders. He was so fluid in the way he moved when he felt comfortable with something, although he fumbled things unexpectedly, like her can opener.

He'd sat at the farthest corner of her couch as though he wanted to stack all her knives between them for protection, but then he'd stretched out those long legs, crossed at the ankle, leaned back, and hooked his arm over the back of the couch. On the opposite side, Natalie tried to keep her eyes on the television because she'd invited him over to relax, not to make him participate in an impromptu episode of The Bachelor.

Bright Stitches opened, and a customer arrived with a skein of yarn in an infinite tangle. Natalie exchanged the ruined skein for an unruined one, then took the new one over to their swift and ball winder. "Why don't I just take care of winding that for you?"

They charged three dollars to wind yarn, but today she didn't because it was worth her time not to end up with a second skein to detangle and then put in the discount bin or else damage out.

Natalie glanced at the damaged skein and wondered, though. Would that make a nice pair of fingerless gloves? Maybe not. It was underspun, so it wouldn't stand up to sustained friction. The yarn at home was much better, plus she loved its color—a soft cream speckled with blue and pink.

Gertie's shawls ought to get done, but Natalie bundled them into a box and set them aside. Instead, she vacuumed and dusted, and she set up the coffee maker. She made the crafting nook more welcoming and straightened the needle and hook display.

Brooke arrived in the store at noon, cheeks pink from the chill and her brown eyes bright. She pulled off her coat but left on her fingerless gloves. "Okay, guys, tell me something good!"

Lilah said, "Twenty-five people signed up for the crafting group already, and they're putting out the word for more! They love the concept."

Brooke shook her head. "They love the concept until it's time to do the work."

"I've got a few volunteers already. A graphic designer mocked up a couple of logos, although without a final name that's a challenge. Another guy built us a landing page on a free website, that way we can start driving traffic to the group's social media. And before you ask," she added, eyes bright, "we already have accounts on four platforms."

Brooke opened her hands. "I stand corrected. Apparently, they love both the concept and the work."

Lilah turned to Brooke. "Also, the shop needs a new rule. We need to charge for finishing and blocking. If you want to know who the people are who don't want to do work, it's the customers who keep dumping their projects on Natalie and expecting her to weave in their ends or block their lace, and it's getting ridiculous. Gertie came at nine carrying a thousand shawls with dropped stitches and all the ends knotted up and snipped off, which she expects Natalie to fix for her by the end of next week."

Natalie sighed. "Four shawls, and she's old."

"Old enough that she should know better." Lilah folded her arms. "I'm dead serious. Fifteen dollar charge for blocking, twenty-five for weaving in ends—and no weaving in ends on colorwork because people bring in things that look like millipedes. I know how long that takes."

Brooke frowned. "Give them back. I've already told her I won't do them anymore because she cuts the ends too close and drops stitches in the middle."

Natalie glanced at the pile in the bag. "They're for people at the nursing home. It brings them joy and comfort. How can I say no?"

Brooke said, "Watch," and pivoted her head side to side. "Grandma taught me a long time ago, and that's how it works. No."

Lilah said, "Every single thing you say yes to is something else you have to say no to."

Like a pretty pair of fingerless gloves.

"Think about a project you'd really like to make, and then compare it to Gertie's self-made disaster that she dumped in your lap." Brooke lifted the top shawl out of the box. "Literally dumped it."

Natalie could crochet something for Colin.

Colin would need dish towels and dishcloths. He probably had no idea you had to wash sponges or else they became bacteria farms. She had a huge spool of kitchen cotton in her stash, so she could make him a set for his own kitchen.

Lilah said, "If you're looking for something to give all

your time to, the crafting guild will take all of it, and more."

Natalie sighed. "Point taken. But Gertie's going to be upset if I don't do hers."

"Boo-hoo." Brooke walked to the register. "I'm not going to cry into my soup."

Soup. Natalie could teach Colin to make soup. Real chicken soup with carrots and celery and lots of garlic, and maybe homemade bread. They could eat in front of the television and watch more of that series, and he'd be right there, in her apartment.

She'd heard him get up this morning to get his shower while she huddled beneath her comforter. His alarm was a series of outer space sounds. He was getting up extra early in order to avoid cutting off her shower water.

It was thoughtful. It was a sacrifice for him.

She could sacrifice for him, too. She could make things for his kitchen.

CHAPTER TEN

Pizza dough, it turned out, required more coordination than Colin had anticipated when he'd blurted it out. He didn't want to buy pre-made dough, although that would have worked out okay. It needed to rise. He also wasn't sure if he could get away with turning up on Natalie's doorstep with a bowl of perfectly risen dough.

He texted her on Sunday during the lull between lunch and dinner. "Dough needs to rise, so I'll buy the ingredients and work out that part myself."

She replied, "Flour, sugar, water, oil, salt, yeast. I've got all that, and I'll get it started."

Colin didn't want to cost her anything, but the dough ingredients couldn't possibly add up to more than two dollars. Well, maybe more if she bought flour in one-pound packages and individual packets of yeast. Even so, not enough to break the bank. Colin was bringing everything else. Speaking of which...

He texted, "Before you reply, please be warned that I take everyone at their word when I ask this question: what toppings should go on the pizza, and what toppings should not?"

She replied, "You want me not to say that I don't care and anything is fine?"

He chuckled. "Really most emphatically not."

She texted, "Fine. Be that way."

He could have fun with this if, despite his dire warning, she went ahead and said she didn't care. "Oh, this was in the back of the walk-in at Fruits de Mer," he'd say, "so I figured I'd try it on a pizza," then dump a bucket of calamari tubes and tentacles into her sink.

What would pair well with calamari?

She texted, "Mushrooms are good. Not a fan of peppers. No pepperoni. Meatballs are okay but complicated to make. Olives?"

He replied, "I hear and obey."

She sent back a laughing emoji.

Then she added, "I should be home around four."

Was she looking forward to seeing him? Was she thinking about him even half as often as he was thinking about her? Would she keep checking the clock on Monday the same way he'd keep glancing out the window at her parking spot?

Austin walked by and chucked him in the shoulder. "I hope you're looking like that about our financial projections."

Colin shoved his phone in his pocket. "*Our* financial projections?"

"Fruits de Mer is like a family. *Our* financial projections, so *we* can keep *our* jobs, and *we* are not updating *our* resumes." Austin headed to the computer. "Alex just called in that he can't do his shift tonight, so we need to rejigger the schedule."

"I'll cover his station." Colin stretched. "Also, I'm thinking of doing something fun for Family Meal. What restaurants around here might want to do a dinner swap?"

Austin studied him. "A what?"

"You know, we cook Family Meal for their staff and they bring Family Meal for ours, and everyone gets a change of pace."

Baffled, Austin said, "Is that a thing?"

Colin shrugged. "It was in Kennebunkport. There's no reason it can't be a thing here, too."

"Sparrows is the other good-ish restaurant in town. Might be worth a shot. There's also the burger place on Main, but they're nowhere near our caliber."

"You mean they make 'real food'?" Oh, right, Austin wasn't in on that joke. "Even so, they might not mind swapping one night. First see if you can track down the owner of Sparrows."

Colin headed into the office. Austin followed, then shut the door. "Who is she?"

Colin stopped in place.

"We started out as the same zygote, idiot." Austin stepped closer. "I know that look, and you haven't had it for a good long time. Who is she?"

Colin faced his brother. "Not an employee, and not a customer. You may never meet her, either, because she isn't... Well, nothing's happened."

Austin sat on the edge of the desk. "Things don't simply happen. You have to make something happen."

Colin flinched. "It's awkward and wild and weird, and I think I've already messed it up."

"You're such a disaster. Move on her." Austin smirked at him. "Haven't we agreed it's a slam-dunk to get a first date if you comp her meal?"

Colin raised his eyebrows. "Doesn't work if she hates Fruits de Mer."

Austin frowned. "That's a challenge."

"Hating Fruits de Mer was the first thing she said to me."

Austin stuck out his hand. "Hi! I'm Jane Doe, and I hate Fruits de Mer! Weird introduction, but I like her already." When Colin laughed, Austin added, "Here's what you do. You bring her for Family Meal on the day I arrange the food swap, and then you can both comp her meal and not subject her to our terrible food."

Colin's eyebrows shot up. "Brilliant! I knew there was a

reason you're the smart twin."

Austin shook his head. "You're too besotted to be any good around here until you get that resolved. Either she'll fall in love with your food, or else she'll slam the door in your face and you can forget about her. But move on her. Do it today."

Besotted?

Every few weeks, Colin used to have the pleasure of escorting a drunken patron to the CharCuties lobby where he and two big guys from the kitchen would stand guard until that person's ride arrived. The whole time, the patron would be unable to think of anything more than his favorite liquid poison.

It hadn't happened yet at Fruits de Mer, but it would, and Colin would need to figure out which of his staff could back him up. According to Dale, Bill had come to the restaurant ten years ago as a work-release from prison, and he'd liked cooking enough that he'd made sure never to go back. Bill had the build and the glower (and the non-skid shoes) to sober a drunk right up.

No one could sober up Colin. Colin thought about Natalie on the drive home Sunday night, and also when he awoke Monday mid-morning. First thing, he reached for his phone to see if she'd texted.

He should have gone back to sleep, but he needed to know. Ten-fifteen. The yarn shop would be open. She'd be thinking about yarns and hooks and patterns, and he was thinking about her.

His breath caught as the lockscreen registered a message, and it also had a photo. He clicked it open, and there was a bowl of dough. Alongside it was one of her handmade dish towels.

He smiled. She'd captioned it, "Tucking it into a warm place with a blanket so it will rise and get airy."

He could have done that for her. Instead she'd mixed and kneaded the dough in her precious minutes between waking up and heading to work.

He had to tell her. This wasn't fair.

Instead he replied, "I can endorse being tucked into a warm place with a blanket." Monday was his only day to catch up on sleep, but his heart was racing.

Today he'd unpack enough to live not-in-squalor until the other apartment opened. Every item incriminated him, from the high-end cookware to the cookbooks to the instructional DVDs to the business management books. Even his artwork. He had posters from Paris and Rome with sumptuous meals in a hand-drawn style. For crying out loud, he had a framed, hand-drawn menu by Jacques Pépin. He'd never pass this off as anything other than what it was.

He hung the artwork in his bedroom where the previous tenants had thoughtfully left nails in the walls. Natalie wouldn't be going in here, at least, and if she ever did get in here, she'd already know the truth by then. Likewise, he tucked a bookshelf into the bedroom and left all the management books and the cookbooks on those shelves.

There was nothing to do about the kitchen, but it had a lot of storage space. He'd leave most of it boxed, and what he really needed could stay in its place all the time. She might not be able to price out cookware at a glance, and he'd hide the oddments he'd picked up here and there. It wouldn't be for long. Just until he could get her relaxed and happy enough that he could say, "There's a misunderstanding I need to clear up."

He glanced out the window, and her car was in its parking spot. Colin's pulse doubled.

The sound of the outer door. The rusty clang of her mail slot opening. Five steps to his apartment. A tentative knock.

He opened the door and beamed the second he saw her.

"You're home!"

"I'm home! Come up whenever you're ready." Her head tilted. "Let's see if the dough did what it was supposed to while I was away."

Her eyes, her hair, her smile. His brain whirled. "I'll get the ingredients and follow in a bit."

She looked like she was about to wait, but Colin shooed her. "I'm not going to make you carry anything. Give me three minutes. You were working all day."

She gestured toward the flattened moving boxes. "As if you weren't?"

He made a pssht with his lips. "I'm working for myself. It's different."

Natalie shrugged. "Working for yourself, you work harder."

Once she was out, he gathered what had to go upstairs, noticing everything she'd have noticed if she were standing behind him. He did have a nice kitchen. After he cleared things up, he'd invite her down here to cook for her. Despite the ancient appliances, he'd dazzle and impress her as if he were Austin, and he'd offer her anything she wanted.

She'd left her door open, so he stepped into her tiny afterthought kitchen. "Hello?" She was in one of the other two rooms, and as with his bedroom, he assumed hers was off limits. He unloaded the sauce and cheese and toppings onto the counter.

She reappeared. "You got the good stuff. I usually just buy generic."

Colin said, "I tried to use my judgment," and she assured him that was fine. "Also, I robbed the restaurant kitchen for these." He pulled a bunch of carrot tops out of the bag. "Propitiation for your guinea pigs."

She laughed. "Will they eat that?"

"I'm told they'll adore that." Colin brought the carrot greens to the guinea pig cage and held them just at the edge, and within seconds the pair of excited, whining guinea pigs had tugged the entire bunch inside and were chowing down.

Natalie's eyes were huge. "That is not something that would have occurred to me."

"If the restaurant considers it trash, and the guinea pigs consider it gourmet, who am I to judge?" Colin stood. "Did the dough do what it was supposed to?"

"I waited for you to check it." Natalie opened the oven door, and there was her metal bowl, covered with her peach towel. "Ready?"

As he stood next to her at the table, she lifted back the towel so he could see the soft, rounded dough where it had grown while waiting in its secret and hidden place. Kind of the same thing Colin's feelings had been doing.

"Looks good," he said. She was right next to him.

Move on her, Austin had said. Prompt her and get a response.

Natalie winked at him. "I was worried that maybe I'd done it wrong, and then I'd have to teach you the best place in town to order pizza."

Colin arched his eyebrows. "I have the equipment, too. Unlimited calling!"

"They have a website, so you wouldn't even have to talk to them, other than tipping the driver." She turned, and again, she was so close. Austin's advice sounded really good. "I like to punch the dough down once more and then let it rise again, but that will take another forty-five minutes. If you're starving, we can skip that step."

And pass up an extra forty-five minutes with Natalie? "Let's do it the right way."

She wiped down the table, floured it, and upended the bowl. If she noticed him staring at her as she got her hands into the dough, at least Colin had an excuse to be watching. "That's your kneading technique, is it?"

She said, "Kneading distributes everything inside the dough, and that makes it rise better."

Kneading actually changed the structure of the gluten strands in order to affect the consistency and enable it to hold its shape better. He kept his mouth shut.

Natalie added, "I like to fold it like this, and push it, then turn it and fold it again."

She had a nice rhythm. Push, push, push. Pause, turn. Push, push, push. Her hips and shoulders were in motion as she worked the dough, and she had just a little bit of flour on her cheek.

What would Austin do here? The suave twin. The attractive twin.

While working, Natalie said, "Do you want to try?"

Colin stepped behind her and reached around either side, putting his hands on top of hers She went still, and he leaned forward, getting right behind her and then pushing forward into the dough. He could smell her skin, her hair. He closed his eyes, feeling her hands beneath his and the dough beneath hers, her body against his, his heartbeat steady even though he was afraid to breathe.

"Like this?" he managed.

She kneaded forward, and yes, she was right there, her fingers woven up into his, tugging him gently against her back. Then she pushed back into him.

He couldn't think. This was a lot, and way too quick. He hadn't thought it through, how close he'd be to her.

In a small voice, she said, "Yes. Like that."

He stepped back, dizzy with her presence and all that contact, yet hungering to do it again. "I'm sorry. That was uncalled for. You're being nice, and—"

She rested her forearms over his shoulders, and then she kissed him.

His hands were floury. Hers were oily. She kissed him without touching, and he had no idea what to do because he didn't want to put his hands on her waist and get flour all over her, too.

As she stepped back, he stared with wide eyes. She said, "Don't apologize."

A smile burned inside him. "You're okay? We're okay?"

She looked aside, and it was sweet, and it was shy, and it was perfect. "I'm okay."

Colin fought to keep his voice steady. "Then let's finish

kneading, because I'd really like to kiss you again. The right way."

CHAPTER ELEVEN

Colin kneaded that dough for five minutes straight while Natalie watched his fluid motions and his mischievous smile.

He said, "Remember what I said about telling me, 'Oh, anything's fine'? In a few minutes, I'm going to be done with the dough, and I'm going to ask if you mind if I kiss you again."

Natalie folded her arms. "Is that so?"

"If you tell me to choose for you...?" He shrugged. "I know what I'm choosing."

She said, "Once again, I consider myself warned."

Colin was magnificent. It had to be an interplay of hormones and infatuation and excitement, but he looked really good kneading pizza dough at her table. He would have looked good shoveling a ditch. Natalie's whole body still tingled from having him come up behind her like that.

She sat across the table and looked at him while he looked at her, although every so often he looked down at the dough.

She said, "Do you kiss everyone who teaches you how to cook?"

"That would be weird. I did kiss my mother," Colin added. "Pizza dough undoes my self-restraint. All that yeast action with the flour, plus it's pretty darned cute that you tucked it in to rest with a handmade blanket."

Natalie said, "You're supposed to cover it to rise."

Colin looked away from her, smiling shyly. "I thought you wanted it to sleep in privacy."

"The pilot light in the oven gives off a little heat, and that keeps it warm."

"I don't think—" Colin stopped himself, then said, "No matter how tired I've gotten at work, I've never tried to nap inside the oven."

He returned the dough to the bowl, then laid the towel over it again. "You do amazing crochet work. It feels like a waste to turn it into dish towels."

Natalie flinched. "Why? They work great."

Colin set the bowl back inside the oven. "You crocheted them with care and beauty, and then you drench them in hot water and scrub greasy pans."

Natalie said, "If, on the other hand, I crochet them with hatred and fear, they cut grease on contact."

Colin burst out laughing as he washed his hands. "I need to remember that the next time I'm on dish duty."

"Do they make you wash dishes?"

He looked uncomfortable. "I do a bit of everything in the back of the house. If dishes need doing, I'll do them." He returned to her and gave a wicked little grin. "Have you considered the question I asked before?"

Natalie narrowed her eyes and looked up. "About whether you could kiss me again?"

"The right way," Colin said. "Not full of flour and confusion."

Natalie stood and looked up into his face. "Were you confused? You didn't seem to be."

"Entirely bluster on my part." He slipped one arm around her waist and put the other on her shoulder. "But if you want me to try again, I'll do better."

She tilted her head, and he fingered the ends of her hair

at her waist, then slipped his hand up her back toward her neck, until he ended up cradling her head with his fingers in her hair. He looked both excited and disbelieving. Natalie yielded to the very slight pressure until she was closer, and he brought his lips to hers.

"Better?" he whispered.

Warm all over, Natalie replied, "I had no complaints before."

He held her so strongly. It was the embrace she'd hoped for—firm, but gentle. He must be hefting and pushing and lifting things all day. Now he was holding her, and he was all warmth. He smelled faintly of aftershave, and in that moment, he surrounded her.

He gave a nervous laugh. "The complaints department will be relieved."

She said, "I'm not going to leave a bad review."

"Five out of five," Colin said, giving a little squeeze before letting her go. "Would kiss again."

He had a look in his eyes that she couldn't decode, whether it was nervousness or relief.

In silence and darkness, the pizza dough rose for forty-five minutes while Natalie and Colin talked on the couch. They talked about everything—and it was amazing and fun and easy.

"Tell me about working in a restaurant," she said, her arm stretched along the back of the couch so she could join her fingers with Colin's. "What's the wildest thing that ever happened to you?"

Colin said, "There was the old veteran at CharCuties who stood up when we had a ball game on TV. Got right to his feet and shouted at the entire dining area that they were playing the national anthem, so everyone had to stand out of respect to the flag."

Natalie exclaimed, "Did they?"

"So help me, they did. Everyone in the front of house stood and laid their hands over their hearts and waited in silence until the anthem was over. Then the guy complained that the waiter had just stood there while his meal was getting cold." Colin's eyes sparked. "That was a day."

She said, "People will complain about anything."

He rolled his eyes. "Hungry people who don't want to pay full price will gripe about more than anything. We're constantly tasting in the kitchens to make sure everything is just right, but then someone wants a discount because their chair wobbled or they asked for no ice and their soda arrived with no ice in it."

She said, "What do you do then?"

"When they eat the whole hamburger and then want a refund because it tasted terrible? We tell them to either give back the food or to get lost." He shrugged. "You figure out early in the conversation who's a comp scavenger and who's genuinely disappointed. For the disappointed customers, you'd be shocked at how thoroughly free cake equates to an apology." His eyes glinted. "The comp scavengers? They'll demand the whole meal free plus a discount for every member of their extended family."

Natalie said, "After they're done with you, they come to the yarn shop and return the yarn they refused to have us wind, but they tried to wind it and turned it into a Gordian knot."

Colin sighed. "I was hoping a yarn store wouldn't have to deal with those people."

"Well, I'm the owner, so I have to deal with these people. At least you don't have to face them down when they're screaming at you."

Colin recoiled. "Screaming? About yarn?"

Natalie rolled her eyes. "A couple of years ago, I got blindsided by what they called 'minkgate,' where an expensive yarn was tagged as one hundred percent mink, but in actuality it contained zero percent mink. Customers brought it back demanding refunds, angry at me as if I were the one who mislabeled it."

Colin shifted a bit closer. "That's disgusting. Crocheting is a hobby. People shouldn't be screaming about a hobby."

Natalie said, "By the same token, Fruits de Mer is high-end food, and not one of your customers is starving."

Colin said, "Do you still think Fruits de Mer is just an overpriced lunch for a tourist?"

Natalie flinched. "You're never going to let me forget that, are you?"

Colin looked abruptly uncomfortable. "What would convert you into a fan?"

"I haven't seen anything that would change my mind." Natalie averted her eyes and pulled back her hand. "I'm a believer in facts, and the facts I've seen are the menu, and —sorry. I know you moved here for them."

He waved her down. "All right, all right."

This wasn't good conversational territory, so Natalie went to the kitchen to check on the dough. "It's rising again. What did you bring for toppings?"

Colin followed. "Mushrooms. Black olives. I avoided pepperoni. I did get ham." He unloaded everything from the paper bag, then handed her a jar of sauce. "What needs doing first?"

The olives came out of a can, but the mushrooms were actual mushrooms. "We need to fry those first," Natalie said. "Can you wash and slice them?"

Colin saluted. "Ma'am, I'm a professional. Consider it done."

She did peek into the fridge to make sure the cheese didn't need to be shredded, but he'd bought pre-shredded mozzarella. He'd also bought a little baggie of grated parmesan, and that was cute. Smiling, she opened the sauce and started it warming, then got the pans she'd use for pizza—well, one pizza stone, and one cookie sheet. "I'm not exactly a brick oven pizzeria, so this isn't going to be great."

"We're doing this together. How could it not be great?" Colin beamed at her. "And as you said, we have phones and the ability to order online. We'll be fine."

Natalie got out her rolling pin, but a thought kept nagging in her head: if Colin wanted to change her mind about Fruits de Mer, why wasn't he offering to bring her there? Maybe that was a no-no in the restaurant business, that you don't eat at the place you worked? Her friends who worked fast food never wanted to walk back in the door after they were done. Some of them had stepped in for a soda only to end up saddled with an extra shift.

Also, after she'd teased him about the takeout, it made sense he wouldn't bring her any.

Finally, the worst thought: what if the restaurant didn't pay him enough to eat the food, let alone take someone else?

Natalie said, "Do you think you might want to work somewhere other than Fruits de Mer?"

Colin straightened. "What?"

"You work long hours, and you don't get a lot of recognition." It couldn't possibly pay that much, not if he was living here. "You told me last time about turnover, how you don't want anyone to be a dishwasher forever. That means you don't want to wash dishes forever either." She looked up. "Or are you doing what you said your brother started out doing, floor manager?"

Colin didn't look at her. "I do some of the same work, but I'm not the floor manager."

He'd finished washing mushrooms and now took her knife to them. He cut in a way she'd never seen anyone do, rocking the knife on its front quarter and flashing it up and down while he moved the mushrooms through, all the while keeping his fingers protected from the blade. And he wanted to use a sharper blade? When he was working that fast? She didn't want to speak in case she distracted him, but the more he chopped, the more she thought, *His brother is taking advantage of him. His brother is relying on him to pick up the gaps while getting paid the higher salary and keeping the job title.*

It wasn't like that with her and Brooke. Natalie and Brooke had sat down before buying the business from Mom and broken down exactly what it would look like to co-own a shop. Brooke had insisted on a business plan with regulations and scheduled hours. That was just how Brooke did things. Brooke loved rules and schedules, and she was a whiz at math—all of which combined to make her a formidable pattern designer, but Natalie had thought it would make her a lousy business owner.

To Natalie's surprise, Mom had agreed with Brooke. "I don't want you doing too much, sweetie," was all Mom had said. Brooke had added, "You need to leave fifty percent of the work for me to do," which wasn't a fair assumption at all. Natalie liked being useful, and Brooke would never take advantage of her.

Colin, however, was being nothing but useful to his brother, and in return his brother was pressing him into hundred-hour work weeks. Natalie had added up the hours between when she heard Colin leave in the morning and when the front door awakened her in the middle of the night. Even if he napped between lunch and dinner, how could he survive on that? Shouldn't it be illegal to work an hourly employee to death? After forty hours, Colin should be getting overtime. With a hundred hours a week, even at minimum wage, with sixty hours of that as overtime, why wasn't he living on Sky Ridge Drive?

He split those mushrooms in nice even rows, doing it twice as well as Natalie in half the time. Then she showed him how to butter the pan and get them cooked up. He'd bought cremini mushrooms. It was cute. She hadn't told him which ones to pick out, so he'd picked anything.

He deserved better than to be worked to death. "If you weren't working for your brother, you'd be working fewer hours. You might get paid better."

"I'm happy where I am." Colin stirred the mushrooms in the pan. "I did long hours at CharCuties, too."

She said, "If you're not salaried, they need to be paying

you overtime."

Colin looked startled. "Nat, I promise, this isn't an issue. Don't go to the labor board."

That sounded more final than she liked, so she opened the can of olives rather than subject Colin to the humiliation of not being able to work the can opener.

He needed an advocate. He wasn't going to step up to make sure he got what he deserved.

She showed him how to roll out the pizza dough, which led to more flirting and him reaching around from behind her to put his hands over hers on the rolling pin. His breath crept along the line of her jaw, and his presence was intoxicating. He murmured, "I had no idea pizza was this much fun."

He was all over her, and Natalie tensed. "Watch out before I poke you with the rolling pin."

He backed off. "Sorry! I should have asked."

Tingling, Natalie said, "I didn't mean— Well, yeah, I did mean that."

Colin raised his hands. "I'm sorry. We haven't even gone on a date, so I need to slow down." When he smiled, though, it was sweet. "Tell me where to take you because I don't know what's good around here. I know where *not* to take you."

Yeah, because Natalie might have it out with the owner.

She spread the sauce on one of the pizzas, then handed him the spoon to cover the other. Repeat with the cheese. Then they distributed the toppings, including his sprinkled parmesan, By then, the oven had pre-heated.

Colin said, "You don't heat the stone first?"

Natalie said, "I'm not sure how I'd get the pizza onto the stone if it was already hot."

He shrugged. "Well, let's get these in there."

"One at a time." She laughed. "I also don't have a coal-fired brick oven, in case you weren't sure."

"Come to think of it, I'd noticed the lack of fire and smoke." Colin gestured to the oven. "Show me how it's done."

He was so effusive with his gestures when he wanted to be. Natalie got the pizza in and turned on the timer. She said, "Thank you for bringing all the toppings."

Colin said, "I said I would."

There was a difference between a guy saying he'd do it and actually turning up with them. She said, "You have a good track record so far, but not everyone does."

Colin's nose wrinkled. "If I want to spend time with you, I'm certainly not going to make it cost you money."

"I figured that out the first day when you hadn't hooked up your router yet, and you didn't ask for my Wi-Fi password."

Colin grinned. "You mean I could have?"

Natalie looked back at the stove timer counting down. "I haven't had the best experience with taking guys at their word, so it means a lot that you promised something and then followed through. You asked what I wanted, and then you didn't do whatever you pleased while ignoring what I asked for. You've been thoughtful. I mean, I even asked you to stop holding me, and you backed right off."

Colin's voice lowered. "I'm not accepting a medal of honor for meeting the most basic standard of decent human behavior."

She looked at him. "But you've been honest with me."

He flinched. "Nat, I need to tell you something."

He looked pained and uneasy, and Natalie put up her hands. "No, stop. Listen." She couldn't stand it when he looked so uncomfortable in his own skin. "You've been honest, and a lot of guys aren't. You don't see it because you're a good guy, but my last boyfriend was a user. He would plead poverty when it came time to go on a date, only then I'd find out he went on a road trip with his friends to watch a Red Sox game. Or he'd tell me he was too tired to go for a walk, but instead he'd spend the day fishing. He wasn't working for six months because no one would hire him, except I found out he never applied for anything."

Colin said in a thready voice, "Yeah, not applying

usually prevents people from hiring you. Natalie, I'm sorry."

"I'm sorry, too. Brooke told me there's something wrong with the way I choose guys, that not all guys are liars and users." She looked up at Colin. "Maybe that's the most basic standard of human decency, but some people fail to meet it. I'm glad you do. It helps me feel secure, knowing when you say something, you mean it."

CHAPTER TWELVE

Colin had never in his life both loved and hated a pizza the way he loved and hated last night's pizza.

At seven o'clock in the morning, he did a walk-through of the front of house, and he ended up with the tool chest fixing a wobbly table. Austin wasn't here this early. That was fine. Colin needed to think.

Natalie liked him. That alone would have left Colin walking on air for months, and when Colin closed his eyes, he could re-create every single kiss from their pizza night. From the first one over the dough to the final one when he returned to his apartment, and the half dozen kisses in between. Oh, the way she felt in his arms. The way gravity faded when she touched him.

Then the way gravity returned when she said she appreciated his honesty.

"I am in so much trouble," he hummed to himself. "This is never going to work."

She'd find out eventually. She would have found out last night if she'd gotten angry enough about the overtime situation that she'd pulled up her phone and visited the restaurant website. Was he on the front page? No, because the things visitors wanted to know were, "What time is the restaurant open?" and "How do I get there?" and "Where's the menu?"

On the page about the restaurant's history, however, was a photo of Dale as the founder, and further down the page was a small square photo of Colin. No one would notice unless they went looking for it. If, for example, they intended to contact the state labor board to report the conditions under which Colin worked.

Of course, labor laws were not exactly a thing when the person forced by the owner to work eighty hours a week was...the owner. The worst trouble Natalie could start would be with Natalie, when Colin came home after eighteen hours onsite to find her standing in his doorway, her arms folded, her eyes narrow, and her trust smashed.

"I'm so in trouble," he continued singing. Natalie's morning song to her pets had worn off on him, but singing like her made him feel as if she were with him. The table no longer wobbled. He couldn't say the same about his spirit.

In his office, he reviewed the paperwork. They had deliveries coming this morning, plus he'd need to get on the phone with one of their suppliers to change how many potatoes they were getting. Last week's specials had sold well, and Colin had swung by a few of the tables to ask what they thought of the *matelote Normande* special. That one might have to become a regular.

Natalie couldn't come here. Not until he'd broken open the truth to her, but when was the right time to do that?

He couldn't just say it anymore, not now that he'd kissed her. Not before they had enough history together that she would understand why he'd let her go on thinking he was a ne'er-do-well who haunted restaurant kitchens and scavenged extra food.

His office was a walk-in closet, and that was fine. The kitchen needed space, and Colin didn't. But walled inside it, he thought again about losing Natalie before they'd even gotten started, and it left him craving escape. He wanted to go to her and secure her affection and get her to care about him and maybe even love him.

Women never did that. They liked Colin until the day they simply didn't. Colin had never gotten the knack of being the person they liked for long enough that they stayed around. Time after time, he tried harder to be like Austin, with flair and assurance. Austin had panache. Austin had enthusiasm. With his flair, Austin had no issues with women ghosting him.

A woman like Natalie—? She'd stick around without expecting endless fun. They'd met in a dark laundry room. He hadn't led off by comping her a seventy-five dollar bottle of champagne. They'd watched TV together and cooked together. She'd acted like six dollars in parmesan and mushrooms was treasure delivered unto her by the hands of a forest elf, and even at that, she said he shouldn't have. Knowing he worked for Fruits de Mer, she still hadn't said, "Use your employee discount and bring me some lobster," although maybe she hated the concept of their food that much.

Now that he and she had something going on, he couldn't disclose. Once he told her, the expectations would change. He'd transform in her mind from "downstairs neighbor" to "owner of the award-winning shoreside restaurant," and he'd lose her.

Wasn't it always that way? Show them who he was, and they weren't interested anymore.

He'd just have to stay Colin Downstairs for a while.

Given that, what should Colin-the-Dishie not know how to cook for next Monday? Colin needed to not know how to cook something that would take a while to prepare, something they'd simmer while standing together, something with plenty of time to talk and plenty of techniques she could demonstrate. It needed to be something "real," and something solid, and something where he could pay for all the accessories so he wasn't like her last useless boyfriend.

Colin wasn't a shiftless lump of manhood, at least. He

brought the food, and he washed the dishes. Maybe Natalie would have fallen for any man who did those things, but he'd like to think she'd fallen for him.

Not for the guy in the chef's jacket with the stand-up collar who stopped by tables and asked what patrons thought of tonight's special. Not for the guy who drove to the fish market at sunrise to price out salmon. Not for the guy who ought to be a lot of fun and instead had a business to maintain.

Risotto. Time to stand at the stove, stirring. Time to talk. Time to hold her and inhale the scent of her and feel her right next to him, and then time to eat together. Risotto was soothing and filling and comforting, and if nothing else, Natalie would have to agree it was real.

CHAPTER THIRTEEN

Gertie returned during the Sit and Stitch to collect her shawls. "I'm sorry," Natalie said. "I haven't had the time."

"Next week." Gertie dumped another shawl onto the table. "Here, do this one, too."

Lilah marched over. "Gertie, your ends are too short. See this one?" She dangled the shawl by one of the yarn tails. "This is an inch and a half long. We've told you repeatedly, six inches. At least the span of your hand. When you knot it and cut it this close, you make it five times harder for anyone to handle your ends."

Gertie shrugged. "I hate to waste yarn, and Natalie doesn't mind."

Natalie said, "I really would prefer if you left them longer."

Gertie sat down to work on another entrelac shawl. "Would you be a dear please and bring me some coffee?"

Natalie got her a coffee in one of the store's ceramic mugs, making it up with a lot of cream and just a little sugar because that was how Gertie liked it. Lilah was fuming, but since Gertie couldn't see very well, Gertie would miss that.

As Gertie reached the end of the row, Lilah walked around the table and slapped her hand down onto the scissors on the table. "Show me with your hands exactly where you planned to snip."

Gertie showed her. Lilah tugged the yarn another four inches. "Cut it there. That's how much you need to leave."

Natalie fought laughter as she set the coffee in front of Gertie. "Here you are."

One of the women said, "Lilah, tell me more about the Brighthead Crafters Guild. Will you be selling quilts?"

"We won't be selling anything. Right now, it's a forum where professional crafters can share ideas and marketing support for one another so we can boost our reach and help the community." Talking about her passion-project, Lilah had brightened up on a dime. "We already have two quilters signed on over at the group, plus the crafting supply store in Ellsworth, and a woman who professionally restores antique fabric."

Natalie said, "The forum is amazing. There is so much talent in Maine."

One of the women said, "Well, naturally. We're hiding from the cold, so we have to do something."

Everyone at the table laughed. Today's Sit and Stitch consisted of four women and one man. The man was working on a Star Wars latch hook rug, and his current task was cutting a skein of goldenrod yarn into six- and eight-inch strands. Natalie wondered if he could teach Gertie to do the same.

Although, half the time, Don would snip, measure, and then re-snip. She'd have to vacuum afterward to clean up behind him.

Lilah ticked things off on her fingers. "We've got pottery and embroidery and woodworking...quite a few painters... and any number of sewists."

"Sewers," corrected Gertie.

"Sewers looks too much like something that goes down the drain," Natalie said. "Sewers...? It doesn't work. They prefer sew-ists."

Gertie sniffed. "My mother was proud to be a sew-er."

Time to derail the conversation before Gertie took offense. Natalie said, "Do you still have anything your mother made?"

Gertie shook her head. "It was years and years ago. It's all fallen to pieces, but oh, the dresses! She could make a dress fit for the Queen of England!"

Natalie said, "That must have been amazing. So much talent, and it was just what people did for their own families and friends. Knitting and crocheting, quilting, cooking—they learned it and perfected it and did it all the time, and now here we are, with all these skills relegated to hobbies."

One of the women said, "It's a shame, isn't it?"

Natalie said, "The guy who lives downstairs from me can't even cook. He was planning to live the rest of his life on takeout."

Don said, "I'm sure his arteries would have something to say about that."

Natalie smiled. "Well, he's learning now. But can you imagine? In *Little House on the Prairie*, Pa built his own house and could slaughter and dress a pig to feed the family, but nowadays a guy can get to nearly thirty and not know how to fry a hamburger."

Lilah said, "How about a hot dog? Poke it with a fork and microwave for thirty seconds."

Natalie said, "He pointed to the stove and said he had no idea how to cook on that beyond maybe being able to boil water, and you've seen my apartment—we're not talking about an appliance designed by NASA for the first manned mission to Mars."

Lilah said, "To be fair, it would be hard to fry a hamburger in zero gravity when it keeps floating off the pan."

Natalie rested a hand over her heart. "The tragedy of a five-year mission with no bacon cheeseburgers."

Lilah exclaimed, "Gertie! Where are you about to cut?"

Gertie snipped before Lilah could get around the table.

Natalie said, "Gertie, please, if you don't leave them long, I can't weave them in anymore."

Gertie said, "You'll make it work. I hate to waste the yarn."

Natalie clenched her teeth.

Don said, "Is your creative group open to anyone?"

Lilah said, "We haven't established membership criteria yet."

Don nodded. "My cousin might be interested. He restores statues."

Lilah gasped. "That's amazing!"

Gertie said, "My son-in-law is a chef. I'll tell him too."

Don said, "Cooking isn't crafting."

Natalie looked up. "Of course cooking is crafting. It's taking raw materials and turning them into something beautiful."

Don said, "Everyone has to eat."

Natalie pointed to Lilah's project. "Everyone needs socks."

Lilah breathed, "Oh, Don, please think carefully before you reply," and while everyone laughed, Don raised his hands in the air and exclaimed, "Objection sustained! I withdraw the question!"

Lilah added, "Life would be awful without crafting and creating. Like that guy who can't cook. Can you imagine going through your whole life without experiencing that little hit of joy when you make something beautiful?"

Natalie looked at her own project and smiled. "Yeah. But I'm helping him learn that for himself."

The first moment the shop was empty, Lilah planted herself in front of Natalie. "Okay, all the details, right now, right here." Arms folded, she tapped her foot. "You, my lady, are nurturing a savage crush on that guy, and I need every single detail."

Natalie stepped backward.

Lilah advanced and pointed at her. "I can read you like a Kindle novel. How cute is Mr. I-Can't-Cook that you're stepping in and teaching him how to live like an adult?"

With a nervous laugh, Natalie said, "Can I at least put this yarn on its shelf?"

Lilah gestured toward the cubbies, and Natalie approached the Malabrigo section. "His name is Colin, and he moved here to work at Fruits de Mer."

"He works at a restaurant, but he can't operate a stove?" Lilah snorted. "He'd better have a whole host of pluses because just for that, I'm giving him wicked side-eye."

"Yeah, I don't get it either. His brother is the general manager, so when the last restaurant Colin worked at got sold, his brother offered him a job." Natalie started shelving skeins of Malabrigo Worsted. "Colin fills in at the restaurant doing anything that needs doing. He's told me about cleaning up, waiting tables, washing dishes, peeling potatoes..." She glanced at Lilah. "And he's got wicked skills with a knife. You should see him chop things."

Lilah frowned. "Go on."

"I offered to teach him to cook. So far we've made chili, tacos, and pizza." Natalie's cheeks heated up as she remembered the pizza-making. "We're going to make risotto next, so I'm looking that up because I don't know how to make it, either, but he said we can figure it out."

Lilah said, "Why is it your responsibility to teach a grown man how to feed himself?"

Natalie shrugged. "It's not. He's funny. He's smart, and he's a hard worker. I like talking to him." She tucked the last hank into the cubby. "I asked him not to get in his shower when I'm using mine, and the next day, he started waking up earlier. He's silent when he comes home so he won't bother me. He's considerate. He's super honest."

Lilah looked unconvinced. "Do you really want to hook up with a dishwasher? He doesn't sound like he's got any ambition. I think he's using you for free food."

Natalie returned to the laptop with their inventory spreadsheet. "Everything we've made, he's the one who bought all the ingredients, and then he washes all the dishes."

Lilah started. "You found a guy who pays for the meal and then washes the dishes? Does he have a brother? Oh, wait, you said he does have a brother—and the brother can cook." Lilah laughed hard. "Maybe you should date the brother!"

Natalie said, "Too late. Colin kissed me after we made the pizza. Maybe *you* should date his brother."

Giggling, Lilah said, "I'm still agog that you got this far without breathing a word of it. You're way too private. You need to take us on the emotional ride with you."

Natalie picked up more yarn. "I wasn't sure. Also, he works a lot of hours. They're taking advantage of him."

Lilah raised her hands. "No. Right there, stop. He's an adult. This is where I get nervous, because you have a radar for fixer-upper guys, and then you set about saving them from themselves. Only, how well does that work?"

Natalie carried the yarn to its shelf. "I do not."

Lilah counted off on her fingers, which once again looked like the hands of a woman who couldn't decide on a color and therefore was wearing them all. "Roll call! Chad: perpetually unemployed human throw-pillow whom you tried for two years to convince to go to college or get a job. Rob: wasn't entirely sure how or when to use a shower stall; never had money for the movies but managed to supply himself with beer and cigarettes for his fishing trips. Ted: effectively married to his mother and would abandon you if Mommy snapped her fingers. And now the ambition-free Colin, who lives in a dump, washes dishes for his brother, and has never figured out where food comes from."

Natalie shook her head. "I promise you, Colin's different. He keeps his word. I mean, I even asked him to back off when he was kissing me, and he stepped away."

Lilah bit her lip. "Have you talked to Brooke? She'll tell you what she thinks."

Brooke had been...well, "negative," about Rob, Chad, and Ted. At first she hadn't said anything, of course, just watched and retained every little interaction as though entering it into a spreadsheet for further analysis. Eventually Natalie had broken down and said, "So, what do you think?" and after that moment, Brooke was always blunt and preachy and, weeks later, smug. Because in addition to blunt and preachy, she'd been correct.

"Brooke waits so long between boyfriends because her standards are too high," Natalie said. "Although Hal is decent for her."

Lilah sniffed. "They have no chemistry. Brooke needs someone with heart and passion. Get the two of them together and they're punching a clock and checking items off a list."

Hal didn't deserve that broadside, but if it got Lilah off Natalie's case, all the better. "I'm worried she'll marry Hal by default."

"Don't turn into Colin's caretaker by default. You're not his mother." Lilah, apparently, was not to be deterred. "I want you to run Colin by Brooke. In fact, bring him to the store and let us get a read on him. If you're not here when he shows up, I'll try to sell him some yarn for you, and we'll see if he can give the maid-of-honor's husband a run for his money."

Natalie said, "Colin appreciates my work. He tells me to make nice things for myself."

Lilah said, "And would you take Brooke's advice if she tells you to walk away?"

Natalie paused. Would she?

Lilah added, "If you want to explore a shipwreck, take a scuba diving class and bring a camera. Don't date a human wreck. If you want to date a *guy*, find someone who doesn't need fixing."

Before Natalie could reply that Lilah wasn't making sense, the door jangled, and they both turned.

Brooke entered the shop, her jacket zipped to her neck, her eyes downcast, and her face blotchy.

Lilah rushed up to her. "What's wrong?"

Brooke kept her shoulders hunched in her jacket. "Is it obvious?"

Natalie dropped the yarn onto the table. "Are you okay?"

"I'm fine," Brooke said. "Hal and I broke up."

Lilah threw her arms around Brooke, but Brooke stood stiff under the embrace. "It's okay. We should have done it ages ago."

Natalie said, "Do you want the day off? I can hold down the shop."

Brooke shook her head. "It's better if I'm working."

Lilah said, "What happened?"

"The same fight we always have. He's too good for me and for everyone else on Earth, and I'm just supposed to shut up when he lords his perfect self over me." She shrugged. "I'm not going to live my entire life with a guy who acts like he settled for me."

Lilah's nose wrinkled. "That's awful."

"And him ending with, 'I was only kidding! Can't you take a joke?' Last night I told him no, I am locally famous for being unable to take a joke, so, off you pop." She unzipped her jacket and headed for the back. "That's a year of my life, wasted."

Lilah sighed as Brooke disappeared into the back room. "That's awful."

In a low voice, Natalie said, "You do not tell her about Colin."

Lilah shook her head. "Agreed. This isn't the time to talk to her about cute guys and fancy restaurants."

Natalie handed Lilah the inventory sheet, and she followed Brooke into the back room, ready to listen and give support.

Chapter Fourteen

For the fifth time, Natalie read Colin the directions off the tablet computer. "We cook two tablespoons of chopped onion in a tablespoon of olive oil."

Frustrated, Colin said, "Maybe we should just start and see how it works?"

Wide-eyed, Natalie looked up at him. "I don't want to mess it all up. You deserve a nice meal."

It was going to be a nice meal. Natalie's commitment to pleasing him (or maybe to pleasing everybody) was sweet, but her hesitancy was frustrating. "Like we said last week, in the worst case, a pizza is a phone call away."

She gave an embarrassed smile. "That's true. It's only food."

Colin couldn't remember the last time something was "only food" unless it was him grabbing a leftover roll to forestall exhaustion. Food had become art and business and creativity and life itself. No "only" about it. Natalie, though, approached cooking with the wonder of a school kid spotting a rabbit on the front lawn.

The onion went into the pot and sizzled. That oil was too hot, and the onion was going to burn. Colin said, "Can

I stir it?"

"Sure." She handed him the spoon, and he pushed the onion pieces to the far end of the pot and shifting the pot off-center on the burner. This trick wouldn't work if she had better cookware, but she didn't.

Still, he needed to get the temperature down. Colin surreptitiously lowered the heat. "Now do we add the rice?"

The grocery store had sold him the tiniest container of arborio he'd ever seen. It was adorable. At the restaurant, he regularly took deliveries of twenty-five-pound bags.

Without giving Natalie the chance to re-check the directions, Colin dumped the rice into the hot pot and stirred the arborio into the oil.

Natalie looked unnerved. "How long do you think until it's toasted?"

"The directions said a minute or two." Colin kept stirring until all the oil was absorbed and the pot had lost enough heat that it was no longer a threat to the onions.

He'd eat burnt onions with Natalie if he had to. It's just —he didn't have to.

Natalie watched over the top of the pot as he stirred. "What does toasted rice even look like?"

Colin said, "Do you think it pops up?"

She laughed. "Should I get a teenie rice toaster?"

"Get the eight-rice toaster, not the two-rice toaster. Otherwise we'll be here all night."

Natalie said, "Not that I would mind."

He wouldn't mind either. She was close enough now that he could have put his arm around her waist. Oh, the temptation.

Instead he poured a quarter cup of white wine into the rice. It sizzled as the alcohol burned off, and momentarily the scent filled the kitchen.

"Nice," Natalie whispered. Colin stirred it again, then added a cup of broth.

That was how it went for the rest of the preparation— add, stir, wait, stir, wait some more, stir, add, stir. In the meantime, he did get to put his arms around Natalie, and she rested against him, and they stood in a still-life slow dance while the kitchen smelled of broth and wine.

Colin said, "Do you want to tell me what has you upset today?"

Natalie sighed. "I didn't want to bother you with this. It's your day off."

His stomach clenched, though, because he couldn't tell what she was about to say. *So, hey, I looked you up online, and do you know what the internet thinks you are?*

He fumbled in his brain for a defense. It had been a good run. Two or three weeks—that was all women ever wanted of Colin, anyhow. Except Natalie was different. He'd thought she was different. It was going to hurt when she ditched him.

Colin prompted, "Wouldn't my day off be the ideal day to bother me?"

She stepped away and added more broth to the pot. "You're so tense."

Colin steadied himself. "Are you dumping me?"

She pivoted, shocked. "No! We're not even dating, are we?" Her brow furrowed. "Why would you leap to that? No."

Colin said, "No?"

"No." She stirred the pot. "You went from zero to sixty on getting dumped."

Colin said, "Then what's making you so upset?"

"I have an entire life that isn't you and is perfectly capable of leaving me upset on its own." Her nose wrinkled. "Are you on the rebound from a bad breakup?"

"No." Colin backed off a step. "But even joking about tiny rice toasters didn't relax you."

"It actually is about a breakup, but it's my cousin." Natalie shook her head. "She'd been dating this guy for about a year, but he acted superior to her all the time. She said it was always the same fight, with him treating her like she was ignorant. She's not. She's one of the smartest people I know, but sometimes she has these gaps in what she understands. He kept using that against her. She ended it, but she's sad. She keeps wondering if he was right that she's stupid."

"She's better off without him," muttered Colin. "Think about it. If he holds himself that high, he should pair off with the theoretical smart woman who's his perfect match. Except he'd be intimidated."

"Yes!" Natalie turned to him. "I keep contrasting Hal to the guy who was married to my maid of honor! He kept saying about her, 'We're an even match.' And so help me, when she walked into the store, you could see it."

That raised interesting questions about why Natalie was wasting her time with Colin, since if she thought him an incapable slacker, clearly she couldn't consider them an even match.

Natalie went on, "That woman knew exactly who she was and what she wanted. He knew her, too, right down to what she'd say. My cousin isn't secure like that, but she's just as smart and capable."

Colin said, "You're smart and capable, too."

Natalie flinched away from him. "Not like Brooke. Brooke is clear-headed. She remembers all these details. Her spatial reasoning is amazing, and if you give her a set of parameters to work within, she'll negotiate exactly what needs to happen and when." Natalie's shoulders sagged. "The problem is, her social skills aren't all that. She tells me I don't know how to pick guys, but then she went and picked *that* guy."

"She believed his press releases." Colin hesitated. "Wait, this is the second time you've said that. If you don't know how to pick guys, it sounds like I should be worried."

Natalie picked up her head. "You're different. You work hard, and you're honest."

Colin busied himself adding more broth.

Natalie went into the fridge to gather what they'd need for the rest of the risotto. She'd told him not to bother buying more parmesan since they had that left from last week (she should have used it on her own pasta during the week—he'd have gotten more) but now they also had butter (the real stuff, thanks,) plus mushrooms, plus shrimp. Colin had bought the precooked shrimp even though that broke his culinary heart. It seemed better to streamline if they were working together rather than in parallel.

It had been much harder to resist bringing in a little shaved winter white truffle to sprinkle over the top. He could have amazed her. Natalie deserved some culinary happiness, but it would just compound the lies. How would he have passed that off? "I asked some guys in the kitchen about risotto, and here's what they said." No.

He had not resisted bringing more treats for the guinea pigs. Over the last week, he'd taken to bringing home a carrot top or seven every day and hanging the bag on Natalie's doorknob. Traditionally, you had to ask a woman's parents for permission to court her, but in the current situation, he'd just get a blessing from her pets. He hadn't yet figured out how to bring home treats for the anoles, but Birdie Holly had tried the carrot greens as well...and approved.

When the risotto was creamy, they stirred in the butter and cheese, then covered the pot to let that melt. Natalie used the time to have him slice the mushrooms (because he did it faster) while she shelled the shrimp.

Colin needed to bring his knife sharpener upstairs next time because this knife was ridiculous. He'd have been twice as fast if he hadn't needed to be three times as careful. Meanwhile, Natalie watched his every move in silent terror.

"I haven't lost a fingertip recently," he assured her.

"If you meant that as assurance, you're misfiring."

Colin glanced at the pan she had preheating, then nudged the heat up. "I'll do these like we did last week, then?"

She said, "Are you okay with that?"

"I'll manage." Butter, in the pan. Momentarily, melted butter. Mushrooms, right after. He'd gotten baby bellas this time. Natalie hadn't specified the mushroom type, but it would be fun if she corrected him. She hadn't last week. How outlandish could he get?

Colin said, "Is that guy at least leaving your cousin alone?"

"She didn't say whether he tried to get her back, although you have a point. If Hal does keep pursuing her, that proves he doesn't believe she's beneath him. That's messed up." Natalie shook her head. "Maybe someday you can explain to me how men think."

"That particular man sounds like the pride-driven kind," Colin said. "Question something they love, and they can't tolerate it. They might do anything. In this guy's case, it sounds like he loves himself."

Natalie's nose wrinkled as she brought over the bowl of shrimp. "What do you love?"

You? That was the right answer, except it wasn't entirely true yet. He was attracted to her beyond reason, but that wasn't quite love.

He loved his work. He loved his restaurant. He loved exploring taste combinations and new cooking techniques and unexpected twists on old favorites. He loved finding bargains at the terminal market and whipping up a special in his head, and then the gratification when guests loved it, too. He loved juggling all the pieces of his business to make everything balance out.

He needed a safe answer. "I love my brother, and I'd do anything for him."

Natalie said, "Yet you didn't bite my head off when I implied he was taking advantage of you."

Colin chuckled. "It's complicated, but he isn't."

Natalie said, "Sometime, I'd like to meet him."

Colin opened the lid on the risotto and added the mushrooms. "I'll just warn you in advance that we're identical twins, but he's the handsome one."

Natalie laughed. "As if you're not?"

"It's happened a number of times that a woman starts off with me and then gravitates toward Austin." Colin shrugged. "I don't blame them. I like him better than me, too."

Natalie turned, eyebrows raised. "What's not to like about you?"

"Austin's more fun than I am. I—" Colin caught himself before saying, "I work longer hours than he does." Natalie would be dialing the Department of Labor before he finished the sentence. "He laughs a lot. He's more outgoing. I'm more of a planner, while he adjusts to things on the fly."

Natalie carried the risotto to the table. "I cannot imagine this. Is he a hypnotist? Because you laugh, and you're fun, and you adjust to things on the fly. How can he just waltz in and take all the attention off you?" She turned. "Which one of you is older?"

Colin gave a mock bow. "By forty-five minutes."

"It's your added experience," Natalie declared in a sage tone. "You need to find a woman who appreciates a seasoned man."

"My lady," Colin said, inclining his head, "I will attempt to impress you both with my wisdom and with my seasonings."

She started spooning risotto into their bowls. "Speaking of wisdom, what did you study in college?"

Ha ha ha, culinary arts? Colin said, "Business," because that was also true.

Natalie said, "My mother says business is what you major in if your soul is in a shoe box at the back of the closet."

Wide-eyed, Colin said, "Wow."

Natalie set his bowl in front of him. "I'm not *saying* there's a shoebox at the back of your closet."

Colin said, "But because I wouldn't let you unpack my stuff, you can't rule it out."

Natalie raised her fork. "*Bon appétit.* Is that what you say at a French restaurant?"

He waited for her reaction as she sampled it, and there it was—that split second when she thoroughly enjoyed the taste, the texture, and the scent. The slight widening of her eyes, the half-smile. He tried some too. "This worked! Thank you."

"I was worried there," Natalie said, unnecessarily because she'd been an incandescent ball of worry from minute one. "The whole process didn't make any sense."

Colin said, "That's the key, then. Follow the directions, and hope the directions are good."

She flinched. "Well, yes, but no. Because if I agree, you'll buy a cookbook, and you won't need me anymore."

Colin waited until he'd swallowed. "I'm uncomfortable letting that stand. I'm not trying to use you."

Natalie recoiled. "How do you mean?"

"You're more than a service provider." Colin pushed back from the table. "I thought we were spending time together. If having me in your apartment is your part-time job, then we need to have a long conversation and change things up. I'd rather eat takeout for the rest of my life than spend time with you because you feel obligated."

Natalie raised a hand. "I was joking."

Colin studied her.

"I mean it. That was just a joke." She looked down at her risotto and forked up one of the mushrooms. "Besides, we both know you can cook."

Colin straightened. "What?"

She wouldn't meet his eyes. "You're not uncomfortable with anything we're doing. You slice and chop like a master. You look a bit awkward when you're stirring or pouring, but you adjust the stove temperature without asking about it, and you aren't afraid of getting burned. You plan ahead. You've got a sense of how long things are going to take, and your timing is excellent."

Relationship ending in three, two, one...

Laughing, Natalie looked up at him. "Don't look so horrified. I'm saying you know more than you give yourself credit for."

Colin tried to steady his voice. "What do you think I know?"

"It's not what you know as much as your willingness to get comfortable with knowing it." She raised her fork again. "*Bon appétit.*"

CHAPTER FIFTEEN

Mid-afternoon. Brooke had come into the shop, and Lilah was behind a computer to get a handle on the nascent guild's paperwork.

Chili. Tacos. Pizza. Last week, Risotto. This week's adventure had been beef stroganoff. Colin had arrived with a whole grocery bag full of goodies—mushrooms, sour cream, onions, garlic—but instead of ground beef, he'd brought beef round. Which he'd tried for one minute to cut with her kitchen knife before saying it was too blunt to work and getting out her kitchen shears. That was horrifying enough, except then he muttered imprecations about right-handed scissors. "You can use the knife," she'd urged. No, the scissors were far sharper, and he insisted. He just awkwardly angled his wrist and managed to make the shears do the job.

Then, oddity of oddities, he'd separated the blades to wash them. Natalie hadn't even known they came apart.

A customer entered, and Natalie directed her toward the fingering weight yarns. Then she returned to the register to review an inventory sheet. They had plenty of Cascade 220, but small quantities of any single colorway. Not sufficient for a yarn customers looking at sweater quantities. She'd have to order more, then flag the single dye lots so no one ended up with an accidental stripe.

The customer came to the register holding three skeins of yarn. "Would you like these wound?" Natalie said.

"No, that's fine." Two minutes later, the woman had paid, but she paused with the skeins in her hand and sighed. "You know? I've changed my mind. Can you please wind these for me?"

Natalie fought annoyance. "There's a three dollar per skein charge for winding."

The woman said, "Can you do it anyway?"

Brooke glared at Natalie from across the room. Natalie said, "Sure. Do you want me to wind all three skeins, or only one to get you started?"

The woman began rummaging in her shoulder bag. "All of them, please."

Brooke hadn't removed her eyes from Natalie, so Natalie opened another ticket on the computer. "That will be nine dollars."

The woman pulled her hand out of her purse holding not her wallet, but two other hanks of yarn. "These too, please. And I don't have any cash."

Brooke strode over to the desk. "I'm sorry, but we can't wind yarn purchased from other shops."

The woman said to Natalie, "Here."

Brooke said, "We can't take the chance of damaging our equipment or there being bugs in the yarn."

The woman rolled her eyes like a preteen. "I assure you, there aren't any bugs. I just need the yarn caked up."

Brooke had no inflection at all. "Nine dollars to cake the ones you bought today, and we aren't going to cake the extra skeins. We're more than happy to charge your credit card a second time for the winding."

The fury in the woman's eyes kept spiking through Natalie. The woman finally turned to Brooke. "I was working with her, not with you."

Brooke folded her arms. Her black lace fingerless gloves

gave her an intimidating air, as though she were a weightlifter. "We co-own the shop, so when you work with her, you're working with me."

The woman raised her voice. "I can't believe you're insinuating that I live in bugs and filth!"

By contrast, Brooke lowered hers. "I can't believe you expect me to believe you changed your mind about having your yarn wound. Not when you brought in two hanks specifically to get them wound."

The woman turned to Natalie. "Are you going to do it, or not?"

It wouldn't take that long. Ten minutes, and she could wind the three skeins the woman had just purchased. It never took that long, except Natalie had a whole day full of tasks that would take only ten minutes to do, or only five, or only three.

Meanwhile Brooke was exactly right. This woman had waited for the transaction to close and then was trying to weasel out of paying a three-dollar surcharge on top of her twenty-dollar yarns, plus get two extra hanks wound for free.

Brooke said, "No, she's not."

If Brooke weren't here, Natalie would already be snipping the yarn ties and setting those skeins on the swift. She didn't want to be mean. She didn't want to risk the customer leaving the shop and telling fifteen people about the nasty hags at Bright Stitches. Invariably those two hanks from the woman's bag would have bug eggs, or they'd be friable and snap during the winding, and then the woman would blame Natalie for that too.

Except Brooke was here, and Brooke had placed herself like an immovable object. They had rules, and Brooke was going to enforce them.

No matter what happened next, someone was going to be disappointed. Either that woman would be disappointed about her unwound yarn, or Brooke would be disappointed at her cousin for once again purchasing peace at any price. No matter the outcome, Natalie would be disappointed in herself.

The woman looked down her nose at Brooke. "You certainly have a high opinion of yourself."

"I have a high opinion of the rules of our shop. Which Natalie can tell you she had an equal share in deciding." Brooke shrugged. "It's up to you whether you pay to have three skeins wound or not."

The woman said, "Then I want a refund on the three skeins I just purchased."

Natalie took back the receipt and started charging it back out without a word. Her hands shook on the keyboard. "May I have your card again, please?"

The woman handed it over. "I hope you realize your partner is the entire reason you lost my business."

Sixty dollars. So much business. Natalie offered, "There's a yarn store about ten miles west where they'll cake yarn sold by anyone, not just their own." She handed back the card. "Your purchase has been refunded. Have a great day."

Her voice trembled just a bit, but Brooke was right alongside, cold as iron.

The woman raised her chin. "I'm going straight to the other shop. And I'll buy my yarn there, instead. All my yarn."

Natalie kept silence, and the woman left, tossing an extra, "Have a nice day!" over her shoulder for good measure.

As the door jangled closed, Natalie said, "Thank you."

Brooke looked awed. "That was a savage parting shot about the other store. I didn't think you had it in you."

Puzzled, Natalie regarded her. "What?"

Lilah added, "Cold as ice. I wouldn't have thought of that."

Natalie turned toward Brooke. "Don't they wind yarn there?"

"Absolutely. For five dollars a hank, they'll wind anything. She gets to burn her gas and then pay twenty-five bucks to get it all wound up, and then our competitors

125

get to deal with her bug-infested yarn that's probably got eleven breaks in it." Brooke opened her hands. "I count that as an absolute win, and it's entirely on your shoulders."

Natalie shrunk back. "I didn't realize any of that."

Brooke side-eyed her. "Pity."

Lilah pranced over. "You know what's not a pity? That horrible customer is going to tell them we sent her over there, and then they'll get to gripe at us next week when we have the first *meeting* of the Brighthead Crafters Guild!"

Brooke turned. "Meeting? It's going to happen?"

"I've got a large enough group of people now that yes, I'm booking us a function room, and we get to show up in the same place at the same time!" Lilah folded her hands and bounced in place. "The jewelry-making duo from Juniper swears they want to be there, plus the furniture restoration guy from downtown, plus an oil painter—and it's going to be a blast!"

Brooke finger-combed the edge of her hair. "That hamburger place on Main Street has paper tablecloths, so if I bring a carton of sixty-four crayons, we can create a visual representation of our first gathering."

Lilah said, "Try a bit more upscale. I was thinking about Fruits de Mer."

Natalie glared at Lilah.

Brooke raised her eyebrows. "They outclass us. I mean, maybe not you, but they outclass me."

"I'll be there, so they won't outclass *us*." Lilah grinned. "If we go for lunch and reserve their function room, we get the same service for two-thirds the price, plus I can negotiate even further because this is the off season." Lilah raised her eyebrows at Natalie. "Don't you want to drop in there and see someone special?"

Brooke turned to Natalie. "Oh?"

Natalie lowered her voice. "I thought we weren't going to bother Brooke about that right now."

"Why, because I dumped Hal on account of his inherent

superiority?" Brooke snorted. "Please. Tell me who 'someone' is and what he's like and when I get to meet him."

Natalie said, "He's not inherently superior to me, so I don't know that we even need to talk about him."

Lilah said, "He works at Fruits de Mer, and Natalie's never been, so I say we compel Natalie to go there by holding our first meeting in their function room."

Natalie said, "And I say we don't."

Lilah made an abashed face. "Actually, I've already talked to them."

Natalie stepped toward her. "Lilah!"

She raised her hands in defense. "I want to meet him! He had you all doe-eyed!"

Brooke frowned. "This is beyond unfair. Even if I was ready to put Hal on a barge and push him out to sea, you needed to be doe-eyed around me too. Give me something to be happy about." She boosted herself onto the Sit and Stitch table. "Okay, maybe I can deal with going to a high class restaurant. Our mystery man will stop by the table with a complementary glass of champagne on a small round platter and set it before you, intoning, 'For the lady.'"

Natalie's cheeks were hot. "He's not a waiter. His voice is amazing, though."

Lilah said, "The general manager is his identical twin, right? Now *that* guy had a voice I just wanted to bottle up and keep in my pocket to sing me to sleep every night."

Brooke said, "Then I definitely need to talk to him. Colin, huh? Is he a sous chef?"

Natalie shifted uncomfortably. "I think he's a dishwasher. He says he helps his brother and fills in doing anything that needs to be done."

Brooke frowned. "You're...dating a high school senior?"

Natalie sighed. "See, it's not like that. He works super hard."

"Is he the ghost of Chad? Zero ambition, waiting for his brother to get a good enough job that he's virtually unfireable?" Brooke wove her fingers together around the gloves. "Well, at least he's not going to backstab anyone with his rampant success."

"You haven't even met him." Natalie's stomach clenched. "He puts in eighty-hour weeks, so if anything, his brother is wicked taking advantage of him. And I know that's the truth because he lives downstairs from me. I hear his alarm go off. He's out the door by six-thirty, and most days, he's not back until nearly midnight."

Lilah said, "How does anyone survive working those hours?"

"That's what I mean! Even if he wanted another job, how would he have time to apply for one?" Natalie shrugged. "Anyhow, that's not the point. I don't know if I want to go to Fruits de Mer and see him there."

In her kitchen, Colin didn't feel like "a dishie" (as he put it). In her kitchen, he was funny and sweet and thoughtful. Even washing her dishes, he felt like more. At Fruits de Mer, she'd see him as the low man on the totem pole, and see him that way in front of so many amazing artists and artisans.

Brooke shifted uncomfortably. "That's two reasons we should find somewhere else to host it."

Lilah turned to Natalie. "You need to go and get it over with." She turned back to Brooke. "Natalie insulted the restaurant the first time they met, before she knew where he worked."

"Oh, then you do need to go." Brooke frowned. "Also, I want to meet this guy, because after a year of dealing with Mr. I'm-So-Much-Better-Than-Everyone, it'll be refreshing to meet a guy who does honest work with rubber gloves and hot water."

CHAPTER SIXTEEN

Colin was hauling a new tray of glasses into position when Austin popped into the kitchen. "I'm rearranging the schedule because we've landed an event booking for Saturday, and we're going to need coverage."

"Nice!" He slid the tray into place and carried the empty tray to the sink. "How many people?"

"At least twenty, maybe as many as forty. They want the event room, and they'll give us a head count on Thursday."

"They should definitely have one dedicated server, maybe two." Colin looked around the kitchen, but everything was smooth. "What kind of function? Rehearsal dinner?"

"It's actually a meeting. Brighthead Craft Council or something like that."

Colin stopped in his tracks. "The Brighthead Crafters Guild?"

Austin pointed at him. "Bingo! Do you know them? Their contact person joked that all our cooks might want to join because food is an art form." Austin paused. "Except you don't look pleased by the prospect of forty brand-new local customers to impress, so what's going on?"

Colin grabbed the black trash bag from the full container. "Come with me."

As he carried the trash to the dumpster, he said, "The woman I'm in a relationship with is part of the group organizing that."

Austin tilted his head. "The one who hates Fruits de Mer?"

"She told me she hated Fruits de Mer because I had our takeout bag on the table. She thought the takeout meant I couldn't cook."

Austin's nose wrinkled. "Perfectly competent cooks order takeout all the time."

"I kind of also said something that made her think I couldn't. Anyhow, I ended up in her apartment to borrow her vacuum cleaner, and she was making dinner, so she offered to teach me how to make white bean chili because that's '*real food.*'" Colin heaved the bag into the dumpster. "I thought she was mocking me, except she was serious as a car crash. '*There's a whole world of good and healthy food when you cook it yourself,*'" he said, miming Natalie's earnest tone. "'*You'll save money, and you'll feel a lot better.*'"

Austin busted up laughing. "At which point you served this woman her own ego, deep-fried and drizzled with balsamic vinegar?"

"It's not her ego!" Colin turned to him, wide-eyed. "She's the sweetest woman I've ever met. She enjoys teaching things to me, like how to use a spatula and how to tell when the noodles are cooked."

Austin guffawed so hard he had to lean against the dumpster. "Bro—? And you still haven't told her?"

Colin opened his hands. "She knows I work here, but she thinks I'm a kitchen porter. When she asked what I did, it was right after she said we were an overpriced lunch for tourists. I thought she meant an owner was a useless appendage who made the GM do everything. I told her I did do a bit of everything."

Austin craned back his neck. "No, stop. I'm going to get

a stitch in my side. You are such an idiot!" He swiped the tears from his eyes. "She thinks you're a dishwasher? You are the only person on earth who'd get into this kind of mess."

"You're not helping!" Colin's fists clenched. "If she comes here with her group, it's over."

"Then make sure it's over before she sets foot in the door." Austin shook his head. "You tell her now, before she's in our dining room and the owner's supposed to swing by the table to say hello to this nice little artist's collaborative—to whom I gave a sweet discount, by the way."

Sighing, Colin stared out across the back lot.

"What you do not do is some weird scheme where I swap coats with you halfway through their meal and step out there pretending to be Arson, our triplet brother who actually owns the place."

Colin snorted a laugh. "Gosh, I miss Arson. He always took responsibility for every single thing that went wrong —as long as no one witnessed either of us doing it."

"Mom and Dad certainly don't miss Arson. Besides, Arson was only useful when trouble was caused, not for getting us out of it." Austin headed back toward the restaurant. "Before you ask, the other thing we're not doing is pretending I was the one sneaking into your house to beg for cooking lessons." He turned to Colin. "Did she not ask things like, where did you work before?"

Staring at the ground, Colin shoved his hands in his pockets. "I told her I came here when CharCuties was sold, and I ended up in Brighthead because you worked here. She drew her own conclusions."

"That's not a relationship. She doesn't know you, so you don't have a relationship." With that pronouncement, Austin banged open the door and strode in, singing to the tune of *Witch Doctor,* "I—told—the dish-wash-er just how he made a mess!"

Colin followed, glowering.

Austin grabbed one of the servers. "Danielle, tell my

brother he's an idiot."

"Sorry." Danielle sidled out of Austin's way. "He keeps me employed, which implies a certain intelligence."

"Good answer," Colin muttered, stepping into his office.

Austin followed him in. "Look, make the woman a chocolate cake and apologize and explain."

Colin opened his laptop. "Like I haven't thought of that?"

"You finally found a woman who likes you and doesn't mind that you work a thousand hours a week." Austin got closer. "She isn't after you for money or prestige, and you're ruining it."

Colin wouldn't look at Austin. "What do we do about her coming here?"

"You blow her out of the water with the food," Austin said. "I don't know what we do about the owner thing if you refuse to come clean. A group of leading artists and artisans—? It would be politic for the owner to stop by and talk to them. If not, I can handle the payment and deal with their contact person." He took a deep breath. "I guess they don't have to know the owner is around."

Colin rubbed his temples. "Do you think we could get Dale to turn up?"

Austin's eyebrows shot up. "Some of their members might know him. And then you can keep lying to the nice woman for the foreseeable future."

Colin frowned. "I don't like it either. It's just that every time I try to tell her, she brings up something that stops me."

Austin said, "Something like, 'Wow, Colin, I love the fact that you're so transparent'?" Then, getting a look at Colin's face, Austin said, "No. No, dude, I love you like a brother for obvious reasons, but this is bad. You're ten feet deep in the pit, and you keep digging. Bring in Dale and you've compounded the lie not only to her but to everyone else."

Colin hunched in his seat.

Austin said, "How can she be worth all this handwringing?"

Colin sighed. "She's gorgeous. She's fully alive, and she relishes everything she does. Her heart is bigger than the entire Maine coastline, and generosity streams out of her heart. She wakes up in the morning and sings to an apartment full of adopted animals. She finds beauty in the everyday, and then she shows it to me."

Austin shook his head. "A woman like that deserves the truth."

Colin's shoulders dropped. "I'm going to lose her either way."

Austin said, "Then lose her for who you are, rather than for who you're not."

CHAPTER SEVENTEEN

A knock on the door made Birdie Holly squawk. With a rod and a shawl in her hands on the living room floor, Natalie called, "Who's there?"

Colin's voice replied, "The cookie fairy!"

"Give me a minute!" It was four o'clock. Colin must be making use of the in-between-time at the restaurant. Natalie put everything down to let him in.

He was holding a grocery bag. "Behold! Flour, sugar, eggs, and a package of chocolate chips." He set everything on the table. "Also baking soda. I assume you have salt. Finally, an offering of carrot tops for the guinea pigs and the bird."

Natalie pointed at him. "Did I, or did I not, tell you that you'd enjoy learning to cook?"

Colin rested his hand on his heart. "You said exactly that. Also that it's cheaper, although I need to say a package of chocolate chip cookies would have cost less than this, so I've identified a slight hole in your logic." He picked up the chip bag. "There's a recipe on the back, so I say we go for it."

"I hope you're not on a time crunch because I'm trying

to block a shawl."

Colin said, "How about I get started, and you catch up after you're done doing whatever blocking is. Which I don't intend to learn how to do."

"Fair enough." Natalie returned to the living room, wondering what would happen with Colin and a chocolate chip cookie recipe if she just left the two of them alone in a kitchen together. She returned to the mats on the living room carpet, along with a pile of pins and steel rods. "Wait, is the butter cold?"

"I took some of the softened stuff from the restaurant. I'll replace it for them." Colin positioned himself near the stove where he could see her. "What on earth are you doing? You said blocking, but that looks like fabric surgery."

"It's the last part of finishing a shawl." Colin knew exactly which cabinet to go into for the mixing bowl, which drawer for the spoon. Once he'd gotten comfortable doing things like opening cans and using a spatula, he'd relaxed right away.

Maybe when you worked in a restaurant where food was an art, you started to think of yourself as a culinary bystander, incapable of the brilliance you witnessed on a daily basis. People did that to Natalie, too: they'd look at her shawls and say, "Oh, I could never," and because they were looking at bullion stitches, they'd assume they couldn't learn to chain stitch.

Speaking of which, she really should make that set of dishcloths for Colin. He'd be cooking his own dinners soon, assuming he was ever in his apartment long enough to turn on the stove.

He'd begun creaming the butter and sugar. "What's with the wires? Are you going to hang the shawl up?"

"The wire isn't a hanger. It's there to give the piece a nice straight edge. Okay, so you know how if you go to sleep with wet hair, it ends up all over the place?" When Colin nodded, Natalie said, "Wool is sheep hair. If you get it wet, it remembers the shape it dried in, at least until the next time you get it wet."

Colin said, "The only time I had a wool sweater, I shrank it."

Natalie wrinkled her nose. "Maybe after this, I should teach you to do laundry."

Colin made a sad face. "Pow! Shot to the heart."

"I wasn't the one who felted your sweater." Natalie had her own list of laundry disasters, but she'd ignore that for now. "Anyhow, when you cast off a knit or a crocheted piece, the fabric is all bunched up around itself. What you do is soak it until it's wet through, then dry it a bit and pin it into the shape you want it to stay. If you had a cotton dress shirt, you'd iron it to make it smooth, and this is the equivalent."

Colin cradled the mixing bowl in his right arm, then cracked an egg with his left hand and broke it one-handed into the bowl. He had to have learned that from watching the cooks because Natalie herself couldn't do that. He cracked the second egg into the bowl, saying, "That's what makes it lie flat?"

Natalie said, "Blocking is what makes the lace open all the way up so everyone can see the full pattern. Otherwise you'd put in all that work, but the best part of the piece is hidden. And that'd be a shame because you don't want to hide what's most important."

Colin looked momentarily haunted, but then he resumed creaming the eggs into the mix. "I can understand that."

Natalie finished threading the steel wire through the eyelet row at the shawl's top border, then bent it until it stayed in a wide U shape. Matching her silence, Colin worked while letting her concentrate. Natalie pinned the wire in place on the blue foam boards, then ran another wire up the shawl's center spine. This one she left straight.

Colin approached. "Here, open up."

She looked up to find him with a chocolate chip in his hand, and she opened her mouth so he could pop one in.

Next, Natalie grasped the points on the shawl's lower edge and tugged until they'd reached a good stretch. Not too strained, but enough that the stitches opened out. When she had it at a nice tension, she set a T-pin through the point. Every few points, she'd measure to make sure she was keeping the tension even.

In the kitchen, Colin finished setting dough balls on her cookie sheet. "I'd rather wash a sink full of greasy pots and pans than do that kind of mad scientist experiment on lace. Your poor, tortured shawl."

Natalie said, "Joke's on you. It's not my shawl."

Colin slid the pan into the oven and set the timer. "Is it your cousin's?"

"She'd never let me do the finishing on one of hers. This is for a customer."

Colin said, "Bringing your work home. Not something a dishie has to worry about."

Natalie looked up. "You wash my dishes."

"Well..." He found a flat pan and started setting cookie dough on that one too. "Don't confound me with sense."

On her knees before the shawl, Natalie kept tugging and pinning, measuring and re-pinning, shifting the fabric, adjusting the stitches.

Colin said, "How much do you charge for that service?"

"This customer was desperate. I felt bad."

Colin said, "Your time is worthwhile."

Natalie said, "Should I have charged you for cooking lessons?"

Colin looked uncertain.

Natalie said, "You wouldn't have done it, would you?"

Colin's voice softened. "No, but there's a reason. I don't want you to think badly of me, but—"

He sounded embarrassed. He was nearly thirty and had no money and a lousy job, and she didn't want to hear it. Natalie blurted out, "It doesn't matter why."

"It does. See—"

Shaking her head, Natalie spoke rapidly. "Look, I don't charge for blocking because a lot of people don't have a lot of money to throw around. I happen to know this customer is struggling. It's not her fault. She's a good person. She's using up her stash because she lost her job, and she needed to give someone a gift. She had the time because she's unemployed. She used the best yarn she had, but she can't afford blocking boards and pins and wires, and she certainly can't afford to pay me twenty dollars to block it. I'm helping her because money isn't the only thing that determines whether someone is a worthwhile person." Natalie made her voice stern. "Okay? I get it. We all have tight seasons. You just moved. And soon, you're going to move again."

Colin sounded tentative. "I'm not sure about that anymore."

Natalie said, "This house didn't get any better. The lights still turn off if you start the washer while the dryer is going."

"I get that. But...well, things are different."

"Things being different" must be that the other apartment cost more. Natalie's cheeks burned. She said, "Well, I'm glad you'll still be here."

The timer went off, and Colin traded the pan on the stove for the pan in the oven. Subdued, he said, "Do you have a cooling rack?"

Natalie had no right to know Colin's finances, so it was good he'd changed the subject. "Alongside the roasting pans."

"Found it." For a minute, the only sound was the spatula retrieving cookies off the pan and onto the rack. But that minute stretched longer and longer, like a shawl pinned out just beyond its full extension, all the holes a little too big, the stitches contorted. Colin's discomfort permeated the apartment more than the smell of fresh cookies.

Sounding uncertain, he said, "I'm going out on a limb and assuming right now isn't the time to give you warm cookies that are gooey with chocolate, so I'll be right back," and he escaped to the downstairs.

Natalie's eyes burned. Colin deserved better out of life. He shouldn't be ashamed of his job or his bank balance.

Birdie Holly squawked. Natalie said, "I know, honey."

When Colin returned, he checked the cookies on the rack, double-checked the timer, and said, "Can I show you something?"

He held up what Natalie would have guessed was a knitting needle case, except it was leather and a lot thicker. He unrolled it and showed her how it contained... knives? Six of them, each with a different color sheath.

"Oh my gosh," she breathed. "That looks scary. Are you planning on murdering and filleting me?"

"I don't have a specialized knife for deboning an entire human." Colin looked so darned cheerful as he said it. "This is my knife roll. Everyone comes into a kitchen with their own."

She said, "Okay...?"

He pulled out what looked like a short, blunt sword. "This is a honing rod. Now watch."

He took a knife as long as his forearm in his left hand, and that honing rod in the right, and then he was running them against one another with a teeth-shivering scraping.

Natalie recoiled, but he just kept doing it—fast and accurate, he ran the rod against one side of the knife from heel to point, then changed the angle of his hands and ran the rod against the other side, again from heel to point. Three on one side, three on the other, fast and accurate.

He was going to hurt himself, except he knew exactly what he was doing with that thing, and at every second it just got sharper and more dangerous. *Don't hurt yourself!* This was so much worse than watching him chop onions. As fast as he was scraping those things together, she was terrified anything she did might make him lose concentration.

When Natalie's heart couldn't possibly be hammering any harder, Colin stopped all at once. He got a wet paper towel and ran it along the blade, then showed her the fine grey residue.

She managed, "That's got to be sharp enough to cut anything."

Colin said, "This is a honing rod, and it doesn't sharpen.

All I did was align the edge of the blade so it's better balanced. We do this every day in the kitchen."

Aligning the fibers...like what happened with a fleece comb. Get all the animal hairs pointing the same way, and then the fleece was prepared for action. You couldn't do anything with an uncombed fleece. Afterward, it was ready to be spun into the most glorious yarn.

Colin put the plastic cover back on his knife, then returned it to the leather knife roll. "Can I please do that to all your knives?"

"No!"

He stepped toward her. "That's not sharpening it. You said you didn't want them sharpened, but at least they should be balanced."

It sure looked like he'd been sharpening it. Natalie spread her hand. "I did this to myself when I was a kid." She traced the white line between her forefinger and middle finger. "I was cutting a bagel. Five stitches. I don't want that to happen again."

Colin knelt in front of the shawl and wrapped his hand around hers. "Can I teach you how to use the knives, then? I can show you what we do in the kitchen. You need to respect what the knife can do, but when it's functioning properly, you'll trust it to do its job."

She pulled back her hand. "I can already stay safe with my knives the way they are. I know how not sharp the knife is. It's predictable, like you said. If you sharpen it, you're going to change everything."

The timer beeped, and Natalie left the blocking mats to get the second pan of cookies. "I appreciate that you're trying to help, but that's not what I want."

Colin trailed her into the kitchen. "If you let me sharpen the knives, I'm actually protecting you."

Natalie huffed. "I'm not that brave."

"I think you're brave." Colin waited until she had the hot cookies on the stove and the other cookie sheet back in the oven. He set the timer. "You kept dealing with me after I was rude the first time. That makes you brave. You help people who are nothing but ungrateful in return, and you keep showing up. Every day, you show up."

She said, "There's a difference between showing up and signing up for more pain. I have a system that works for me. My knives aren't great, but they're predictable. I don't care if I have to work a little harder with them. I'm not asking for anybody's help, and I don't want any surprises. Leave my knives alone."

He wrapped his hands around her hand, then traced the old knife scar. "You offered to teach me to cook. My offer stands." He gestured to the cooling rack. "In the meantime, would you care for some cookies?"

CHAPTER EIGHTEEN

Pre-shift meeting. Colin and Austin called the back of house and front of house staff together to review the impending disaster.

First Colin ran down all the specials. "Aggressively push the mussels and any dish that has them," he said. "I may have overbought."

Next, Austin reviewed a scheduling issue, which they settled quickly. The line cooks always complained about working extra shifts, but when offered, they always took them. Money's money.

Finally Austin said, "Now for the function room. It's from one to three, thirty-two covers. Danielle and Ally will handle that room, so be aware of this while seating. Also, we're going to need to space the front of house tickets so we don't slam the kitchen while we're trying to get the function serviced."

Colin reviewed the menu for the crafting guild lunch. "I'm probably going to send out an *amuse bouche* as well," he added. "I'm not sure what, yet, but I'll figure it out."

"Mussels," muttered Bill. "Lots and lots of mussels."

Austin said, "Also, there's a complication."

Colin braced himself.

"For the duration of that meeting, we're going to pretend Colin isn't the owner." Austin pointed to Colin. "Allow me to introduce Colin the Dish Dog."

The Dish Dame snorted. "As if."

"I mean, fine, you do wash dishes," said Danielle, "but what's going on?"

"Is this a sting operation?" Alex said, and the BOH guys started to laugh.

"We've got what, a health inspector coming? A secret shopper?" Danielle opened her hands. "If I'm out there serving a restaurant critic, I need to know."

Austin said, "Guys, calm down. I'd tell you if it was something like that. This is far more dangerous. Our esteemed owner is dating one of the guests, and he didn't tell her who he is."

Uproarious laughter. Bill trumpeted, "Special on the menu—catfish!"

Colin shook his head. "Worst catfishing in history."

"Man, what are you doing?" Alex exclaimed. "Show her a good time! This is like the opposite of a secret shopper."

Danielle said, "With a party like this, used to be Dale would have gone through and talked to the folks."

Austin said, "I wanted Dale to swing by the meeting as if he were still the owner, but he's out of town."

Colin said, "I plan to tell her, but not here and now. When I mentioned I worked at Fruits de Mer, she wasn't impressed with the restaurant. If I tell her I own the place, she's not going to truly experience the food or the service. If she thinks I'm washing dishes, she'll judge the food and the service based on you, not on me."

The Dish Dame said, "Sounds nice, but dumb."

Austin raised a hand. "Two points to the Dish Dame."

Colin said, "This is a ridiculous situation, but here we are. For today, in front of the guests, act like I'm not the boss."

Austin said, "In the meantime, I'm in charge, so don't go insulting my brother."

Danielle said, "Well, that's easy to do. It's not like most diners ever go to the back of house to see the dishies."

The Dish Dame sniffed. "The feeling's mutual."

Colin shifted. "I've told her I do a bit of everything, like a floor manager but without the title. Also, a group that big —I am going to want to stop by and see how things are going."

Austin said, "There are fifty ways this could go wrong."

"Fifty ways things could go wrong is just another day in back of house." Bill huffed. "This is stupid, but I'm in."

Danielle said, "I'm in, too, but I want hidden camera footage when you unveil who you are."

Austin said, "Maybe we need to bring her into the kitchen afterward, so you can stage your big reveal."

Colin scanned the room. Bill. Danielle. The Dish Dame. His smirking twin brother. His kitchen family.

Austin pushed him on the shoulder. "Be brave and bold. Wow her with the food, and afterward, we'll reveal you're the genius behind it all."

Colin shook his head. "I'll be the one to tell her, and I'll do it when she's ready."

CHAPTER NINETEEN

Brooke trailed Natalie into Fruits de Mer, and Natalie talked her through the change the same way she'd introduced Brooke to all sorts of new places when they were kids. "I like the low lighting," she said, or "The tables are arranged so nicely." Brooke stuck close while Natalie confirmed with the host that they were with the crafting guild, and then the host threaded them between tables to a room at the back.

Just as overwhelmed as Brooke, Natalie tried to center herself amidst the grey and blue tones, the tables set for eight, and the buffet station at the back. The restaurant had adorned each table with a flower arrangement that had a candle inside a glass lantern.

Lilah waved them over to the two men she was already talking to. "Brooke! Come here, you need to meet these guys. This is Adrian Lim, a sculptor who relocated to Maine from Singapore ten years ago, and this is Emerson Charles, a landscape painter from Boston."

Emerson had brown skin and deep eyes that looked all the way through Natalie as he shook her hand. "A pleasure to meet you," and then he turned to Brooke and did the same.

Brooke said, "What part of Boston did you escape from?" and Emerson laughed.

"*Naa-at!*" Lilah singsonged. "I need to talk to you." She darted between Emerson and Brooke and snagged Natalie by the arm. "I met the mysterious evil twin, and honestly, he's amazing. You say they're identical?"

"I haven't seen the brother, but yes?"

Natalie glanced at Brooke, who seemed uncomfortable with her surroundings, but she kept talking to Emerson.

Lilah giggled. "Talk about easy on the eyes. The evil twin introduced me to the servers and consulted me about a last-minute change to the buffet, but we're good to go."

Natalie looked around. "Is Colin here?"

"I saw only one copy of the dreamy guy, so I have no idea."

Probably for the best. Natalie imagined Colin working flat out in stained jeans, sweating through a t-shirt under that black coat, his hair covered in a protective cap, and a soaked apron over his chest. Rubber gloves, hot water, soap, and a stainless-steel brush. It didn't feel right. Not when she knew him midday as clean, trim, and always a little exhausted.

Artists and artisans arrived for the next fifteen minutes, and Lilah kept exclaiming, "That's you!" Natalie knew how she felt. After weeks of getting to know everyone via their profile pictures, it was a shock to see their faces and hear their voices. Natalie spoke to a basket maker who had exchanged thousands of words of private messages with her, and it was a cognitive effort not to keep thinking of her as a sleepy otter floating on its back with a flower on its chest. For a while, Natalie had to not look directly at her.

Colin caught her eye, and Natalie's head jerked toward him, but then she realized it must be Austin. He carried himself differently, and he made a beeline for Lilah before getting her attention away from Emerson and Brooke (who still hadn't stopped chatting) and asking her a couple of questions.

Austin laughed. His laugh had a different tenor. It wasn't exactly performative. More that Austin realized he was "on" and was comfortable with the spotlight.

Of course Colin would get used by someone like this. Colin always sidled out of the spotlight. Even Natalie's acknowledgement of how quickly he was learning always left him distressed. He'd demurred when she pointed out that he'd made amazing cookies on his first attempt. Even alluding to his new confidence left him looking guilty.

Lilah called, "Natalie! Come here!" and Natalie braced herself to talk to her boyfriend's white-coated nemesis.

Austin shook her hand. "It's a pleasure to meet you." Even to her, he sounded performative without being insincere. He did want to meet her. He also was displaying the image he expected she would expect to see.

Natalie gave a measured, "Yes, Colin told me about you."

Austin beamed. "All lies."

Natalie raised her eyebrows. "He told me you were the handsome one."

Austin grinned. "That's my brother, honest as the day is long." When Lilah laughed, Austin turned to her. "We're getting out the drinks now and then we'll give everyone another five minutes to get settled before we lay out the first course. Salad and rolls, followed by soup, followed by the buffet."

Lilah said, "Thank you for setting up the room so nicely. The centerpieces are adorable."

"*Someone* insisted we pull out the stops." Austin looked sidelong at Natalie. "As long as at the end of the day, you're impressed."

Natalie's skin crawled. She liked Austin despite herself, but after so much exposure to Colin, everything seemed just a little off. He existed a smidgen outside the margins of himself, as though he'd never learned to color inside the lines. No—more like a crocheted-on border in a different color. Colin didn't need that extra spark of extraversion to make himself likable. Austin was used to dealing with the public and had in some respects accustomed himself to facing forward with what they expected to see.

It was like a beauty contest, where beautiful women changed their appearance to match the style of beauty they thought the judges were looking for. Still beautiful, but not their natural selves.

With Colin, at least, Natalie got to see the real person. The vulnerability, the curiosity, and the appreciation.

The pair of servers, Danielle and Ally, began delivering drinks to tables. Natalie took a seat between Lilah and Emerson. Brooke sat on Lilah's other side, but she and Emerson kept bantering with one another. This was good for Brooke. Emerson's quick wit and an easy smile were helping her relax.

Lilah breathed into Natalie's ear, "Okay, so we get you established with Colin, and Brooke with Emerson, and then I'll die happy."

Natalie murmured, "You can take Austin."

"Fine, I'll pick up the spare." Lilah snickered. "Except I'm a bit too busy to do that right now, so bookmark him for me."

Natalie pretended to look sly. "Can we arrange a convoluted scheme where we lead Austin to the shop at midnight for an emergency pair of knitting needles, and you can just happen to be there to sell them? Then—I don't know—you give him knitting lessons and by some hilarious mishap, you're both tangled up in a skein of DK weight?"

Lilah said, "Better make it acrylic so we can't just break out of it. Wait, what's this?"

Danielle set a Japanese soup spoon before each of them. "Complements of the owner. *Amuse bouche.*"

Lilah said, "We didn't order that."

"Complementary," the server repeated. "Just something fun ahead of the actual meal."

It was a bite-sized and very pretty bit of frippery. Lilah said, "Any guesses?"

Emerson said, "*Amuse bouche* means bite-sized

appetizers. Always strange, and no one ever repeats them."

Natalie examined it again: a fried cube of something, topped with a curved slice of mushroom cap and dotted with a dark sauce. Emerson ate his in one bite, so she did the same.

The flavor burst on her, and her eyes flew open.

Lilah said, "Well, that looks like an endorsement."

Natalie nodded as she chewed and swallowed. Everything blended together so well, but it was just that one piece, and then gone.

Emerson said, "Chefs experiment with these and don't make them twice. They're never on the menu. You get them because the head chef wants to play with the food."

Brooke said, "My grandmother spent ten years telling me not to play with my food."

Emerson shot back, "Imagine if she'd spent ten years encouraging you, and then you'd own the restaurant."

Natalie said, "All that work for fifteen seconds of enjoyment? It's a shame."

Emerson said, "How long do people enjoy a painting for, though? And that's weeks of work."

Natalie said, "Crochet isn't like that. I put a lot of work into making it, but then it's reusable over and over again."

"Same with dyeing yarn." Lilah's eyes were bright. "It takes time to come up with the right color combinations, and there's idea generation, but then people take hours to use the yarn. Afterward, the creation is available for reuse over and over again."

Emerson said, "The ones I feel bad for are musicians. Unless their work gets recorded, it doesn't stay around. We have paintings by Renoir, but we don't have the actual sound of Beethoven's piano playing."

Brooke said, "Which may be for the best. He used to destroy pianos trying to get the right sound from them."

Emerson said, "I'm sure that made his sponsors happy."

Brooke quipped, "The Eddie Van Halen of the pianoforte," and Emerson snorted a laugh.

The volume of chatter grew low with the arrival of the salads. As Natalie would have predicted, each bowl contained five varieties of greenery as the backdrop for the assortment of vegetables you'd anticipate, along with a tiny pitcher of dressing which tasted of dill and lemon. Not bad at all. The tables had baskets of rolls, with the option of seasoned olive oil to dunk them in, or a pat of butter carved in the shape of a flower.

Natalie leaned over to Lilah. "Are we supposed to eat the buttery rose?"

"It's a shame either way," said Lilah.

Natalie would have to apologize to Colin for calling the place an overpriced lunch for tourists. It was that—but the food was good. "Real food," as he kept reminding her.

After the salad, Danielle and Ally whisked away the bowls while the kitchen staff rolled trays to the buffet on carts. And there, finally, among everyone else, was Colin.

Distracting a man hefting gigantic bins onto serving frames seemed like an idea of the worst caliber. Natalie kept quiet, but her eyes were riveted to a black-coated Colin. So were Lilah's. A moment later, Brooke must have realized where they were looking, because she turned as well.

This was Colin in his element, he and two other members of the kitchen crew exchanging little by way of words but communicating constantly with gestures and actions. Everything went onto frames poised over baseball-sized canisters of fire, and then Colin distributed the serving pieces before setting tiny nametags in front of each food.

The last thing he did was step back and study it. One of the black-shirted guys chucked him on the shoulder, but Colin returned to the table and adjusted the positioning of the white plates holding the serving pieces.

The other two wheeled the carts back out of the room while Colin followed. As they passed the table, one of them was saying, "Nice to have you actually doing work for once."

Colin replied, "Shut up," and then caught Natalie's eyes.

The smile overtook her before she could wonder whether it was professional.

Colin leaned toward her on the table. He smelled intoxicatingly of smoke and roast beef. "Are you having a good time so far?" When Natalie nodded, he said, "What did you think of the *amuse bouche*?"

Natalie said, "Everyone really enjoyed it."

Colin said, "I'm not actually concerned with everyone. What did you think of it?"

Natalie squeezed his hand. "I loved it, too."

Colin winked at her. "Good." He returned to the kitchen, leaving Natalie surrounded by the scents and flavors of a meal she'd never imagined.

By the time the luncheon came to a close, Natalie's head was full of ideas for the creative guild, and her belly was full of an assortment of high-end everything. High-priced everything, too, except apparently the owner had cut them a break.

Pan-seared salmon in a tangy white sauce. Sous vide beef tenderloin with a garlic and mushroom sauce. *Moules farcies*, a kind of mussels with a buttery parmesan stuffing. Asparagus. Roasted Brussels sprouts. *Pommes Anna*, which was a casserole of thinly sliced potatoes and butter. And then an entire dessert cart of petits fours, replenished several times while Danielle and Ally patrolled the function room with coffee refills.

Austin reappeared to speak to Lilah. "I know you wanted to meet the owner, but that's not going to be possible. It's kind of a shame. Dale started the restaurant about twenty years ago, and he's a huge fan of the arts. One of the things I would like to talk to you about later this week is whether the culinary arts fit your paradigm."

Lilah said, "The membership is divided on that."

"Consider this, then," said Austin. "What about auxiliary membership for organizations that are peripheral to your core membership, but who want to participate?"

Lilah's eyes widened. "I like that!"

Austin's eyes gleamed. "Either way, we're trying to bribe you into saying yes that our head chef can join, so we've got a treat coming from the kitchen as soon as I get back there."

Natalie folded her arms and tilted her head. "In that case, it's to our benefit to postpone telling you our decision even if we already know what we're going to say."

Austin recoiled. "Wow, Colin didn't warn me you were ruthless! But you've correctly identified a hole in our strategy. The other matter to discuss is our lobby, and whether you could use our walls to showcase some of your visual artists on a rotating basis."

Lilah's eyes widened. "Are you kidding?"

"Dale and I had discussed something like this last year." Austin slid his hands into his pockets. "The owner and I aren't sure what that kind of arrangement would look like, but we would love to set up a gallery situation where an artist displays a few pieces in the waiting room and the dining area. Especially during the high-tourism months when we have people waiting up to an hour for a table, a rotating exhibition might benefit both the restaurant and the artist. If a diner wants to buy one of the pieces, we can put them in touch with the artist."

Two notions crashed together in Natalie's head, and neither one of them could detangle itself from the other.

First, that this wasn't the kind of behavior she'd expect from a restaurant owner who demanded Colin work eighty hours a week doing everything a general manager should do but without the title or salary of general manager.

How could a chef or a restaurant owner value oil paintings or charcoal sketches above the actual human beings sweltering in his kitchen, scrubbing pans and chopping onions? From what Colin said, the owner didn't even provide them knives.

But secondly, Natalie's brain caught a little nagging thought—that Austin would refer to the owner by name in one sentence, and by title in the next. It was jarring. And that didn't sound like a restaurant industry thing because Colin had never referred to Fruits de Mer's owner as Dale —nor, now that she thought about it, had he referred to the owner at all. Whenever he talked about the restaurant management, he'd talked about Austin.

Their landlord Denny owned five properties in Brighthead—two strip malls and two buildings he'd carved up into apartments, plus his own home. A management company took care of four of the five, and Natalie had assumed the same for Fruits de Mer: an absentee owner who'd bought a restaurant for the investment, hired Austin to run the place, and then phoned in once a week from Bermuda.

By contrast, Austin referred to Dale ("the owner") as if they spoke regularly. She'd have to ask Colin what that was all about. Maybe Austin wasn't so bad after all. He might be positioning himself as a human shield to keep the brunt of the owner's exploitation off the staff.

Ally and Danielle reappeared with more of those deep white spoons, passing one to every diner. Austin said, "Dessert *amuse bouche*. Tell me what you think."

In the bowl of the spoon was a melon-ball sized bit of sorbet, crowned with a chocolate-filled raspberry and drizzled with a ruby-colored sauce. Lilah took hers, and she sighed, but Austin was waiting for Natalie's verdict. In point of fact, he didn't seem to care what Lilah thought.

Natalie enjoyed her one-bite dessert, and she closed her eyes. "So good."

Austin took back the ceramic spoons. "That's our culinary bribe. Let us know if our head chef can enroll in your creative collaborative."

CHAPTER TWENTY

With the luncheon over, Colin sealed himself in his office, shaking.

Having Natalie in the building had keyed up all his nerves to their maximum output. Showing off for her this way—the invisible chef behind the curtain—left him shivering. He kept hearing the ticket printer even though the front of house was empty and no tickets were coming in. His team was simultaneously giving him a hard time and doing their best work, and he found no fault with anything they'd done. If anything, when Bill had made suggestions, Colin had followed them because his team knew what they were doing.

"Two *amuses*, though...?" Danielle had muttered as she loaded her tray with the tiny ceramic spoons Colin had hand-washed and then refilled for a second trip to the function room. "Honey, I'm not sure any woman's worth that."

Colin said, "My mom's not around to approve or disapprove, so I need your input."

She'd only glancingly caught the sarcasm. "Roses are red, violets are blue. If you mom doesn't like her, she isn't for you."

Danielle and Ally were getting tipped well, regardless. Both for the table service and the spy service.

Colin returned to the kitchen, where the Dish Dame was grumbling about Alex burning one of the pans. Danielle called, "Corner!" and entered the kitchen with a tray of plates, then set them down exactly where the Dish Dame demanded.

Alex said, "What's it like being surrounded by artists?"

Danielle laughed. "I don't understand half the conversations. Those quilters? They got in a fight about sewing machine models."

Colin joined Danielle. "I'll scrape the dishes and get you out of here sooner."

"Thanks." Danielle stepped back, sing-songing, "I told the dish-wash-er, the meal was a success! I told the dish-wash-er, the woman never guessed."

Colin laughed, except Danielle stopped abruptly and blurted out, "Oh, crud."

"Corner!" Austin's voice rang out above the kitchen cacophony. "Civilian under escort. Watch for flying knives," he said more softly.

Looking up from scraping plates, Colin found himself face to face with Natalie.

This was one hundred percent the cover he needed, and yet here she was, impeccable in her heels and dress and jewelry and makeup, and here he was, scraping half-eaten food into a trash barrel.

Natalie shifted her weight. "I hope you don't mind. The meal was wonderful, and Austin offered that I could see the kitchen."

Colin said, "Hang on," and dashed to the hand wash station.

The Dish Dame muttered, "Sure abandon me."

Austin said, "You were going to re-scrape half of them anyhow."

"No one messes with my dish pit," shot back the Dish Dame.

Colin said to Natalie, "If you don't mind dodging people, I can show you around."

Natalie looked afraid to move, so Austin nudged her toward Colin with a hand on the small of her back. "I'll pass you over to him. But remember, I'm the charming one."

Colin guided Natalie to the far end of the kitchen, saying, "Be careful," a caution to her but also to himself because having her here was a minefield, and a reminder to anyone around him that they needed to keep their mouths shut.

Natalie said, "What do I need to know?"

Bill murmured under his breath, "Oh, where to begin...?"

Colin huffed. "Well, here's where the tickets come out when the server inputs an order. And by coincidence, here's a machine that gives everyone a heart attack when we hear it grinding for three minutes at a time."

Natalie laughed, and after that, it was easier. Here were the sixth pans and ninth pans, and this was the good sixth pan because it had rounded edges and everyone competed to get to it first. Here was Bill, the sous chef, drinking out of a takeout container the same way Colin did. Here was the prep station, and here was Eric who would always *mise* the butter the wrong way because why not? Here was the sauté station, and there was the fry station. "This is Alex, who works the broiler because he's the only one who understands this beast, since the broiler is the second cousin of the mouth of hell."

Alex added, "It's all about zones. I put the rares and medium rares right in the back where it's hottest, and no one ever understands that."

"You've met the Dish Dame," Colin said. "She's the most important person in the kitchen because the best food in the world isn't going anywhere if we don't have a clean plate to put it on."

"Darned straight," muttered the Dish Dame.

Natalie said to Colin, "Sounds lucky you're allowed to touch the sinks at all."

The Dish Dame snorted, but at least she didn't say anything else.

At every one of the stations, Natalie responded by admiring it, how clean, how efficient, how amazing the equipment—everything Colin had felt on walking into his first kitchen as a line cook and then every single time he'd moved up the ladder. Fruits de Mer was the pinnacle of kitchens, with everything in its place, gleaming and ready. Chaos in motion during the busy hours, but a model of potential energy while at rest, dancers during a pause in the performance.

Colin introduced Natalie to the servers, "You already know Danielle," he added.

He showed her the sous vide stations, too. Meanwhile the line cooks had resumed joking with one another, and Bill was scraping down the grill with a brick.

Colin walked Natalie back to the dining room. "So, what do you think of the back of house?"

Natalie said, "I liked it. This kitchen is amazing."

It was. The gleaming stainless steel. The robot coupe food processor. The grill and the walk in and the sauté stations—well, not that monstrosity of a broiler, but even so.

Colin said, "Every day, I walk in here, and I'm amazed too."

"Compared to this, it's a wonder we can cook at all in my kitchen." He'd said the same thing, but she missed the coincidence. She held his hand, then let go. "Everyone had a great time, so make sure you tell the cooks again. It was impressive."

Colin said, "Even the little chocolate-filled raspberries?"

"Especially those." When she smiled her eyes lit up. "Did you get to try one?"

He shook his head.

"See if you can convince the chef to make one for you, too." She kissed him on the cheek. "Thank you for showing me the restaurant."

He walked her to the car, his hand in hers, a confession

burning on his lips. "I'm glad you liked the raspberries. That was my idea." He steeled himself. "This is unnerving. I don't want you to think badly of me."

"I don't." She hugged him. "If anything, talking to everyone and seeing the restaurant, I figured out exactly what's been going on."

Colin's heart hammered.

"It's all so complicated back there—fights like how to *mise* the butter and which part of the rebellious broiler is for which kind of steak?" Natalie's eyes practically glowed. "No wonder you didn't learn to cook. They made it seem like black belt artistry. I'm glad I was able to show you it's not."

Whatever Colin's next sentence would have been, the words scattered out of his head like pigeons in front of a bounding Labrador Retriever.

"I can see how everyone in the kitchen feels like family to one another. When everything's flying fast and furious, you must be operating on trust every step of the way. Trust that things are where you left them, or trust that someone isn't going to step in front of you, or trust that no one took the last baked potato out of the warmer."

Colin looked aside. "You're right. We all have specific roles, and we all need to trust that other people will uphold their end of the bargain."

Like not calling him out as the owner, for example. Although he was going to get a whole lot of good-natured flack for it the moment he stepped back inside. Even without turning his head, he knew there would be Alex and Bill and maybe Danielle with cameras pointed through the windows.

"I'm glad you've got people like that with you." Natalie put her arms around his shoulders, and he pulled her toward him. In the parking lot, she kissed him. He probably smelled like grease and hand soap, and she was a vision of beauty, but she held him tight and kissed him anyway.

CHAPTER TWENTY-ONE

The crafting guild discussion group erupted with new conversations the next day, and Natalie took over everything in the store so Lilah could drive a thousand different trains of thought.

"Good news!" Lilah exclaimed. "Per vote on the forum, chefs are allowed into the creative collaborative. Do you want to tell Austin, or should I?"

"You can tell him." Natalie would much rather speak to Colin. "Remember, we were supposed to set up Austin with you, since he can cook."

"He's not the head chef." Lilah ran her rainbow fingertips through her hair. "I'll take care of telling him when I talk to him about a mini showcase, because everyone's all lit up about that, too."

Natalie swept while Lilah did paperwork, and Natalie checked out a customer while Lilah set up a website. "The group needs bylaws." Lilah paced the shop while Natalie readied the table for Sit and Stitch. Later, "We're going to need officers," she said, while Natalie showed a customer how to crochet a foundation chain.

By the time Brooke arrived mid-afternoon, Natalie was

desperate for five minutes to herself so she could eat her sandwich, and Lilah had come up with enough schemes to take over the world.

Brooke pointed to Natalie. "Eat. You're pale and exhausted." She pointed to Lilah. "Stand in one place and give me the address of every single castle you've built in the sky."

Lilah hopped onto the edge of the Sit and Stitch table. "It's not a castle in the sky. We can do every one of these things."

"Castles need foundations under them. Start with the foundations."

Natalie unwrapped her sandwich. Colin must have crawled into her head because how much better would this be if she had a way to toast her slightly stale bun in a pan with butter, then melt the cheese onto the ham, maybe add some other topping...?

Lilah said, "We need to elect officers. I've registered for an EIN, and as of this morning, we have a business license. I've started the process of applying to become a nonprofit. We'll need bylaws, and I've already put up a document and asked for comments. Once we have that set up, I'm going to open a bank account. Then we can ask people to register and pay dues, and we'll have a sliding scale of how much you pay versus what category you're in. Hobbyists will pay less than semi-pro, and then there will be professionals."

Brooke said, "Volunteers should get a break on their membership cost."

Without answering, Lilah typed that onto her tablet screen.

Natalie just kept working on her sandwich because Lilah hadn't yet gotten to the point where Brooke would laugh and then stop as if she'd witnessed a train derailment.

Lilah said, "Our main thrust will be combining our marketing efforts, but our secondary thrust should be overall community outreach. That way, we can increase artistic representation in Maine."

Brooke's nose wrinkled. "What exactly do those last five words mean? Because we have a lot of artists in the state already."

"We want them in the spotlight. We can make people think of coastal Maine the same way they think of Truro or Marfa." Lilah was glowing. "We should make sure we're present at all the town fairs during the summertime."

Given that every town had its own Town Spirit Day, that was a tall order in and of itself, but not yet the point where Brooke was going to step in and write Lilah a reality ticket.

Lilah said, "We're going to reach out to a number of coffee shops and restaurants to see if they'll do what Fruits de Mer offered to do, and showcase artists. We'll slate the higher-ticket artists to the higher-priced venues, though, so the landscape artists aren't displaying their work at a lunch counter."

Brooke said, "Reach out to the local libraries as well. Every local library has displays, and sometimes they allow the artist to give a presentation."

Lilah typed again, and then, "Also, we want to start an artists' colony!"

There you had it. The moment Brooke pulled the emergency brake. "Excuse me?"

Lilah set the tablet on the table so she could gesture wildly with her sparkly blue fingernails. "We get a piece of property, right? Large, but not too far from everything, and then we get twelve of those tiny houses and move them onto the property, and then we divide the property so it's affordable to an artist, and the artist can live there and work. We can have one large studio on the property as well, where they can work together and combine their disciplines! We could have a kiln, and maybe a loom, and easels for the painters, and work desks with great lighting! There could be a shop on the premises too, so we could sell the work!"

Brooke folded her arms. "No."

Lilah shook her head. "You're not listening to me. I'll

bring it to the economic planning board because if we can get it in Brighthead, we can stimulate the local economy. We'll become a destination for people looking to find locally sourced art, and at the same time, we'll be providing affordable housing for artists."

Brooke said, "You're talking about setting up a co-op but also zoning it for commercial use and requiring variances to install multiple small single unit dwellings and then dividing the property. That wouldn't happen in ten years, and we certainly can't start with it out of the gate."

"Say what you want, but I'm going to make it happen." Lilah turned to Natalie. "Wouldn't you rather live in a tiny house than in a drafty apartment where you reflexively say 'Bless you' when the downstairs tenant sneezes?"

Natalie frowned. "I'd have to see the layout of the tiny house."

"They're adorable!" Lilah laughed. "You can get them with lofts so your bed is over the kitchenette and the bathroom, and then you have a sitting room with a table that folds up—"

"And enough zoning violations to keep the collaborative in court every day for six years." Brooke waved her off. "Please don't think again about this scheme. If we ever form an artists' colony, a better plan would be to choose one of the subdivisions and start quietly buying out every townhome that comes on the market. Or build our own condominiums.

"You're such a downer. This is workable!"

"This is a huge time-waster. Let's talk more about the classes." Brooke leaned against the sock yarn shelves. "*How to knit if you're a member of the general public*, kind of classes? Or *how to market if you're a guild member*, kind of classes?"

"Oh, good point. We'll want some continuing education for each other, not just outreach to the public." Lilah resumed typing.

Natalie said, "Half the point of crafting is to spawn new crafters."

Brooke said, "Although I would love a class on how we should not be teaching the public to undervalue our skill set. Things like, *Thou shalt not take our customers' work home to block it for free.*"

Natalie snapped, "It's not that hard!"

"Yes, but you fill your entire day with work that isn't that hard to do. Which brings to mind, how much work has Lilah done today in the shop while she was setting up pipe dreams about artists' colonies? Not that I mind," Brooke added to Lilah. "The point is, Nat, you keep picking up the slack when you don't have to, and you're getting taken advantage of."

Natalie said, "So when someone comes in with a shawl that just needs a little blocking—"

"We will start charging for that service."

Natalie said, "She wasn't going to pay for it. She didn't even know what blocking was!"

"So you wait for them to ask and be willing to pay. Better yet," Brooke said, "we offer a class that's free for anyone who buys blocking boards and T-pins from us, and we teach them how to block."

Natalie's eyes widened.

Brooke said, "Doing work for free undervalues your skills, but it also takes income away from the shop, and it opens us up to risk. If something happened to that shawl while you were blocking it, how understanding would the knitter be?"

Natalie said, "Like what?"

"Like Birdie Holly attacked it, or like her bind-off was too tight and the edging snapped—which you know has happened before."

Specifically, it had happened to Brooke when Natalie was teaching her to block. They'd fixed it, but things had gotten tense.

Brooke faced Natalie with folded arms. "I'm serious. Stop stepping in to solve everyone else's problems. If you don't value your time and your skill, no one else is going to."

CHAPTER TWENTY-TWO

Natalie called, "Come in!" in response to Colin's knock, so he entered into a kitchen that smelled of tea.

Warm already, he set his bag down on the table. "You look like a woman with a plan."

"I have a plan!" She gestured that he should join her on the couch. "Ready?"

She had a website open on her tablet, and he joined her, but while looking over her shoulder at the screen he got distracted and kissed her cheek, then ended up kissing her lips, then ended up sitting away from her breathless because he didn't have a lot of time before he needed to get back to work.

Flushed, Natalie tried to regain her balance. "I found this recipe, and I thought we'd give it a try because they said it looks fancy, but it's cheap."

Colin nodded. "Two points in its favor. How do we start?"

They read the recipe together, and it turned out to be a poor man's version of chicken with thirty cloves of garlic. "Vampire vaccine!" Colin exclaimed. "Not a lot of chopping and dicing, and I'll only owe you ten bucks in supplies."

"You can let that go now. We're beyond cooking lessons, unless you ordinarily kiss the teacher."

Colin gave a helpless smile.

They relocated to the kitchen where Colin set everything on the counter, eventually overflowing to the kitchen table. Natalie had stopped asking, "Why do you do that?" when he got it all out at the same time. She believed in just-in-time retrieval of every implement and ingredient, but Colin wouldn't work that way. He separated and peeled all the garlic cloves, and then Natalie followed the instructions to roast them in oil in her cast iron pan. They removed the garlic, and then in went four chicken thighs, skin-side down.

Colin said, "Here's a trick," and he made tiny cuts alongside the thigh bone. "They'll cook faster."

Natalie seasoned the chicken thighs with salt and pepper while Colin wondered what else he could scavenge from her spice cabinets. They added the garlic back into the pan, then tucked the whole cast iron pan into the oven.

"Twenty minutes," Natalie said. "Come here."

He followed her back to the couch, where maybe they could continue what he'd started before—except she handed him a battered cookbook.

Colin's eyes widened. "A *Settlement Cookbook*! It really is the way to a man's heart."

That was the subtitle: "The way to a man's heart."

Natalie laughed. "This was my great-grandmother's, and she gave it to my grandmother, who gave it to Mom, who gave it to me."

"And now it's the way to my heart." Colin handled it like a relic, willing his spirit to connect with four generations of cookery, through times when the food supply was uncertain and the money supply even less so. "I'm in awe. Do you use it?"

"Not often. Some of the recipes are a bit strange."

Colin stroked the cover. "This book is a slice of American history. It was initially written for immigrants, showing them how to integrate their own history into

American culture. So it has instructions on how to set a table or how to light a fire, but you also have recipes for lemonade, biscuits, borscht, and roasted chicken."

"I had no idea." Natalie cuddled up next to him and opened at random. "Apple fritters. Pineapple fritters. Queen fritters—I hope not made with an actual queen!"

Colin quipped, "That's worse with a Caesar salad."

Natalie laid a hand on her heart. "The age-old problem of the chef's salad—after he's made one, you need a new chef."

"Or she," Colin corrected.

Natalie said, "I've always heard men make better chefs."

Colin shot back, "And I've always heard that's sexist nonsense, from a time when men cooked for powerful men in prestigious locations, whereas women cooked 'only' for their families in their own homes." He snorted. "At CharCuties, two of the owners were women, and they were brilliant."

Natalie said, "You could have had the owners there teach you."

"Oh, I learned a lot." Colin flipped to another page. "'Invalid cookery.' Oh, wait, *in*-va-lid, not in-*valid*. Cooking for people who are sick."

Natalie leaned over. "'Serve food in the most pleasing manner possible. Use dainty dishes. Put a flower on the tray.' Aw."

"That is kind of *aw*." He wrapped his arm around her. "Also instructions on pasteurizing milk."

"Eggnog!" Natalie pointed. "We could try that next Christmas."

She intended to be around next Christmas. This was hopeful. "Followed by toast water. I'm not seeing the appeal." He squeezed her to his side. "Have you ever heard of a toast sandwich? Because it exists."

"I'm sorry to hear that." She flipped again. "Fish! How to skin a fish, how to bone a fish, how to treat a frozen fish." She set down the book and looked at the fish tank in the corner. "Sorry, guys. I do know how to treat you. Not with tartar sauce."

"Fish suitable for boiling," Colin said. "None. That's pretty easy."

Natalie laughed.

He muttered, "Honestly, are you going to buy a salmon and plunk it into a pot of boiling water? And then smother it with, what, gingersnap sauce?"

Natalie's eyes widened. "My apologies, Colin. I thought you were making that up, but gingersnap sauce is a recipe right here on the page." She rested her hand on his. "I should have known to trust you. You would never lie about food."

Oh, boy. Colin flipped a bunch of pages again for distraction. "Potato dumplings! That sounds good. And... Mock asparagus?"

Natalie said, "I would never mock an asparagus."

"Neither would it. It's all pointy, and tastes good with lemon." He studied it. "Well, mock the 'mock asparagus' all you like. It's another potato dumpling thing."

Natalie read, "'Roll into the shape and size of an asparagus.'"

"And dust with cracker crumbs. I'm...moderately horrified." Colin frowned.

She put her hand on his thigh, and warmth shot up to his throat. "We'll get past this somehow."

He rested his hand on her hand and then threaded his fingers between hers. "I'm not sure. Some traumas are too great to be borne."

They cuddled and read recipe titles to each other, or sometimes the instructions. "Macaroni pudding," with an accompanying shudder, or "creamed chicken in potato boats," followed up by, "Well, that might not be so bad."

"Creamed chicken in avocados," Natalie said. "I'm not sure."

Colin nuzzled her. "Avocados are a nightmare. Let's not."

"Salad dressings," she said, flipping pages. "I never even thought about where salad dressings come from."

"The stork delivers them? When you're ready, we can make our own mayonnaise. It's much better than the store-bought stuff."

"Tomato roses," Natalie said.

He murmured, "Do you like roses?"

"Love them. I love the way they smell."

"I love the way they taste," Colin said. Natalie laughed, and he didn't correct her.

"Washington's Birthday Salad."

"Ooh, a special for Fruits de Mer on July 4th." Colin flipped ahead. "General rules on how to make a sandwich. That will come in handy."

Natalie snuggled up against him. "See? It's good. You've opened up a whole world of food now that you can cook for yourself."

Colin tightened his grip. "I need to tell you something."

She looked up.

He couldn't quite meet her eyes. "When I kept coming back, it wasn't that I wanted you to teach me to cook."

Natalie said, "I know."

Colin's head jerked up.

She said, "You were trying to flirt with me, but you didn't want to be creepy about it."

Colin shook his head. "It's more complicated than that. I —"

Natalie cut him off. "You have a birds-eye view of all the chefs, so any time you wanted to learn, you could have paid attention to them. Even if you had a mental block about it, you were coming back because of me."

He said, "I kept coming back for you. But—"

The timer went off in the kitchen, and Natalie kissed him. "You wouldn't be the first person to pretend to be helpless just to spend time with their crush."

He followed her into the kitchen. "You're not quite mad enough. You should let me finish."

"You kept bringing me food." She winked at him. "I prefer the way you did it."

She hefted the cast iron pan out of the oven, filled with

crispy chicken and a garlic sauce.

Colin said, "The thing is—"

She exclaimed, "No! Quit trying to apologize and let me show you how to deglaze a pan, because this is like magic."

She removed the chicken, then poured broth into the hot pan so the steam loosened the cooked-on bits of chicken and grease.

Colin muttered, "That's not magic. Magic is for deceiving people. You show them exactly what you're doing, and somehow they still see something else."

She rubbed the base of the pan with a silicone scraper. "People see what they want to see, but that's not what cooking is. Food is real. There's no deception."

Six o'clock in the morning. Natalie awoke to the sound of Colin's space-themed alarm, and she burrowed further under her comforter.

Her apartment was chilly. The blankets were warm. When she closed her eyes and concentrated, she could remember all the tastes and textures of the guild meeting's meal, and she wanted to head back in time to re-sample those delicious bites.

The best part of the buffet had been not needing to choose between good things. On her first trip, she'd taken tiny portions, mindful of Mom's constant admonitions not to grab more than you'd eat, and even smaller samples if you weren't sure you'd like it.

Then to discover she did—she loved it all. Everything had been combined with such care and precision that it was no wonder Colin hadn't dared learn to cook.

Beneath her, the pipes knocked, and the murmur of his shower started.

He'd been a good sport on her about-face on Fruits de Mer. The restaurant was still frivolous, but not overpriced. It was only beyond Natalie's means and exceeded her allotment of class. And the way he'd tried to confess yesterday that he'd come back for cooking lessons because he was crushing on her and not because he wanted to learn...? He'd been so awkward, and she'd had to spare him the pain of confessing. Even after she'd told him she knew, he'd been unable to meet her eyes.

So cute. So sweet.

She drifted back to sleep, remembering the table settings and the waitstaff passing out those ceramic spoons with the one-bite "*amuses.*"

Her alarm went off, and she awoke to hear Colin's shower had ended, so she got out of bed. Birdie Holly sang when she turned on the light, and she whistled back at him. Birdie Holly kept singing, and Natalie joined him.

Good morning, Sweetie.
Good morning, Sweetie.
Wake up and eat breakfast.
Sweetie, wake up.

As she put food in Birdie Holly's cage, she heard another voice, diffused as it emerged through her floor from the downstairs apartment

Good morning, Sweetie.
Good morning, Sweetie.
Feed the bird so he won't starve.
Sweetie, feed him.

Natalie laughed, then sang back,

Good morning, Sweetie.
Good morning, Sweetie.
That bird is a liar.
I promise, he's fed.

From below, laughter. Natalie fed the other animals, then turned on her coffee maker.

She could make coffee for Colin, but he was always out the door so fast. By the time she dug out a mug with a lid, he'd be gone.

Half the time, he drank out of a quart-sized takeout container with a hole punched for a straw. He did own mugs—she'd seen one on his kitchen table—but she had no idea how well the rest of his kitchen was apportioned. He'd never had her inside his apartment long enough to see it. She'd never forced the issue. She couldn't deal with how embarrassed he must feel about his empty cabinets.

Even so, he was seldom there. If he ate breakfast, he ate it at the restaurant. "Last night's rolls toast up nice and crispy," he'd said once. "And it's good coffee. I could live there."

But he didn't. He was still living downstairs.

If someone turned Natalie loose in a restaurant kitchen for breakfast, what could she do? She'd be able to whip up pancakes with the ingredients they had on hand. There was that huge griddle, and Colin already knew how to work the coffee maker.

She texted him, "If you sneak me into the restaurant kitchen, we could cook you a full breakfast."

Colin replied, "Bacon, eggs, hash browns?"

She said, "French toast."

He added, "Breakfast sandwiches toasted up on last night's slightly stale rolls that we're only going to turn into croutons anyhow."

She said, "That sounds fun."

He replied, "That does sound fun. I'd love to see what you could do on professional grade equipment."

She shot back, "Not the knives."

"You don't need a chef's knife to butter pancakes. I'll slice the baguettes and shred up the potatoes so you don't have to." Then he added, "Do you like omelets?"

She said, "I can totally show you how to cook those."

He said, "Cheese? Mushrooms? There's all sorts of leftovers for fillings. Steak and eggs? Say the word. I have keys."

She texted, "Sneak me in at five in the morning, and we'll cook until dawn."

A pause, and then he sent, "I'd like that. We could sit on

the deck and watch the sun rise over the bay."

She texted, "When?"

"I'll have to adjust Austin's schedule so he won't walk in on us."

Natalie went cold. "Wait, would you get in trouble?"

Colin replied, "No."

She added, "Because I'm not doing it if you'd get in trouble."

"I will not get in trouble."

A minute later, his door shut, and she heard his steps in the entrance. But instead of the front door opening and closing, there was a knock on her apartment door.

Natalie was still in flannel pajamas, but she opened anyhow. When Colin leaned in and kissed her, it went through her like a rush.

"I will not get in trouble if we cook breakfast," he said. "If you want to do it, I just need to make sure we have what we need, including time."

Natalie said, "Austin entrusted you with the keys. And that Dale guy—?"

"That Dale guy doesn't care. As long as we're *mise en place* when the morning shift arrives, no one would mind if I slept in the dining room and shaved in the guest bathroom." Colin tugged her into his arms and pivoted with her as if dancing. "Keep seducing me with breakfast talk, though, because I'm enjoying it more than you think. Why would anyone want a woman who brings donuts when he could have a woman who plies him with talk of omelets and breakfast sandwiches?"

She traced a finger over his cheek. "You're going to be late for work, and I only suggested French toast."

He nuzzled her neck. "Oh, do go on," and she laughed.

He stepped back. "Well, if you ever want to know the way to my heart, you found it."

She said, "Through the taste buds? Brooke says the best way to reach a man's heart is with a metal size ten straight needle, between ribs five and six."

Colin made his eyes sad. "You'd ruin your needle."

Natalie said, "Crochet hooks probably aren't pointy enough, anyhow."

He mimed wiping sweat off his brow. "Safe for another day." Then he grinned. "But plan on that breakfast—because I need to know when to bring my sleeping bag to work. This time of year, we'll want to cuddle up close on the deck to stay warm."

CHAPTER TWENTY-THREE

Colin's headlights were the only brightness on the road as he pulled into Fruits de Mer's back lot, and despite being five minutes late, he'd still beaten Austin to the restaurant.

Oh, the idea of sneaky breakfast with Natalie. That would be the time to tell her. Bring her in, turn on the griddle, get her settled, and then make her everything. Colin had worked a breakfast grill one summer and had mastered all the tricks, plus this flat-top griddle was much better than the one he'd learned on.

After he showed off, when she was surprised, he'd bring her coffee plus eggs, bacon, and hash browns, and he'd say, "There's something I really need to tell you, and I've put it off far too long."

Just, not in the morning before he left for work and she wouldn't see him for ten hours. And not right after she'd told him she could trust him, or that he'd never lie about food, or anything like that. He needed to get her happy and pleased and full of coffee and giggles, surrounded by butter and stainless steel. He needed her to stop leaping to conclusions so she could rescue him from his own admissions. Then he could tell her.

A second car pulled into the lot, but not Austin's. Odd. Had Austin borrowed someone else's?

Colin stepped out of his car, and a driver exited the other vehicle. A woman, short and dark-eyed, her face set like flint.

She felt familiar, maybe one of Austin's conquests, or maybe an employee Dale had fired months ago. Maybe someone hoping for a free meal? She strode across the chilly parking lot braced for a fight, and Colin steeled himself against whatever happened next.

Colin took the fight to her. "We're still closed. May I help you?"

The woman stopped in front of him and extended her hand. "Colin Young? Owner of Fruits de Mer? My name is Lilah Marcille."

Before he could place her name, she added, "I'm acting president of the Brighthead Crafters Guild, and I'm Natalie's employee at Bright Stitches."

Sometimes when you worked in a kitchen, you could see disaster about to strike—a container with thirteen gallons of tomato sauce set on the wrong part of a prep table, about to topple to the floor. There wasn't anything you could do about it.

Just in case it wasn't disaster time, Colin tried to shake her hand. "Thank you for having your meeting in our restaurant."

"I was going ask Austin to give the owner some good news," Lilah said, folding her arms, "except I decided I'd go the extra mile and look up the owner myself. I learned Dale sold the place. To you, in fact."

Colin pulled out his keys. "Let's go inside."

"Let's not go inside. What are you doing to Natalie?"

"I'm not doing anything to her." Their breath frosted up with every sentence. "She broadsided me with a couple of ridiculous statements the first time we met, and I played along until I realized she was serious."

"Except you've known for a while that she thinks you're an incompetent man-child who never figured out how to

175

microwave a potato, so now you're taking advantage of her good nature." Lilah's brow furrowed. "She's head over heels for you, and you're using her."

Austin's headlights swung over the lot as he pulled in. Colin said, "I promise you, I'm not using her."

"Is it revenge? You got mad at her for making whatever assumptions you think she made, and now you're stringing her along with this elaborate scheme?" Lilah stepped closer. "It didn't take long to figure you out, either, so you're pretty brazen."

Austin got out of his car. "Lilah? Was there a problem with the catering? Or is my brother attempting to convince you he's the handsome one?"

Colin waved him off. "Not now."

Lilah said, "There's a problem with your owner being a manipulative swine to one of my best friends."

Austin frowned at Colin. "Natalie? I thought you cleared that up."

Colin said, "I tried, but then she reached an entirely different, and also incorrect, conclusion."

Austin rolled his eyes. "How can you be such an idiot?"

Lilah had fire in her eyes. "He's not being an idiot. He knows what he's doing." She glared at Austin. "Is Colin incapable of communicating with the rest of your kitchen staff? With your suppliers? With your marketing people? You want me to believe it's only Natalie he can't communicate with?"

Colin flinched. "I've been trying to break it to her easy, but I mean it—it's like she doesn't want to hear me out. She leaps to the next weird conclusion instead of listening to what I'm saying, and I never know how to stop her."

Austin said, "I'd think you could stop her by saying, 'Please, let me finish.'"

Lilah did a double take. "Wait, even the handsome one agrees with me?"

Austin huffed. "I told him to come clean ages ago."

Colin muttered, "A week ago."

"Four minutes after you told me what was going on."

Austin turned to Lilah. "My brother is a lot of things, but he's not a scammer. He's been walking around on cloud nine ever since he got together with Natalie, and that's legit."

Lilah snorted. "That's how he treats people he likes? How can you work for him?"

Austin said, "Easily. The question is what to do about Natalie."

"There is no question." Lilah turned to Colin. "Here's what's going to happen. You have twenty-four hours. Somehow before tomorrow when I see her at the yarn shop, I expect you to have told Natalie exactly who you are and what you're doing. The whole truth. Your exact reasoning. Every misunderstanding, although I don't think for a second you misunderstood what was going on. You're going to beg forgiveness on your knees if that's what it takes, and if she kicks you out of her life, then that's also what happens."

Colin raised his hands. "Agreed."

Lilah said, "Because when I walk in the door at Bright Stitches, I'm telling her. It's up to you whether I'm the second person she hears it from, or the first."

Austin put his hands in his pockets. "Sounds generous to me."

Lilah's eyes bored into Colin. "I'm armed with any number of pointy metal implements, but I don't need them to take you down. Not when I've got the truth."

Colin's thoughts kept exploding like roasting chestnuts. As they walked through the terminal market, Austin gave him space in the best way possible: by handling all the purchasing and making all the suggestions and simultaneously taking no risks with the menu. Lots of old reliables here. They'd re-do one of their previous specials. Lots of flexibility with this one ingredient. Not as much lobster this week because prices were high.

Colin had damage control to do.

Austin rejected the beef from one vendor, who gave them a filthy look as they moved on to the next one. "Never mind him," Austin murmured. "He and Dale had this thing going where the dude would keep lowering the quality without lowering the price, until Dale would start buying from someone else. Then the dude would bring back the quality but mark it up too high, so again Dale would buy from someone else. Then he'd make nice, and after a month, the same cycle returned."

Colin narrowed his eyes. "That sounds like a reason never to buy from him."

"It was a game. You had to catch him on the downswing and be able to walk away. Which, considering the amount of competition, we can." Austin shrugged. "Also, why are you ruining your life?"

Colin smirked. "I was waiting for that."

"Yeah, except there's no third twin we can blame it on this time, so enlighten me, because I'm puzzled."

The second vendor had much better beef, although the prices were up there. Austin placed the order anyhow.

The next stop was a produce vendor. "I'm not ruining my life."

"You're ruining a relationship. All you have to do is admit that she underestimated you from the start. I could understand if a guy seduced her by saying he was a billionaire doctor, but this isn't a case of stolen valor." Austin snorted. "This is more like buried valor. You're hiding all the good stuff."

"She'd have rejected me on sight for the good stuff. I'd never have gotten to know who she is."

Austin said, "Except the way you did it, she never got to know who *you* are."

"No one wants to know who I am." Oh, the winter leeks were amazing. Colin said, "Winter leek and potato soup—I think we should do that all week as a special."

"I'm on it," Austin said. "What kind of potatoes?"

These decisions were easiest. Hey, Brussels sprouts! No, avoid those shrimp. Nice escarole!

Austin finally said, "I'm having an issue with that last thing you said because you shouldn't need to hide who you are. Who are you really?"

Colin said, "You're the handsome twin, the outgoing twin, the smart twin, and every other twin I can think of. That doesn't leave a lot of room for me."

Austin snorted. "Even if I'm the honest twin, that doesn't mean you have to be the dishonest twin."

Colin blew out his frustration. "Something's missing. Whenever I'm dating someone, after a few weeks, she ghosts me."

"I'm going out on a limb though and saying that's ridiculous." Austin paused at the shallots long enough to order some, then kept moving. "What happens at the two-to three-week mark that makes them leave?"

Colin said, "They get to know me. They're over the initial rush of *'Fancy!, this guy runs a restaurant!'* That's when things start getting real, and whenever I'm real, the tide turns."

Austin rubbed his chin. "You've dated women for longer than a couple of months. You dated Jen for nearly a year. Ellie was with you a couple of years, and I thought you'd marry her."

Colin shrugged. "Not since I bought in to CharCuties."

They stopped at the seafood counter, which would be today's biggest expense. The vendor came right over to them, pushing his own assistant out of the way. "I have something for you," he said, and showed off the crabs. Nice legs.

Colin nodded, and Austin started haggling for him.

The vendor headed over to his assistant, and Austin said, "Okay, so instead of leading off with the almighty restaurant owner schtick, this time you went for the opposite. Your neighbor bangs on your door and tells you the house is a dump and warns you about the awful restaurant up the road. But she's hot, so you listen."

"You saw her. You'd have listened to her, too." Colin scanned the bin. Scallops. That's what they needed. "Except she poisoned the well by calling Fruits de Mer an overpriced meal for a tourist."

"What exactly is wrong with that?" Austin flagged over the vendor and pointed to the scallops. "Thirty pounds."

Colin regarded him. "What's wrong with that?"

"Yes, what's wrong with that? The majority of the restaurant's income comes in during tourist season. Why? Because that's when Brighthead gets flooded with people who want a day at the shore. Guess who those people are? They're tourists."

Colin rolled his eyes. "Do go on."

Austin did go on. "They look at the lighthouse. They take a photo with the Myth Brightman statue. They climb on the rocks. They walk on the causeway. They buy glitzy souvenirs. And then what do they do?" Austin opened his hands. "They eat. Guess what we sell? And yes, we mark it up because they're paying for the location, the presentation, and the style."

Colin kept looking through the glass case. "The shrimp look small."

"Yeah, they've been fudging the sizes lately." Austin sighed. "But again, this is like what we do: they know we need shrimp, so they're going to charge just a bit more because we're paying for the necessity and the availability."

Colin stepped across to a different vendor to look at the artichokes, which were amazing, and considered what specials they could add just to put some of these babies on the tables. He returned to Austin, murmuring to himself, "Let's say she's right. How do we also reach out to the locals?"

Austin said, "Not like that place we went to in Rome."

Colin laughed so loud that two people turned to look. "The speakeasy?"

Austin rolled his eyes. "It felt like it, right?"

"Oh, and the irritation on that guy's face." Colin and Austin's friend Emilio had brought them to a hotel where they'd get the best meal of their lives—or so he said. They'd met in the lobby, but then the friend brought them down the stairs away from the restaurant, through the laundry, and back up a service staircase. They'd emerged in the kitchen, where Emilio had then led them to this wooden door where a thousand-year-old man was smoking a filterless cigarette. Emilio said something Colin's pidgin Italian translated as, "Dinner for three for a hundred euros," and the old man left his cigarette burning in an overfull ashtray. He led them through two shoulder-width hallways to a wooden table without any tablecloth and no menu. The rest of the place was dotted with families chowing down and laughing loud—and no tourists. It was the back end of the hotel restaurant, and for a third of the price, the three of them enjoyed dish after dish of the restaurant's top-rated specials—plus a bunch of secret items that weren't even on the main menu.

Colin said, "Secret menu items. That's what we've been missing."

"You've been missing them. There's a few people who if they know Alex is on, they order an 'electric burger.'" When Colin raised his eyebrows, Austin hefted a crate and carried it out to the truck. "Hamburger cooked rare, coated in batter and then dropped in the fryer for a minute along with a few onion rings. Slap it all onto a toasted brioche roll along with crab meat, provolone, and Thousand Island dressing."

Colin blinked. "Why didn't I know about this? Because now I want one."

"And then there's Bill's lobster melt sandwich, which he refuses to tell the rest of us how to prepare. He insists he learned how to make it in prison, where I assume lobster is a regular on the menu, right?" When Colin laughed, Austin added, "Danielle pretended a customer ordered it last summer so Dale and I could dissect and reconstruct it, but we decided it wouldn't work on the regular menu."

"That sorts out the secret menu items, then." Colin shook his head. "So, back door from the parking lot, and a couple of tables in the basement? How do we determine who actually lives in Brighthead?"

Austin snorted. "Hire one longtime local from the Oddfellows Club. He'll gatekeep for you," and Colin laughed even harder.

Austin pulled out his phone and made sure everything they'd ordered was in the truck. "All of which is completely a dodge on your part. You need to walk in there and tell Natalie."

Colin hesitated.

Austin sighed. "Skip Family Meal like you do when you see her. Walk into the apartment and look grave. Lead off by asking her to forgive you for what you're about to say because it got out of hand."

Colin frowned. "It's manipulative to set her up like that."

"It's manipulative to lie to her, too." Austin got into the front seat. "At this point, you have to tell her, so you need to do it the best way possible."

Colin sighed. "Yeah."

Austin started the engine. "Brave up, man. All these chances you've taken in your life, but you can't tell a woman your job?"

Colin rubbed his temples as they pulled out of the lot. "It's just that every other chance I've taken, it didn't matter if I failed."

CHAPTER TWENTY-FOUR

Mid-morning at Bright Stitches, Lilah was in a foul mood but insisted she wasn't. Even the Sit and Stitch customers kept asking where her pretty smile was, and Don couldn't make her happy with his Star Wars latch hook rug.

Natalie said, "If it's about the artists' colony, we'll make something work."

Don said, "Tell me! Is a ship of artistic refugees even now crossing the ocean, carrying nothing but their acrylic paints, linseed oil, and a few pre-stretched canvases?"

Lilah's head jerked up. "How do you know about painting?"

Don shrugged. "Art therapy."

One of the women said, "Whatever you do, don't ask him to explain his painting with the grape hyacinths."

Natalie swallowed hard. "Thanks for the warning."

The door jangled, and Lavender Paul entered, her eyes tight and her face pinched.

"Lavender!" Natalie said. "Welcome!"

Lavender went directly to the collectibles section. A knitter muttered, "Please don't have any new lawn ornaments for her. The solar dragonfly swarm was bad enough."

Natalie sighed. Lavender picked through the gift section, then settled on a stained glass light catcher.

"At least that goes on the inside of the house," said the knitter.

Natalie said, "Why is it a problem if she enjoys beautiful things?"

Lavender paid cash and refused the handful of change, so Natalie put it into the "have a penny" bowl. Another sparkling conversation with Lavender Paul.

Shelly showed up before the end of Sit and Stitch. "Guys! Look at this swatch!" She pulled a palm-sized square from her knitting bag. "Natalie, you have to see!"

Shortly everyone was clustered around Shelly to gush about the lacy test pattern. "I'm doing it! I'm knitting my own wedding dress!"

Natalie sighed. "This is going to look amazing."

Lilah added, "This is the yarn from your maid of honor, right?"

Shelly nodded. "I'm still so surprised how you guys pulled that off. But wow." She was nearly bouncing. "I wound all my yarn last night, and I printed the pattern, and I swatched, and then I swatched again." She laughed. "I cannot believe it. I can't believe I'm getting married, and I can't believe I'm making the dress."

Natalie said, "Do you still need beads for it?"

She said, "I need to figure that out still," which doubtless meant she was ordering beads online.

Natalie said, "If you want someone to help match the beads to the yarn, bring your swatch to Bead and Breakfast over in Hartwell. They'll do right by you."

Shelly started. "Are you serious?"

Lilah said, "I'll text you their contact info. They're going to be part of the creative guild. The owner makes artwork out of just beads, like paintings? She ended up with so many tubes of beads in her workshop that her husband got snarky about why she didn't just go ahead and buy a whole bead store, so she did."

Shelly snickered. "Don't say that too loud, or Lucas will suggest I buy a yarn store."

Lilah exclaimed, "Don't you dare! I don't want to be in competition with you," and Shelly patted her hand.

Natalie said, "We don't have a huge bead selection at Bright Stitches, but you'll find a literal ton at Bead and Breakfast. It's easiest when you've got a professional who can pour the actual beads onto the swatch."

"Good point!" Shelly looked at her phone. "Okay, got their address. Next stop, Bead and Breakfast."

Natalie spent most of the Sit and Stitch teaching a woman how to crochet cables but not working on her own project. She ought to be making those dishcloths and towels for Colin now that he was getting up to speed on cooking. By the time he was planning his own meals, she wanted them ready for his dishes.

Natalie's stash had plenty of cotton. She could even make them this week, except that she still had a baby blanket to finish for the family shelter's "baby shower" drive. And the hats for the homeless. Also, the hospital had put out another call for shawls and wraps because chemotherapy patients tended to get cold, and they liked handmade shawls better than the sterile hospital blankets.

Natalie sighed as her cabling student called her over again. There was never enough time to crochet the things she wanted to, and so much beautiful yarn at her house that remained unworked.

Colin was right: she should make something beautiful for herself. She hadn't done a "selfish" project in so long— a shawl as light as a feather, soft as a kiss from a cloud, delicate and sweet, warm to the skin and pleasing to the eye. She had so many patterns in her stash, and so many yarns, and in some cases the pattern bundled with the yarn—waiting. Just waiting.

Except if she were to do that, she ought to get Colin's dishcloths done first. They wouldn't take too long. And before that, she had to finish the baby blanket.

Sit and Stitch broke up for the day, and Natalie rang up

two customers. As they were leaving, Brooke entered the store, grinning ear-to-ear.

Clinging to her foul mood, Lilah muttered, "Well, aren't you just the happiest person alive?"

Brooke flung out her arms. "I will have you know, this is the best day! It's a day that our store will consider a landmark for all time."

Lilah said, "Have you scored a date with a man who can assemble his own lunch?"

Natalie shot Lilah a dark look, which Lilah met with a glower.

Brooke shook her head. "Far surpassing a date—and I don't feel like dating anyone, anyhow. Do you know the yarn-store-that-shall-not-be-named, the one ten miles from here?"

Natalie stepped out from behind the register. "Our yarn-winding nemesis? What about them?"

"Their bitter shop owner started a fight with a crocheting customer who happens to have a social media following of thirty-six thousand yarnies." Brooke dropped her work bag on the table and followed it with her jacket and hat. She didn't remove her fingerless gloves. "Either the owner or one of the employees told this customer that crochet is what you do when you're a little girl, but knitting is what you do when you're mature. They got into a fight, and then the shop ended up refusing to sell her any yarn at all if it was for a crochet project."

Lilah exclaimed, "What?"

Brooke rolled her eyes. "Here's the thing—I don't care why anyone buys our yarn. If they want to buy our yarn and keep it as skein yarn forever, I'll be sad that it never fulfills its destiny, but I'll take their money."

Natalie sighed. She had far too much "skein yarn." It needed to fulfill its destiny.

Brooke continued, "If they buy yarn and stuff it into their couch cushions before setting them on fire, I'll be even more sad, but I'll still take their money."

Lilah said, "Wool doesn't burn."

"Yeah, yeah, quit being pedantic." Brooke unzipped her bag. "But speaking of fires, this social media fight is hot, and fiery, and ongoing, and you know what? I intend to pick up a few dozen disaffected customers. So Natalie, I need a pattern test from you. By tomorrow."

Brooke dropped her graph paper notebook onto the table. "Pick three skeins of Lilah's yarn, two tonals and one variegated, and charge it to me. I need this finished and blocked by tomorrow, because I've set up a preorder and I'm going to make an offer: anyone who buys three of Lilah's yarns gets this crochet pattern for free—and I'm naming it after our shunned internet crochet queen."

Natalie laughed out loud. "Are you serious?"

"Serious as a car crash." Brooke's eyes glinted. "If the yarn shop whose name we refuse to say is going to alienate crocheters, then guess what? I am more than happy to welcome every single crocheter in Maine into this building, sit them on a comfy chair, and hand them a cup of coffee."

Lilah's eyes widened. "I'd better dye some more tonals."

"DK weight, if you have the base."

Lilah's mood had picked up all at once. "Show me the pattern, and I'll try to coordinate some kits."

Brooke snickered as she handed it over. "Honestly. Even if the shop owner hates crocheters, it's beyond stupid to alienate a customer who automatically uses thirty-five to fifty percent more yarn per project."

Reading over the chart, Lilah's nose wrinkled. "Is it physically possible to test this overnight?"

Brooke said, "I'm testing the shawlette version myself, but I need a second pair of eyes on the chart. Plus, Natalie crochets wicked fast. It's only about what, eight hours of work?"

Eight hours of continuous work—assuming the pattern had no mistakes and she never put down her hook for any reason. Natalie looked at the pattern over Lilah's shoulder. "I can get this done. Once I've passed the first section, the next two are pretty similar, so I only need to test the first bit."

"Except we need a demo piece to photograph and blast on social media." Brooke didn't at all look like someone asking for the moon. "I've already set up the preorder, and I'm getting ready to up our online advertising. The crochet community is furious at the whole 'mature yarncrafters' comment. Internet fires burn hot, but they also sputter out fast. That's why this needs to be done tonight. I want them to have proof that both shop owners can crochet, and, well, if we sell kits with Lilah's yarn, we all benefit."

Natalie side-eyed Lilah. "Well? Are you going to say what I know you're thinking?"

Lilah shifted her weight. "It's a bit...well, opposite the values of a crafting guild, to try to destroy the yarn store whose name we do not say."

Brooke huffed. "It's also opposite the values of a crafting guild to insult an entire swath of the yarn community, so I'm not going to worry my pretty head too much."

Lilah looked uneasy, but she didn't object further.

Brooke said to Natalie, "I know you're going home now, but I can send you updates about anything I should change."

Natalie shook her head. "I'll stay to work on it. That way, if there are questions, I can show you what's messing me up."

Brooke sighed. "Thank you. That would make it easier, and you can give me input on the final rows of the chart."

Lilah said, "Oh, good grief, you're still designing the bottom of the shawl while she's crocheting the top?"

Natalie studied the pattern with its semicircles, diamonds, and the mesh backdrop. "This is going to be gorgeous. Imagine it in black and silver."

Lilah dropped three brightly colored skeins onto the table in front of her. "Now imagine this as if you're a marketer. It's the dead of winter, and everyone's craving springtime. Envision it in creamsicle tones, or a subtle orange with a pink-orange tonal for the contrast color."

Natalie offered, "Gold and cream?"

"Won't stand out enough," Lilah said. "Brooke needs something that's going to pop in the photos."

Brooke nodded. "Good thinking. The one I'm working on is a green with a blue-green contrast color." She leaned toward Natalie and smiled. "Please, Nat?"

"Fine." Natalie carried all three skeins to the swift and ball winder. "This probably won't kill me."

Staying here meant she wouldn't be making Colin anything for his kitchen, at least not until this was done. She wouldn't be able to see Colin this afternoon at all. By the time she got home tonight, he'd be working.

Natalie started winding the yarn and sighed. He'd be working—but so would she.

CHAPTER TWENTY-FIVE

Colin got a text during lunch cleanup. "I won't be home this afternoon, so you should eat Family Meal at the restaurant."

With a ticking clock, this was unfortunate. More than unfortunate. Or had Lilah gone ahead and warned Natalie away from him preemptively? He texted back, "Is something wrong?"

"I have an emergency yarn situation here at the store."

"I wasn't aware emergency yarn situations existed," he texted. "Are you okay?"

"About to be worked to death." She sent a smiley face. "For once, I get to work the same hours you do."

He texted, "Is Lilah there?" but then backed up and changed it to, "Are Brooke and Lilah with you, at least?"

"Both of them. I'll tell you about it tomorrow."

Time to send a message, then. "Tell Lilah and Brooke they're keeping you away from me."

After a pause, Natalie replied, "Lilah says to tell you, 'Acknowledged.' She actually specified that you'll just have to wait until tomorrow."

Colin hoped that translated as, "You now have a 24-hour

extension," which would only drag out the pain further.

On the other hand, it freed him up for Family Meal. He headed into the kitchen where the line cooks were prepping for the dinner rush, and Bill was scrubbing hard with the grill brick.

Austin said, "And you should be leaving...?"

Colin said, "Plans changed. My 'appointment' got pushed to tomorrow."

Austin's eyes narrowed. "Does the executioner know this?"

Danielle looked up from rolling silverware. "You have an appointment to be executed? Can I watch?"

"We're live-streaming it," Austin said. "Kind of like the *Tale of Two Cities*, except at the end, you'll never figure out which twin got executed."

Colin said, "Of course she'll figure it out. The smart one survives."

Austin said, "Maybe just the charming one?"

Colin said, "Or the decent one. Regardless, it will be obvious."

Danielle blew at the hair on her forehead. "I hate this job. It was bad enough with one of you."

They set up Family Meal in the function room, three of the catering trays and everyone with their own drinks from the soda machine. Meeting Natalie for "cooking lessons" meant Colin missed Family Meal a couple days a week, but it always seemed to help the kitchen staff bond better when a restaurant had that. Sometimes he'd cook the whole thing himself, just because.

Today they had pasta carbonara, rolls, and roasted Brussels sprouts. Austin loaded a plate and sat opposite Colin at one of the round tables. "How'd you get an extension?"

"Natalie's working late on a yarn emergency. Lilah's with her."

"How on earth can yarn be an emergency?" Danielle said, joining them with her plate. "Does she still think you wash dishes, or have you 'fessed up yet?"

"He was supposed to be *'fessing up* right now," Austin said.

"Have you noticed we finish one another's sentences?" Colin said.

Austin shrugged. "We started as one brain."

"Let me borrow it sometime."

Danielle snickered. "You two are like an old married couple."

Austin added, "Without the expectations. He knows all the ways I'm a jerk."

Colin said, "Yeah, I'm going to have to agree," and Austin laughed so hard everyone at the other table turned.

Danielle said, "You were supposed to say something supportive, like, 'Yes, my dear brother has seen me at my worst.'"

Colin gasped. "I was?"

Austin said, "I'm the people person. He's the chef."

Bill slid into their table with his plate and a takeout container full of something green. Please, let it be green tea, not pure lime juice. "So this woman? Has she dumped you yet? Because she was hot, and I need to know when to show up at her doorstep with comfort food."

Austin said, "That's a terrific idea, and I suggest you keep it to yourself."

Danielle added, "She dumps him tomorrow, when Colin gets executed. At least, that's what I figured out by eavesdropping."

Colin raised a glass. "Classy!"

Danielle said, "I've gotten good at piecing conversations together from snippets. You have no idea what people will talk about when they're eating because to some folks, the waitress doesn't exist. You and Austin talking about your scheduled beheading wouldn't even make the top ten."

Bill huffed. "Well, if you don't exist, I exist even less. Steaks just broil themselves. Unless they're a little overdone, when it's perfectly fine to scream as if someone murdered your mother."

Danielle said, "They don't scream at you over that. They

scream at me."

Bill said, "Because I don't exist."

Colin said, "How can we make you exist?"

When they both looked up, he opened his hands. "How do we make you exist in the minds of the patrons? What do I, this establishment's esteemed owner, do in order to convince our guests of the humanity of the cooks and the servers?"

"You do a pretty good job already," said Alex from the other table, proving it wasn't just servers who could eavesdrop.

"Backing us up is the best thing you can do," Danielle added. "Austin doesn't back down just because they're ranting about something ridiculous, and whenever you've gotten involved, you keep a straight face and then make a reasonable response."

Austin said, "Ten years ago, Colin and I both worked at a restaurant where the owner was a bitter old man who fired one or both of us every week for some perceived infraction."

Colin added, "The fact that we're twins helped the owner get away with it for so long, because if someone saw Austin working again the day after his firing, they'd just say it was me who got fired."

"Between the two of us, we got fired, what—?"

"Twenty times that summer?"

The Dish Dame said, "If you messed up that bad every day, why didn't the both of you get fired for real?"

Danielle said, "You don't hear the front of house, but people complain for all sorts of things. My napkin isn't folded right—I want a free meal. My salad is too cold—I want you to comp my lobster."

Austin said, "We had a great act. The owner looked like an angry Methuselah, and he'd drag me from the kitchen by the shoulder, shove me in front of the customer, and order me to apologize because the pre-sliced olives were sliced off-center. Then, while I was wringing my hands and pleading my sorrow, he'd fire me for being an incompetent miscreant who'd never hold a job in the restaurant industry again because he was putting me on a list. *A list, I tell you!* I'd hand him my apron and slink to the back to get my things, then put on a new apron and go back to chopping mushrooms."

The Dish Dame snorted. "You put up with that?"

Colin said, "Austin neglects to mention that Methuselah was our grandfather."

Bill slapped the table. "Dang, boss! That's amazing."

Colin set down his fork. "He had this greasy pizza place and salad bar over in Portland, and he could never keep the thing staffed for some reason. The customers were all tourists, so no matter what the problem was or who'd caused it, he'd fire Austin or me, and then go out back and smoke a cigarette in front of whichever of us he'd just chewed out while we got a fifteen-minute break. When the guest had strutted off, proud that they'd crushed a high schooler's culinary career, we'd go back to work. The other staff wouldn't have taken that treatment, but us? We were sacrificial lambs because it was a given that we'd stick around."

Austin said, "The work was good. He taught me everything about management."

Danielle said, "Except how to fire your incompetent server."

Austin sniffed. "He taught me everything about how to fire an incompetent server: do the opposite of what he did. I'd do it in the back room at the end of the shift, pay out your final check, and let you know not to show up for your next shift."

Colin said, "In other words, not as a floor show for the entertainment of bloodthirsty tourists."

Danielle raised her eyebrows. "Good to know."

Austin added, "There's a reason you didn't already know."

Bill said, "And when the hot pretty girl dumps you?"

Colin said, "When the hot *woman* dumps me, I suspect it's going to happen the same way."

Austin said, "Minus paying out the final check."

Colin sighed as he returned to his pasta carbonara. "Oh, I'm going to pay all right."

Colin pulled into his parking spot at midnight, and it took a minute to realize he was seeing Natalie's apartment lights on.

He hauled himself out of his van, aching and reeking of "kitchen," as well as vaguely dizzy. Why was Natalie still awake? Was she still sorting out her yarn emergency?

He left his bag in his apartment, but he could hear her voice through the ceiling, alternating with Birdie Holly's. She sounded upset.

Colin headed upstairs and knocked on her door. "Nat? Is everything okay?"

She opened the door, again dressed in flannel pajamas, but this time with a bathrobe over them. "No, everything is awful. I'm sorry I woke you up."

"I just got back." Colin was too aware of the stains on his pants and the way his hands must reek of cleaning fluid. "We did the once-a-week deep clean because the front of house was dead after nine-thirty." He tilted his head. "I could hear you talking to the bird."

"Birdie Holly wants me to go to bed." Natalie's eyes were red. "I don't blame him. I want to go to bed, too, but I can't. Come in."

He followed her into the living room, where she had a triangle of fabric, a hook, an assortment of graph papers, and two balls of yarn. (Cakes. She called them cakes when they were in this shape—he needed to remember that.)

"Is that your yarn emergency?"

"Yes, and I need to get it finished by the time we open tomorrow because Brooke had this ridiculous idea that's going to be terrific for the shop." She planted herself back on the couch. "I hope you don't mind, but this thing isn't going to crochet itself."

"It's gorgeous," Colin offered.

Natalie spread it out across her lap, then extended her legs and her hands to expand the full triangle. "Isn't it? If I weren't trying to get it done in one day, I'd really enjoy it."

Colin said, "Why do you have to do it? If it's Brooke's brainchild, why can't she?"

"She's doing another one herself. I should have had her come here for a sleepover and made her listen to me griping about it." Natalie's hook started flying in and out of the project, the yarn in her left hand feeding over the hook and through the loops and back over the hook like a crazed ouroboros that couldn't find the tip of its tail. "I'm faster, so she gave me the larger version. As in, she worked out exactly how long it takes me to crochet so many yards of yarn, and she worked out how much yarn each stitch would take—don't even get me started," she replied to his wide-eyed stare. "She's a professional, and she was so breezy. 'Oh, it will take Nat eight hours to make this.' Which, it probably would have, except I've had to rip out sections because she made a mistake in charting, or I made a mistake in reading, and it's a nightmare."

Colin picked up the chart closest to him, the one with the most whitespace. It was hand-drawn and full of arrows, Ts, crosses, and half-circles. "If I found this on the street, I'd burn it, thinking it was a summoning incantation for an Etruscan deity."

"It's not hard to read once you get the hang of it," Natalie said, the same way Colin would have said, "It's not hard to make a Scotch egg once you've been in culinary school for two years." "But it takes a while, and my arm hurts, and I'm exhausted, and I'm making dumb mistakes because of that. At some point, I'm going to fall asleep and impale myself on my hook, and that will be a disaster because I'll get blood on the yarn."

Colin added, "Also because you'll be dead."

Natalie muttered, "At least then I'll be able to rest."

Colin stood. "No, unacceptable. I'll be right back, and I'll stay with you and keep you awake."

Natalie looked up. "You go back to work at six o'clock in the morning."

"Six-thirty. I'll be fine."

"You're already only getting six hours a night." Distress crossed her face. "Don't do this to yourself. It's just a shawl."

"I don't care about the shawl. I care about you. You need moral support, so I volunteer."

Natalie shook her head.

Colin added, "You take on every burden so everyone else can have an easier life. This time, it's on me. Let me help."

She bit her lip.

Colin pulled out his phone and hit the voice activation. "Send text to Austin. I need you to open solo tomorrow. It's going to be a late night."

Austin's reply came momentarily. "Are you with Natalie?"

He replied, "I am."

Austin sent a surprised face emoji.

Colin replied, "Calm down. It's not what you're thinking."

Austin sent, "I'll hold down the fort. Don't worry about being here until the pre-shift meeting."

He replied, "Thanks, man."

Austin sent back a thumbs up.

Colin showed Natalie the screen. "There. I've just given myself four extra hours, so I can stay. Give me five minutes, and I'll be back and armed for bear."

Natalie sighed as she returned her attention to her hook. "Maybe bring the bear, too."

When Colin returned, he set up camp in her living room. "Everything I need to keep you awake and entertained while you work." He paused. "How much concentration do you need for this? You're usually crocheting while watching TV."

"Not full concentration, not once I get a feel for the row I'm on. Here." She showed him what looked like a raised ridge down the center of the shawl. "That's the center spine, and I need to pay more attention to what's happening there, and what's happening on the beginning and end of each row. I need to make sure I know what the row is doing and whether I change colors. The borders are the same each time, though." She sighed. "The stuff in between, it's pure mechanics."

Colin said, "Stop me if I'm distracting you. Just be blunt —'Colin, pause.'"

She laughed. "Got it. Do you have a caffeine supercharger in that bag of yours?"

"After years of pulling all-nighters for catering, I've found caffeine after a certain point is counterproductive. It just makes you jittery, and that makes the exhaustion worse. What has helped is camaraderie, and I'm here for you tonight."

Natalie put on a brave face. "Then talk to me. Tell me a funny story about working in the kitchen."

For the second time today, Colin told the story about him and Austin getting fired repeatedly by their own grandfather. She laughed about how the pair of them used to take turns groveling for the chance to keep their jobs, and how once Austin nearly did get fired because he over-acted a bit too much. "My grandfather was a real card trick," Colin said. "He's the reason we both ended up working in restaurants. By the time he was done with us, he didn't even need to show up. I could run the back of house by myself, and Austin knew everything about management and the front of house."

Natalie flipped the work, changed colors, and then frowned as she did the first few stitches. When she picked up speed again, she said, "Your grandfather could have given the place to you two."

"After he died, my grandmother sold it to some guys who installed new ovens and updated the decor. It's still there, but it's not like it was." That was a bit too close to business ownership, so he steered the conversation away. "Anyway, like I said, my grandfather was a firecracker. You did something bad in the kitchen, and boy, you'd hear about it. He fired us so well in front of house because he'd perfected his invective in back of house."

She looked up, sad. Her hook was still going, but it was nearly independent of her. Maybe crochet was magic after all. "Is that why you had a mental block about cooking?"

Colin drew a deep breath, and then he couldn't say it. Not while she was already at the end of her rope. *Natalie, I lied to you.* It didn't matter how he explained it. Her sensitive, beautiful, sweet, and perceptive heart was going to hear that she'd put her trust in a faithless man. She'd bury it deep, but her hands would tremble, and she'd lose accuracy. She'd lose concentration. It would take twice as long to finish the project that already spread long before her. Her arm was in pain. It wasn't fair to plunge her heart into pain as well.

Colin said, "My grandfather was a forceful personality."

She said, "After all that, you kept getting jobs in the same field?"

Colin said, "The restaurant industry can be fun. The good ones are like family. The best ones build you up. You work as a team. The back of house achieves a rhythm like a troupe of dancers. We read one another's minds. We reach for something before the other person has even put it down. We set aside something half-finished and know exactly who will finish it and when. We know whose dominion is whose, and we keep everything in its rightful place."

Natalie said, "You deserve a better place in that dance."

Colin replied, "Right now, I'm concerned about your place. You keep working. I'll keep talking."

They tried watching TV, but that wasn't helpful.

Colin showed off his complete knife roll and told her all the special things about it. That scared her, and while fear was good for raising adrenaline, adrenaline wasn't good for accuracy.

He did show off his oyster knife. "I'd walk into the kitchen to prep and find crates of oysters for shucking." He shuddered. "Five thousand oysters? More? I hated it... until I found a pearl."

Natalie smiled. "What did you do with it?"

"I showed it off, and the manager told me I couldn't take it home because it would be stolen property." Colin rolled his eyes. "As if it was worth anything."

Natalie said, "Aw, *shucks*?" and waited for Colin to respond, but he only raised his eyebrows at her.

Natalie looked back at her crocheting. "That's not fair. I can't see how it would be stolen property."

"I've found plenty of pearls. They're never worth anything."

"Of course they're worth something." At the end of a row, Natalie flipped the shawl. "I love pearls because if you wear them, they turn into you."

Colin laughed. "That sounds science-fictiony. Like your mom gives you a strand of pearls, and then you become the pearl monster stomping up and down the seashore taking revenge on seafood restaurants."

"And freeing all the live lobsters?" How she could read that weird map and dart that hook back and forth and carry on a conversation all at the same time would never cease to amaze him.

Colin said, "And then you hand it down to your daughter, and she becomes more like you? Is that how the child-parent curse works?"

"*Someday, I hope you'll have a child just like you!*" Natalie laughed. "No, you've got it backward. When you wear pearls, they're porous, so they pick up oil from your skin. That's why young women used to sleep wearing their pearl necklaces. Over time, the pearls retain enough oil that they actually have the same tone as you do, and then they'll look good with your wedding dress."

"Oh, that is neat!" Colin sat back and wove his fingers around his legs. "And I like you, so if I give you all the pearls I find from now on, there will be more of you in the world."

Natalie sighed. "I'm pretty sure no one wants that."

"I do. Plus, you said something about putting beads on your crocheting projects sometimes. What if you had a thousand pearls to put on this shawl?"

Her eyebrows raised. "That would take a long time. Not tonight."

"I'd also have to shuck enough oysters to get a thousand pearls." He snickered. "Oh, and sometimes we find little fish inside the oysters. Gobies, I think they're called? Those we just pitch out."

Natalie exclaimed, "Alive?"

"Sometimes. We also find pea crabs living in the oyster gills. That's good luck because it means you've got a high-quality oyster—and they taste great."

He let Natalie think about that for a moment, and then she said, "The oysters taste great—or the tiny crabs?"

Colin raised his eyebrows. "Both."

Natalie's nose wrinkled. "How do you cook those? They must be minuscule."

Colin said, "They're soft-shelled. You just eat them."

She shuddered. "Colin!"

He nodded. "Sure, we could sauté them in butter, but why? They're tiny, sweet crabs. Just pop them into your mouth."

She bit her lip. "That's disgusting."

He smirked. "You're saying, if I bring you the pearls, I

can keep the pea crabs?"

She said, "Bring me the gobies, too. I'll put them in my fish tank."

Colin retrieved the *Settlement Cookbook*, and he started reading the non-recipe sections aloud while she worked. The later it got, though, the less they bantered. It was two-thirty in the morning when he finally fetched his copy of *The Making of a Chef* and started reading that instead.

She said, "It's taking about ten minutes per row, and I've got fifteen rows left."

Colin said, "Then you keep working, and I'll keep reading."

He took her through the opening, through the basics of culinary school, and through a long discussion of broth and how to make clear stock versus dark stock, how to peel a carrot, and all the versatile wonders of food preparation and food presentation. This was dangerous. They were both exhausted, and a lie stood between them the size of the Culinary Arts Institute of America.

Sometimes she ripped back a few stitches, and that hurt because it felt like negative progress, but then she ripped out most of a row. And then two minutes later, she ripped it out again. And then there were tears in her eyes when she ripped it out a third time.

Colin shut the book and sat in front of her. "You need a break."

She said, "I'm so close. Five more rows and then the border. It's just that I keep messing it up, and I don't understand why. I've done this a hundred times."

He said, "Is there a mistake in the recipe?"

She blinked at him a moment, then said, "No, I'm sure the instructions are written out right."

Colin said, "Sorry. Pattern."

"Pattern, recipe—I knew what you meant." She wobbled. "There's been a row like this before, so I know I'm doing it right. It's just not working out. There's not enough stitches. I can't even fudge the stitch count, but I know what I'm doing, and I don't understand."

He wrapped a hand over hers, still gripping the crochet hook. "Breathe. When this happens to me, it's because no single part is difficult, but the combination of all of them one after the next after the next is too much. Like tilapia burritos over at CharCuties, you had to toast the tortilla, fry the tilapia, add the fillings, roll it all up, and stick it on the grill to get it closed. It's not hard to roll a tortilla or fry tilapia, but keeping everything in order when you're already exhausted and people are shouting 'sharp!' and 'hot!' and that printer keeps going off—some part of the process would slip. You'd pull this perfect burrito off the grill, and there's the fried fish sitting next to it—or you'd have the rest of the plate assembled except you forgot the burrito on the grill and now it's charred...and then you'd have to start over."

Natalie closed her eyes and slackened into the couch. "I'm so close."

"I get it." He got up onto the couch and held her. "At this point, if you get four hours of sleep, you'll wake up at your regular time. You can finish after you've rested a bit, right? The store doesn't open until ten?"

She buried her face into his shoulder. "I want to get this done."

"You're beyond the end of your rope. You need to sleep."

She looked up, and as distraught as she was, he couldn't resist kissing her. Kissing her long and slow and with a deep burn inside that said he'd do anything to protect her —even protect her from herself.

He struggled to get steady. "You talk about my brother taking advantage of me, but your cousin took your whole night. Trust me on this: it's okay. Lie down and close your eyes, and when you wake up, you'll be better able to focus."

She murmured into his neck, "I'm having trouble getting the hook into the right spots, too. I'm missing yarn-overs."

"You're exhausted." He reached over to the lamp alongside the couch and clicked it off. "Lie down. See what happens." He pulled the throw blanket over her. It was crocheted, and that was sweet. Everything in the apartment bore Natalie's stamp.

He started toward the other side of the couch to get that light, too, but she squeezed his hand. Squeezed it tight.

He moved back to her. "Send me a picture tomorrow, because I want to see that shawl when it's done."

She said, "Are you going back downstairs?"

He'd been about to. "Do you want me to stay?"

He wouldn't object to staying, but nothing was going to happen. Not with both of them a mere five seconds of darkness away from pure unconsciousness. Then she'd wake up and get right back to work, and nothing would happen then, either.

She released his hand. "No, I guess you should go."

Although disappointed, Colin would never push her to let him stay—and until he confessed to her, it would be unfair to her even if she wanted it. Keeping her hand, he kissed her again. "I'll be right downstairs. You'll finish it off in the morning."

She said, "And you'll get to work?"

"I'll arrive by the pre-shift meeting. I promise. I'll set five alarms." He squeezed her hand tighter. "I need to talk to you tomorrow. Will you be home at three?"

Her voice pitched up. "What do you want to talk about?"

"I'll tell you tomorrow. I need to be sure you'll be here. You weren't here this afternoon, and I didn't want to distract you by talking about it tonight." He straightened away from her. "I just feel like—everything's going so well, and there's something I need to tell you."

She hugged him, and he closed his eyes.

"I love you," she said.

He pulled her tighter.

"There. If that's what you were going to tell me, I beat you to it. I love you, and you're being so good to me." She rested her head on his shoulder. "I'm too tired to play games. I love you."

He kissed her cheek. "I love you, too."

She stayed still, eyes closed. "Now you don't have to have wait another day."

Colin slumped into her. "Can I talk to you tomorrow, anyhow?"

Tomorrow. He'd tell her tomorrow.

She nuzzled him. "Yes. I'm always available to talk to the people I love."

CHAPTER TWENTY-SIX

Colin loved her.

It was the first thought Natalie had on awakening. She didn't sing, though. She shut her alarm and dragged herself out of bed in silence so she wouldn't awaken Colin in his bedroom below hers. He'd started out sleep deprived, and then he'd given her another three-and-a-half hours. And then he'd told her he loved her.

She didn't sing to Birdie Holly or the fish or the anoles. Birdie Holly warbled, but Natalie quickly fed him. She gathered her nearly finished shawl and the pattern, and then she crept down the stairs. She'd pick up coffee and a muffin on the way to Bright Stitches.

The drive-through was open, so she got in line, placed an order, and idled up to the window.

That story about Colin and Austin at the pizza place was wild. Both of them getting fired every couple of days, getting a quarter-hour-long vacation until the tables turned over, and then getting back to work. Colin had said that got both him and Austin started in the restaurant business. Just went to show, whatever you learned first would rule the day. Natalie had learned crochet first, from her mother. Grandma had been the knitter, and she'd taught Brooke. Natalie had lived the rest of her life surrounded by yarn.

The drive-through cashier handed Natalie her coffee and breakfast sandwich, and Natalie handed her two bucks in tip.

That's where the brothers diverged, though. Austin had taken over in management, and by the time it was over, Colin could do everything there was in back of house.

Back of house being the kitchen. She'd picked up some restaurant terminology from him in six weeks.

As she drove back to Bright Stitches, though, she thought about the pizza place and what went on in the back of house—and wouldn't he have been making dough? Except he'd wanted her to teach him to knead.

In fact, she'd shown him how to assemble a whole pizza, which of course he'd have done if he'd done "everything in the back of house" at a pizzeria. He'd have known how to use a pizza stone—or, well, maybe he wouldn't because they'd just push the pizza into the oven on that big flat spatula.

Natalie pulled into her space in the Bright Stitches parking lot, then gathered her project and her breakfast. She had five rows left, and not much time to crochet them.

She ate while working, but that next row was having issues again. Had Brooke made a mistake? That's why you did pattern-testing, of course—to find mistakes. Brooke had been crocheting a shawl herself last night, but Brooke knew what she'd intended to do. Natalie had only the results of what Brooke had written—that is to say, the pattern. Sometimes you assumed something was there when it wasn't.

Natalie started composing an email asking about the issue that had made her rip out the same row four times, and then she backed up and started figuring out the stitches she was working into. And then she backed up one more row and re-read the pattern—and there was the error.

Maddie Evans

Three rows back, on the transition from the border to the body, she'd skipped a stitch she was supposed to crochet into, omitting two stitches. And on the next row, that meant she'd omitted the multiple stitches that should have gone into those stitches. By the time she'd reached the current row, everything was off by enough stitches that she'd never make the row work. With a sigh, she ripped backward.

Then she texted Colin, hoping he'd silenced his phone. "You were right to make me go to sleep. I'd made a fatal error three rows back. That's why nothing was working."

She set back to work. Last night, she'd been so tired she hadn't seen what was right in front of her. Those missing stitches had distorted the shape of the shawl, and she hadn't been looking at the big picture.

So it hadn't been a "tilapia burrito" issue, or whatever Colin had called it last night. Natalie wasn't even sure why you'd want to make burritos or tacos out of tilapia, except that he said the previous restaurant made things kids liked. But again, given how urgent he'd been, it sounded like something he'd experienced, not something he'd overheard.

Was he now working as a line cook for Fruits de Mer? Except tilapia burritos would be Mexican—not their speed.

Natalie filed that away and kept working on Brooke's shawl. Progress was faster this morning, maybe because she was caffeinated and had a few hours of sleep under her belt. Maybe because she was still flying high from Colin saying he loved her.

Full of coffee and bedazzled with emotion, Natalie reached the troublesome row again and flew through it. She forged forward and knocked out the remaining rows before nine o'clock, and by the time Brooke arrived at ten, Natalie was finishing the picot border.

She held it up, and Brooke gasped. "That's amazing!"

"I'm going to die," Natalie pronounced, spreading it out on the table. "I'm in pain and delirious, but it's nearly done. I want to steam block it quick before you photograph anything."

"Get on it!" Brooke urged. "Actually, can you do mine too? I crashed last night before I finished blocking."

Natalie started pinning both head-to-tail on the blocking boards and then readied the steamer. Usually she wouldn't block wool this way, but they needed it fast.

Lilah arrived while Natalie was still pinning. She whistled. "Well, that's astonishing."

Brooke said, "Did you make some kits to sell?"

"What do you think I have in the bag?" Lilah snorted. "Or did you think I was bringing my laundry and planning to wash it in the sink?"

"No need to be rude." Brooke took a couple of pictures to start teasing the reveal. "None of us got enough sleep."

Natalie took a picture and sent it to Colin, since he'd asked. Asked because he loved her. Then she went to work with the steamer, watching as the wool relaxed and all the lace eyelets opened.

She'd told Colin that blocking was like truth being revealed. Add heat, and the finished garment would show itself for what it had been all along, all the beauty as well as all the mistakes.

Brooke watched over Natalie's shoulder. "That's beyond amazing. Even I didn't think the pattern was going to work up that gorgeous."

"You picked good colors." Natalie smiled. "Colin liked them too."

Lilah turned from where she was hanging yarn kits. "You saw Colin last night?"

"He came upstairs when he got home from closing. Which was sweet because that was around midnight, and he's always exhausted from all the work he does."

Lilah muttered, "I bet he is."

Natalie looked up at her. "He works long hours there."

Lilah said, "And did he tell you why he works such long hours?"

Natalie paid attention to steaming the center spine. "Because of Austin, but Austin's not so bad. Colin texted

Austin last night and asked for the morning off, and Austin said that was fine. That way, he could stay with me and keep me awake."

Lilah said, "And...he stayed the whole night?"

Natalie huffed. "Not like that. I was crocheting. He was reading to me, and we talked a lot. He told me stories about his life."

Lilah edged nearer to the blocking boards. "What did he tell you...? Anything huge?"

Brooke said, "Lilah, seriously?"

Lilah's voice lowered. "He spent three hours talking to you. What did he tell you?"

Natalie maneuvered the steamer along the border, watching the wool relax under the warmth. "He told me about his grandfather being bananacrackers and making a show of firing him or Austin whenever someone messed up at the pizzeria. He told me about mishaps in the kitchen."

Lilah prompted, "Anything bigger than that?"

Natalie looked up, surprised. "Did he tell you what he was going to say? Because yes."

Lilah nodded. "And...? Are you okay with that?"

Brooke looked up from the laptop where she was composing her announcement post. "Why on earth would Colin talk to you about something he was going to tell Natalie? You'd never even met him before the crafting guild had that get-together."

Lilah folded her arms. "Because I wanted him to do right by Natalie."

Brooke frowned. "I'm missing all the subtext. What did Colin say?"

Natalie said, "Colin told me he loved me."

Lilah slammed her hand on the table. "Blast it, no, that's not what he was supposed to tell you! He wanted more time because you weren't home yesterday, but he's a snake and he slithered right out of it!"

Natalie backed away from the blocking board while clouds puffed from the steamer in her hand. "What are you talking about? I told him I loved him. He said he loved me, too. Why would you be involved in that?"

Brooke was on her feet. "What did you discover, Lilah? Is he married? Wanted for murder?"

Lilah whirled toward Brooke. "Colin's been forcing Natalie to give him cooking lessons since the day they met because he convinced her he didn't know which end of the stove was the hot one."

Natalie went numb, head to foot. She should put down the steamer. Her ears were ringing.

Colin had worked in a pizza store. He'd made tilapia burritos at least once, in a rush, while several other things were on the grill and the restaurant kitchen twirled like a dancer.

Lilah said, "The reality is, Colin's not just washing dishes at Fruits de Mer. He's the *owner.* He graduated from the Culinary Arts Institute. He's been working as a chef since practically childhood, and before he came here, he was part-owner of a charcuterie chain in Kennebunkport."

Natalie's mouth went dry.

Lilah looked at her. "He's Chad all over again, only without the couch. He's been lying from day one. He swears it's not some kind of sick joke, but it looks like a sick joke from where I'm standing. Even Austin said Colin's behavior was reprehensible."

Natalie returned to steaming the shawl. Her hands were shaking. "I don't believe you."

Except she did. Everything had made sense to Natalie when she believed Colin couldn't cook, but it made a lot more sense believing he could.

How comfortable he'd been with her stove. How he knew all the lingo. How he'd wielded that knife. How he'd gone downstairs and come back with a memoir about culinary school. How he'd improved her tacos "by accident." How he'd asked for meals that took a while to prepare but kept them working the whole time—working and talking.

"I had something to tell you," he'd said, and she'd leaped right ahead to what she'd thought he was about to say—what she'd wanted him to say. The same way she'd assumed he couldn't cook because he'd said he couldn't.

Natalie's eyes were blurring. She kept moving the steamer over Brooke's shawlette, getting it hot and then letting the wool cool rapidly so it would stay in the strained position she'd forced it into. All those holes, wide open for the world to see. Every stitch, visible. Every beautiful and intricate detail of its construction obvious to everyone who looked. Everyone except Natalie.

She blinked. Lilah was right next to her with the phone, saying, "He didn't even try to hide it. He's on the Fruits de Mer webpage, and when he bought the restaurant, they blasted publicity all over the place."

Lilah took the steamer and thrust the phone into Natalie's hand.

From the other side of the table, Brooke said, "Why didn't you tell Natalie right away?"

"I didn't find out until the guild voted that chefs could join. I figured I'd talk to the owner myself rather than going through Austin."

Natalie's voice sounded distant. Small. "Austin said some other guy was the owner. Dale something."

"Dale was the previous owner. It's in the article."

Natalie couldn't read an article now. She could barely read the caption under Colin's smiling face.

Brooke's keyboard clicked, and she said, "Wow, that son of a dog."

Lilah said, "I gave him twenty-four hours to come clean, and he didn't."

Brooke said, "Is that why he texted Natalie to tell us that we were keeping him away from her?"

Lilah said, "And that made sense because if she was here, that wasn't his fault. But he stayed with her three hours last night. He could have told her anything."

Natalie spoke almost to herself. "Except I was upset. I was freaking out because I had so much to do, and I was afraid I couldn't get it all done." She blinked hard and handed back the phone. "He said he had something important to tell me today, but he didn't want to hit me with it when I was exhausted. I thought he wanted to tell me he loved me, so I told him I loved him." She trembled. "He said he loved me, then. And I thought that was the big reveal, not that he was lying to about who he was."

She started pulling pins out of the blue-green shawlette, plinking them back in the metal tin where they belonged. "Everything in its place," Colin said when getting ready to cook. See, now that made sense. It wasn't just a kitchen thing. He'd been taught already. He'd been taught you put everything in place, and you put it away again afterward, and you don't leave a mess. All along, she thought they'd been bonding, and instead, he'd been mocking her.

The only sound in the shop was every pin as it fell into the tin. One at a time, Natalie released the shawls from their stabbed-out torture and gave them their freedom.

She turned to Brooke. In a thin voice, she said, "Where do you want them displayed?"

Brooke's eyes were wide. "The dress forms in the windows."

Natalie wrapped them around the shoulders of the headless wire bodies and secured them with beaded shawl pins made by a jeweler from Juniper.

Colin wanted to see the pink/orange shawl once it was done. She'd said she'd send him a photo, but instead she wanted to get that container full of T-pins and stick all of them in his heart. Pin him out at a full stretch on his carpet and leave him there to dry.

Then, with the shawls on display, Natalie returned to the back room and got her jacket, her purse, and her car keys.

Brooke gave a tentative, "Nat? Are you going to be okay?"

Natalie forced a cold smile. "I'm going home for half an hour. I need to move something out of the frying pan and into the fire."

CHAPTER TWENTY-SEVEN

When someone banged on the door, Colin's heart stopped.

Because that was anger.

He buttoned his chef jacket on his way to the door, calling, "Hello?" as if he didn't know exactly who it was and why she was here and what was about to happen.

Natalie said, "It's me," and even that sounded furious.

She'd loved him last night. Last night, he'd said the same, except he'd also said five other things she could have put together to work up into a full story, the same way she'd worked out the mistake in that shawl—one small mistake that compounded every time you advanced a row, and every time more impossible to correct without destroying the whole thing.

Colin opened the door and met Natalie's fierce eyes.

She stood with folded arms, her mouth set, and her stance rigid.

Colin said, "I guess we're going to talk now?"

"I guess we are." She walked past him into the apartment and went right for his kitchen cabinets. "Clever. You didn't fully unpack everything. I would figure the kitchen of a world-class chef would be like the devil's toy box, but you needed to hide everything in case I ever wandered in here."

Colin fought a tremble in his voice. "I'm hardly world-class."

She turned to him. "You see, this is what I don't get. After the first time you had your fun with me, when you mocked me for putting cream cheese in the chili, you could have laughed in my face and told me that was itty-bitty baby cooking. But instead you doubled down and asked how to make tacos."

Colin's breath caught. "Can I explain?"

"No, because you have to get to the restaurant for your pre-shift meeting or whatever it is a restaurant owner does, and finally I'm piecing it all together because I'm not actually stupid."

Colin raised his hands. "I never thought you were stupid!"

"Then what was this all about?" Her eyes gleamed. "Because from where I stand, it looks exactly like mockery. Oh, let's show up the cute little lady and take advantage of her and make her think she's so special and maybe get taken care of like a little kid, and all along you're riding high with the powerful job and the money and the fun."

Colin choked out, "Natalie, no, that's not—"

"And you took me through the kitchen, where you said everyone is like family, so that means they're in on it, too?"

"They're unanimously of the opinion that I'm an idiot," Colin said. "Everything snowballed, and I was going to tell you yesterday. It's just that—"

"Yesterday was one day!" Natalie stepped toward him. "You had *six weeks* when you could have opened your mouth and said, hey, you know this thing we have? That it's entirely built on deception?"

Colin raised his hands. "I didn't start out by deceiving you!"

Natalie made mid-air twisty fumbles with her hands. "So hey, cookie lady, is this a can opener? Do you use it to open cans?"

Colin clenched his fingers. "You had a right-handed can-opener, and I'm a lefty! I legitimately couldn't reverse it in my head!"

"You spent six weeks sandbagging me!"

He squared his shoulders. "You were dragging my restaurant for not making real food, so when you offered to teach me to cook—and I'm not world-class by any means, thanks—I figured sure, she's as sarcastic as I am, so I can play along. I'll put the cream cheese in the white bean chili, and you'll teach me how real Mainers eat when they're invited to the grown-ups' table. By the time I figured out you were dead earnest, I wasn't sure how to get out of it anymore!"

Natalie said, "By opening up your mouth and saying, 'Let's have tacos next week, but how about I cook them because by the way, I went to culinary school'!"

Colin's heart pounded. "It wasn't that easy! It was an honest mistake. I said something sarcastic, and you took it literally."

She said, "It's not about the mistake. At some point, you made the decision to persist. And then you persisted six weeks while you let me think you liked me!"

"I do like you!" He loved her, and he was losing her. "You'd never have kept talking to me if you knew what I did."

Her eyes were fire. "Wouldn't I have?"

"You only kept dealing with me because you thought I was a hapless ne'er-do-well you could save from himself!" Colin's heart hammered. "Whenever I did try to tell you, you leaped to some other conclusion before I could finish, and I didn't want to hurt you."

She folded her arms. "Oh, so it's entirely my fault that you used me for six weeks?"

"Stop right there." He nearly stepped toward her, but he needed to de-escalate her, not herd her toward the door. "I never used you. I was buying the groceries, and I cleaned everything afterward. Okay, so I didn't need the lessons, but I made darned sure that I paid my own way."

"And the mental work? And the emotional work?" Natalie's eyes spilled over. "And the relationship that was real for me, but was a charade for you?"

Colin stepped backward.

"You don't see that? That even now you're making it my fault that you pretended you were someone else so I would interact with you beyond moving your forgotten laundry to the dryer?" Her whole body was trembling. "You just said it, that I wouldn't have fallen in love with you if you weren't pretending to be someone you weren't. So who did I fall in love with? And what does that make me?"

Colin managed, "You wanted someone to save. You needed someone to rescue."

Natalie took a deep breath. "Well, then drown."

She walked out of the apartment. Colin caught the door before she could slam it and raced into the hallway.

She didn't look back as she walked past the mailboxes. "You need to get to your pre-shift meeting, Monsieur Chef."

"Not like this!" Colin caught up to her, but he didn't touch her, and he didn't block the door. "Natalie, I'm sorry. I'm sorry because I dug a hole for myself, and then I didn't want to risk losing you because you're very sweet, and you're so genuine, and you're so giving—and the whole time, I kept digging it deeper."

"You finally hit the water table." Natalie faced him. "I accept your apology. I completely and truly believe you are sorry that you got caught, and now you're distraught that you have to face the consequences of deceiving me. You won the game. I don't know what the prize is, but you can claim it now."

She opened the door and walked out.

He followed her onto the porch. "You know what the prize is? Confirmation that I was right."

She pivoted. "You were right about what? That I'm a fickle girl with a Messiah complex who has nothing better to do than talk down to her betters?"

"I never thought I was better than you! Will you please listen?" Colin's head was pounding, and for a moment he wished he'd dumped all this on Natalie last night when she was beside herself and she'd have cried over everything at once: the shawl and him and her heart and the whole world. "The minute you saw who I was, you walked out the door. I could have set a timer on it. I gave myself six weeks with you so maybe you'd be able to tolerate me over the long term, and then exactly when you found out who I was —"

"A liar," she snapped.

"A restaurant owner," he corrected. "As soon as you found out about that, bam, you're out the door. Literally out the door. Not because I'm better than you, but because as soon as you knew I worked with heavy cream instead of Campbell's soup, you shoved me into another category of human being, the lordling who passes judgment on everyone and plays games with people's heads."

Natalie opened her hands. "And? Was I wrong?"

All the neighbors must be sitting with their windows cracked and their ears against the sills. "You keep attributing malice to me where there isn't any."

"And you keep attributing stupidity to me. I'm not an emotion charity for helpless men." She headed to her car. "You and Chad should look each other up."

She was nearly at her car. He shouted, "You know, I actually liked the cream cheese."

She called back at him, "And I actually liked you, but it turned out that was never you in the first place, so whoever you really are, you can go to the devil."

She got inside and slammed the door.

All the things he could shout at her—plead at her—they fell apart in Colin's head. If anything, the breakup was slightly less dramatic than he'd thought it would be. She wasn't going to listen to reason, and she wasn't going to let him apologize.

He stayed on the steps until she'd pulled off the block, just in case she had anything else foul to shout out the car window.

One hour. An hour ago, she'd texted with gratitude that he'd prevented her from making a bigger mistake, and she'd sent him a picture of the pink/orange crocheted triangle crucified on a rubber mat. An hour later, she wanted him dead and on fire.

Natalie never got angry at anyone. Even the relentless users over at the yarn shop—she made excuses for them and then tidied up their lives. How sweet that she saved her invective for Colin.

He finished getting ready for work. He'd still make it for the pre-shift meeting. He put his knife roll back in his bag, then remembered that last night he'd left his book upstairs. Maybe Natalie would throw it out the window so he could fetch it from the lawn. Whatever. Not worth asking for it back for at least a week. Maybe a month.

He texted Austin. "Looks like I'll be there for Family Meal today."

Austin replied, "Dumped you, did she?"

Colin didn't bother replying.

A minute after, Austin sent, "You're such an idiot," and Colin didn't need to reply to that, either.

CHAPTER TWENTY-EIGHT

Even though Colin had expected to get dumped, this was so much worse than he'd anticipated. For three days, whenever Colin closed his eyes, he could remember the hurt on Natalie's face the moment she'd flung open his cabinets.

When he'd heard her wake up these past two mornings, she hadn't sung.

Fruits de Mer's kitchen was full of song during prep, and always during close. The line cooks picked the music, but sometimes they'd just start singing as they worked. Austin did it too, making up words to familiar tunes. The music made it fun, and once the front of house was empty, they'd blast it in the back.

Colin's days ended with music, and his mornings used to begin with it.

"Dude, forget her," Bill had said, as though it were that easy.

Denny still had that other apartment. It would be worth the hassle just to give Natalie what she wanted—which was Colin gone from her life. She'd forget their six-week culinary fling, and he wouldn't have the constant reminder of breaking her heart.

Tonight, Colin focused on working the broiler because the kitchen was in the weeds. As with Natalie, he'd had a six-week fling with Fruits de Mer's kitchen, and he already knew the quirks of all the equipment: this broiler got wicked hot in the back, less so on the right side. In the middle of the dinner rush, the kitchen printer kept grinding out tickets. The line cooks called instructions to one another, and Colin fought to turn off his emotions.

At least the broiler required all his attention. He had less time to think of Natalie hating him when he was wrapped up in getting proteins in and out without scorching them.

"Behind!" called Ally as she rushed past his back.

The printer growled again. Colin had awakened hearing the printer in his sleep, and he heard it in the white noise of his car engine, and he heard sometimes in total silence. When Natalie hadn't sung this morning as she cared for her animals, he'd heard the ticket printer in the spaces between the floor creaking.

"Six-ounce ribeye," he called. "What's it wearing?"

Someone shouted back, "Baked potato and mushrooms," so he plated it and dropped it under the lights. The ticket rail was a white-out, and he checked the next one, then back to the broiler.

Too bad none of this was "real" cooking. You know, real like dumping cream cheese into five bland nights' worth of white bean chili.

A filet in the back was about to go from rare to medium, that nebulous "rare plus," so Colin yanked it out, and his arm glanced against the broiler top.

Hissing in pain, he plated the steak, grabbed the next one that needed to come out, and plated that, too. "Hold for asparagus!" He checked the rail for what needed to go in and shoved three more proteins into the broiler, then pulled out an appetizer.

The heat blasted his arm, and he glanced at it. Nice burn. He'd need to do something about that.

It hurt, but that was just what he needed right now—real

pain, real injuries, real food. Reality. Heat and protein and hunger and satiety. Those were real.

Natalie was real, but Natalie had nothing left for him.

Twenty minutes later, they'd cleared enough tickets that they could see the rail again, and the general noise level calmed. Colin checked his arm again. It didn't look good—angry red, nice blister forming.

The ticket printer went off again.

"Behind!" Austin came by, then stopped. "Dang. Go take care of that."

"Hang on." Colin flipped two steaks, shoved in a tray of stuffed mushrooms, then headed for the printer.

Austin yanked him back. "Who's available for relief?" He shoved Colin out of the way and put Alex in front of the broiler. "First aid kit. Now."

At the corner cabinet, Colin ran his arm under cold water. Austin found the burn gauze and antibiotic ointment, then wrapped his forearm and taped everything in place. "That's an urgent care visit."

"It'll be fine."

"It's this big." Austin made a circle with his thumb and forefinger. "You'd send any of the line out the door with that."

"I'm not on the line. I'm staying."

Austin stepped closer. "Your head isn't in the game. There's a lot in here that'll kill you."

Colin shrugged. "I'm not the one who dropped his phone in the fryer and reflexively reached after it."

"That's why I know. It takes one distracted second to grab a 550 pan with your bare hands, and even less time to slice off your fingertips with the mandolin." Austin's eyes were sharp as Damascus steel. "Bro, go to urgent care and get antibiotics."

"I'm not going to urgent care." His arm stung, but he could deal with heat. He'd dealt with pain before.

The kitchen was out of the weeds now that the first seating had gotten their meals. Colin pulled off his apron and checked the front of house. Mostly couples, but there in the corner was a table of three young women, one of whom looked kind of cute.

He could take two minutes to straighten up, then swing by their table. *Is everything to your satisfaction?* They looked happy as they chatted—all the better. That table had the earmarks of a "girls' night out," and odds were at least one of them was single. The trick would be figuring out which one that was (although usually one of the women would do the work of volunteering another for him). Tonight he even had a "war wound" courtesy of the broiler, so that would win him pity points. He'd focus on the single gal and send out free slices of chocolate cake. Then he could write his phone number on the back of his business card and hand it to her, saying, "Call me if you want a dinner where I'm not working."

It wasn't smooth, but Austin made it work, and it used to work for Colin. If the best he could hope for was a string of month-long relationships, he might as well embrace it.

Except...not tonight. His arm hurt, and his heart hurt, and when he thought of starting something with someone else, his brain hurt, too.

He should call Denny and get that other apartment. Maybe Natalie didn't actually know Colin, but Colin knew she'd be better off without him in her life. She needed real food. And a real boyfriend.

Colin tracked down Austin. "Just so you know, the idiot twin is going to urgent care."

Austin shook his head. "You're not an idiot. Just... Quit making bad decisions."

Colin grabbed his coat from the office. "It wasn't a bad decision. I got burned because I wasn't paying attention."

Austin said, "At least don't make it worse."

Which, Colin thought as he went into the parking lot, had lately become his forte: stumbling into a bad situation, and then making it worse.

CHAPTER TWENTY-NINE

And that was how the relationship ended. Natalie had known Colin six weeks, been in love for maybe two, and admitted it for six hours before it was over. Now there had been five days of feeling stupid, feeling empty, feeling restless. Wanting. Just wanting.

Wanting him to admit he'd been a jerk. Wanting Colin to knock on her door so she could tell him off again. Instead he was creeping around like a mouse in his hole. He'd taken to showering at night after he got home and in the morning darting out the door without making a sound, and maybe that was pure cowardice. Maybe he was setting up something else and hadn't figured out yet the best possible way to humiliate her.

She didn't sing in the mornings because he'd hear. And what if he joined? She'd want to stamp on the floor until he stopped, so instead she crept around maintaining a sphere of silence. He had no right to join her song any longer. He never should have tried joining it in the first place.

She had his book, though. He had to come back upstairs sometime to get it, and then he could start stringing her along again. "So, hey," he might say, "since I julienned your heart, I might as well sharpen all your knives to make sure you slice apart your fingers."

Lilah kept sneaking glances at her. It was annoying.

"Are you okay?" Brooke asked.

Natalie shrugged as she opened a box of Cascade yarns. "I'm fine."

Lilah said, "Well, you shouldn't be fine. You should be furious. He acted like a first-class twit."

Brooke said, "Should we review-bomb Fruits de Mer? 'Five stars to the restaurant, but one star to its dog of an owner.'"

Natalie said, "Don't hurt the restaurant. He's not that bad."

Brooke said, "He's merely a higher-grade user than Chad."

Lilah wove her fingers together. "He wanted a live-in servant."

Brooke added, *Bang maid.* That's the term you're looking for."

Miserable, Natalie checked off inventory. "But he did pay for everything. And he did clean up. And he wasn't getting the other half of that, either."

Lilah slow-clapped. "Man of the year, right there. Let me go look in my closet for a trophy we can award him for doing the dishes."

Brooke snorted. "No trophies for liars."

Natalie swallowed hard. "But—"

"Oh, and you can quit defending him." Brooke turned toward the door as it jangled open for a customer. "I get it that you want to protect the world, but he doesn't need it."

Every day was like this now. No looking forward to dinner. No browsing recipe sites hoping to find something that would make Colin's eyes light up. Instead it was Brooke's anger, Lilah's indignation, and the customers' demands.

"What needles do I need for a Weekender sweater?" followed by, "It's a very popular pattern. How could you not know that?"

"What color choices match with teal?" followed by, "Well, maybe I won't work with teal after all."

Natalie ended her shift by mailing out five packages of Lilah's yarn kits coupled with Brooke's pattern. The whole time she stood in line at the Post Office, she watched the door, just in case. Colin wouldn't come here, though. Colin would be at the restaurant, using that laser knife to *brunoise* a parsnip.

The clerk rang her up with a smile. "Have a great day!"

Awesomely great, thanks. The only thing left was to go home and make dinner, except cooking felt wrong. Every time Natalie turned on the stove, she thought about Colin judging her stove-turning-on technique or hating her cheap nonstick pans or mocking the way she put cream cheese in her chili.

She could get takeout, but takeout was how this fiasco started in the first place.

She still had leftover dinners prepped in the freezer. Colin had said meal-prepping was exactly the same as takeout, but Colin could go jump in a creek. Maybe the best revenge would be to prep an entire month's worth of delicious meals and not cook again until spring. Meatloaf. Meatballs. Chili. Teriyaki chicken. Lasagna.

Who did he think he was to take her fun away? Natalie had actually liked cooking. What right did he have to smear it all up for her?

Sitting in her car, Natalie searched Colin up on the internet. He was all over the place, of course. She could have ended this on Day Two if she'd bothered opening a search engine, except why search for a kitchen porter? His whole life was online, his history with a variety of restaurants, including a summer-long stint at a Michelin-star kitchen. That charcuterie restaurant sounded like a fun place, but it must have been a nightmare with four owners. Sometimes Natalie wanted to strangle Brooke, and Brooke doubtless felt the same way about her co-owner—but they were cousins, and there were only two. Imagine if there were more, and they could gang up on one another?

Also, Colin had written a culinary column for a regional newspaper. The articles were about things like how to handle ordering from a restaurant when you have allergies. Here were tips for dining out with small children. Colin had never discussed having kids, but he seemed to like them.

According to him, he'd prefaced the CharCuties children's menu with, "We welcome our littlest diners, and our servers love when they use their restaurant manners." He'd included five "restaurant manners" that made one an excellent little diner. Sit tall. Use your indoor voice. Stay in your seat because the servers are carrying heavy trays of hot food. Use your own plate and utensils. Say please and thank you. On their first pass, the waitstaff would compliment something about the child's behavior, ("Oh, you're sitting in your seat! You must already know all about restaurant manners!") and this helped the kids live up to expectations. "I always wonder at restaurants with nasty signs that threaten unruly children with removal," he'd concluded. "Model the behavior you want to see."

Natalie started her engine. *So hey, Monsieur Restauranteur, what behavior were you modeling? Pure helplessness? Mining people for narcissistic supply?*

Colin had done well for himself, and he was going to keep doing well for himself. So would Natalie. She'd go home and finish weaving in Gertie's stupid ends. She'd volunteered to block a shawl for some hapless customer who didn't know how to fit foam board pieces together, had even made the offer to block while she was winding yarn for that very same customer. Someone had asked to take the display shawl when the shop was done with it, so probably, yeah. Natalie could be helpful. Everyone knew Natalie was helpful, and they didn't even have to trick her into doing it.

At home, she found Colin's apartment door open and a bunch of cleaners at work.

Denny was there. "Hey! Looks like you're going to have

the place to yourself for a bit."

There you go. Once Natalie was no longer free entertainment, Colin had no further use for her.

Denny said, "We should be out of here in a few hours. Sorry about the noise."

Natalie muttered, "At least you won't have to clean up the kitchen. I know he never used it."

She still had his book on her end table. She'd been waiting for him to be home so she could give it to him, but now it made sense why she'd never heard him. He'd lit out of the place like a black-hat cowboy riding out of Dodge under cloak of midnight.

CHAPTER THIRTY

Sit and Stitch was a joy, and Natalie didn't mean that in a good way.

"Can you remind me how to do the popcorn stitch again?" said the woman Natalie had already taught the popcorn stitch four times.

Natalie said, "Do you have your cell phone? I showed you a video last time so you'd be able to remind yourself whenever you wanted, not just when you're here."

From across the room, Brooke picked up her head and caught Natalie's eye. Her expression had a warning to it—a warning that wasn't a scolding, but more like a caution.

Natalie snapped, "What?"

Brooke said, "Nothing," which was a lie if Natalie had ever heard one. Which she had. From Colin, in fact. She was getting better at catching them.

The door jangled as Lavender Paul entered, her face pinched and her eyes narrow as always. One of the Sit and Stitchers sighed, and Natalie burned with fury. They needed to leave that woman alone. So what if Lavender had five hundred lawn ornaments? What would be different after the five hundred and first?

The popcorn-stitch crocheter said, "You did show me on the phone, but I don't remember how to find it."

For crying out loud. Natalie said, "We bookmarked it."

Gertie entered the shop behind Lavender Paul, lugging a bulky shopping bag. "Hello, everyone!" She settled herself in at the table. "Such a sunny day!"

"Too bad about the wind," said Don, snipping gold yarn for his latch hook rug. "Thought it'd blow my car off the road."

One of the women said, "Brooke, dear? You were friends with Jonathan Levesque, weren't you? That nice seminarian?"

Brooke raised her head. "Yes. I heard his great-aunt Millie died last week. It's sad. She was a wonderful person."

The woman shook her head. "Is he coming to town for her funeral?"

"He said he's going to, and I think the priest at Saint Lucy's is going to let him serve at the funeral, too." Brooke smiled. "Next year, he'll be Father Jonathan. He's looked forward to that a long time."

The would-be crocheter set her phone back on the table. "Natalie, I simply can't find the bookmark. Can you show me again?"

There was no reason this woman couldn't figure out how to find her own bookmarks on her own phone, let alone a reason she couldn't remember how to do popcorn stitches when she'd already done eighty of them over the past several weeks. And watched Natalie do them. And watched a video about doing them. Natalie said, "I'll get to you in a minute," and headed to the coffee maker.

Lilah approached, and Natalie shot her a glare. Instead of speaking, she backed off.

Behind Natalie, one of the new customers said, "Here, I can show you how to do a popcorn stitch."

They'd picked up so many crocheters in the past week. Brooke's intuition had been spot-on about the pattern release, and how they'd needed to get that pattern out the next day. They'd sold several dozen kits, and Brooke had sold well over three hundred copies of the pattern. She'd been right, but in the end, Natalie lost everything.

When she looked back, it did feel like Colin would have told her in the afternoon. Maybe she was using rose-colored glasses, but that bit about him saying he needed to talk to her—and him being unnerved that he wouldn't see her during the mid-day break—that seemed legitimate.

How he would have told her, though, she couldn't imagine. There wasn't a good way to say, "By the way, I've lied for the duration of our relationship." The most important part of his life was something he'd hidden. He might as well have been hiding a second family back in Kennebunkport.

Natalie returned to the table where Don was snipping his already snipped yarns to be a little shorter. Quarter-inch snips of yarn were scattered on the table, and beneath him a number of gold snips danced on the floor.

Irritated, Natalie said, "Don, would you mind keeping those all in one place?"

"Sorry." He grinned at her. "They do kind of wander."

Natalie said, "Maybe you need a sheep dog?"

He said, "Except these are acrylic, so I need a robot dog to herd the plastic."

Not funny. She turned away.

Gertie said, "Oh, Natalie, dear, I have two more shawls for you." She hefted her shopping bag onto the table, and there were two more entrelac shawls peeking out. Along with their ends.

Tiny, tiny ends.

While she watched, Gertie reached the end of a row, and she got out her scissors.

"Stop!" Natalie exclaimed. "Just stop!"

Everyone fell silent. Gertie went ahead and snipped the yarn.

"No!" Natalie advanced around the table. "Do you see this? I cannot weave in ends that short. I can't do it any longer. We've asked you a dozen times not to snip them that close to the last stitch because it makes weaving in the ends five times as hard."

Gertie said, "You never said that."

"Then you have never listened to me!" Natalie opened out the top shawl. "Do you see this?" No, of course she couldn't, she was legally blind. "Every time you work an entrelac shawl, you drop stitches, and these ends are two inches long. Less than two inches."

Gertie said, "I hate to waste the yarn."

"And don't tell me nobody ever said it," Natalie went on, "because both Lilah and Brooke refuse to do these shawls any longer because of the dropped stitches and the short ends. You do remember that because you don't ask them to do it—and now you can stop asking me, too, because I'm done. I'm done being used just because you don't want to listen to a very basic instruction."

Lilah came up behind her. "Gertie, I showed you six inches and had you snip it that far away. We did that two or three weeks ago." She edged Natalie away from the table. "Six inches isn't that much yarn waste, and it gives us leftover yarn to pick up loose stitches."

Gertie warbled, "You never told me any of this before!"

Natalie said, "Then why won't Lilah and Brooke finish your shawls any longer?"

Gertie shook her head. "I... I guess they're busy."

Natalie dropped the shawl back on the table. "Then I'm busy, too. I'm too busy to clean up everyone's loose ends when no one is even slightly concerned about making things easier for me to do it." She turned. "And Don, those yarn bits are going everywhere!"

Brooke approached the table. "Nat, I'm having trouble with the ball winder. Can you help me?"

Nope. Not exiting this one gracefully. Not this time.

Gertie said, "I don't understand why you want me to waste yarn."

A hand landed on Natalie's arm, and she turned to find herself face to face with Lavender Paul. "Check me out. Now."

Lavender's eyes were piecing. She held Natalie's gaze for a New York second, then marched over to the register. She thrust a pinwheel lawn ornament at Natalie, who rang it up in fury.

The table behind her was silent other than Gertie muttering to herself about yarn waste.

No, Gertie, those four inches of yarn aren't going to add up to anything. Every nine rows would make one yard. What are you going to do with a yard of yarn? It takes a hundred yards of worsted to make a hat, so are you planning to snip off the ends nine hundred times? And they're all different yarns, so it's not even like you'd have a hundred yards of the same color.

Natalie handed back the card, and Lavender narrowed her eyes. "Carry that to my car."

Oh, good. Natalie had managed to torque off one of the old townies. See if Natalie ever set aside sparkly solar outdoor decorations for Lavender Paul again.

She carried the package to Lavender's overstuffed station wagon, and the townie turned to her.

"Good for you," Lavender said. "Blasted biddies, ordering you this way and that. You tell 'em. You're not their maidservant."

Natalie blinked.

Lavender took the package from Natalie's hand. "I been listening. Now you listen. There's people will take advantage of you because you're nice and they're not, and then there's people who take advantage of you because they don't think. Don, he's one of them who don't think. Had a mother who swept up after him and then a wife who swept up after him and now a daughter. Never occurred to him where his trash goes because it's never there when he comes back." Lavender poked Natalie in the shoulder. "Gertie, she hears what she wants to hear. You ask her to change, and it's not what she likes, so she does what she wants. You did right."

Natalie looked over her shoulder at the shop.

Lavender said, "You make pretty stuff. I want that shawl

when it's done being on the stand. I want it for two hundred dollars, and I'm not giving less. You tell Brooke, she's not giving away that shawl. It's mine."

Natalie looked back at Lavender. "You don't have to do this."

"You're not looking out for yourself. You get so used to people treating you wrong but you say to yourself it's okay, until then you can't tell when people treat you right."

Natalie closed her eyes.

"Don never learned about cleaning up because he never had to solve his own problems. Let him figure it out. Gertie never learned to listen because everyone was busy making her excuses for her. Let her figure it out when no one's excusing her." Lavender put her package in the car and slammed the door. "You've got to be what I call 'smart-stupid.' If they sigh and huff and hint, act like you're too stupid to notice. If they don't say it direct, act like you don't hear what they want you to hear—because you didn't. Be stupid in a smart way. Don't jump in and offer. Stop assuming what people need, and let them grow up for once."

CHAPTER THIRTY-ONE

Natalie didn't go back to the Sit and Stitch table. Instead, she dusted the gift section with her back pointedly turned toward their silent stitchers. Natalie was not going to re-teach a stubborn crocheter the stitch she couldn't be bothered to remember the first eighty times she worked it. Natalie was not going to deal with Don's yarn fuzz, and Natalie absolutely was not going to try to prove to Gertie that she'd said something everyone had heard her say three dozen times.

A few of the attendees purchased yarn before they left. Don did get down on the floor to pick up quarter-inch pieces of yarn. Gertie left without saying goodbye, but carrying her shawls.

Brooke said, "You can knock off early if you want."

Natalie said, "Because I'm driving away customers?"

Brooke snorted. "I darn near applauded when you told Gertie to get stuffed, but Don was mortified. Still, we're stable here, and we're not supposed to get any deliveries. You might as well take off."

Sure, go home and play with her pets. The animals took advantage of her, but at least Natalie had known what she was signing up for when she opened her heart to them.

Natalie pulled in at her house to see an unfamiliar SUV in the driveway, so apparently she'd be needing to break in a new tenant already. Only this time, the downstairs tenant could starve, and then after maintenance found their emaciated corpse, Natalie would have her third new neighbor in a year.

She opened the door and ended up face-to-face with Colin. Gasping, she nearly slammed the door until she realized, wait, not Colin. Wrong twin.

"Austin, are you moving in?" She backed up a step. "Move right back out again."

Austin bowed. "My pleasure. I'm retrieving a package Colin forgot to have redirected because he's an idiot. Only, despite his idiocy, he knew you didn't want to see him."

Austin flipped the box in his hands so the address label faced her.

"How very perceptive." She looked him up and down. "Although for all I know, you're actually Colin."

Austin stepped to the side and held the door for her. "I assure you, I'm the smart one."

"You know, I hate that." She folded her arms and didn't enter. "I hate how you and he have this running joke that whatever quality it is, you're the *whatever* one. Why couldn't Colin be the decent one?"

"Not fair." Austin's voice sharpened. "My brother is a lot of things—for one, we've established he's an idiot—but he's not indecent. I understand if you despise him, but at least despise him for who he is."

"Gee, if only he'd ever shown me who he is." Natalie walked past. "Actually, wait here. He left his book in my apartment back when he was still treating me like dirt."

Austin exclaimed, "And you didn't burn it?"

Natalie hurried up the steps. "I'd never harm a book."

Birdie Holly sang a greeting, and as Natalie grabbed *The Making of a Chef* off the end table, she whistled back.

Downstairs, Austin was leaning against the porch rail. "Did you actually introduce yourself to him by saying

Fruits de Mer was an overpriced lunch for tourists?"

She handed over the book. "Of course I did."

Austin grinned in a way that left Natalie off-balance because he looked so much like Colin. "That's awesome. And did he sharpen every knife in your kitchen?"

She frowned. "I wouldn't let him."

"You should have. It's his love language. When we visit our mother, I'll be still hugging Mom at the front door, and then from the kitchen, *Zhing! Zhing!* He's sharpening her knives."

Natalie laughed. "Priorities."

"No kidding. And don't touch them." Austin fanned the edges of the book pages. "I mean, *his* knives—you don't touch those. Yours? Those are in his hands the moment he sees them. *Hey, is that a forged boning knife? Rockwell hardness 57? I always wanted a Damascus blade. Get me a rack of lamb I can French trim just to feel how it works.*"

Natalie bit her lip. "And does he give a running commentary on all your kitchen tools?"

"Don't get me started." Austin rolled his eyes. "Did he complain about your cheese grater?"

Natalie laughed. "You mean, before or after he used my scissors to cut steak?"

"And then he asked which is your best microplaner for truffles? And it was a total shock that you have neither a single microplaner nor fresh truffles?"

Natalie leaned against the wall. "He accidentally called my crochet pattern a recipe, which I guess is fair. Also, he read me my cookbook for fun."

Austin raised his eyebrows. "And was it fun?"

"It kind of was," Natalie admitted. "Out of his mouth came this mini-essay about how the author used food to create community, and how these different recipes had a goal toward assimilating an immigrant population." She bit her lip. "He was so sarcastic with me the first day that he came right out the other side and sounded sincere. Anyone that angry was clearly self-conscious. I wanted to help."

Austin raised his hands. "You acted in good faith the

whole time."

"Now it's obvious why he'd be asking questions when he washed my dishes. 'So...is this your only colander?' Except he did love my dish cloths. He was awed that you could scrub glass with them." She arched her eyebrows. "Hello—that's why I made them."

Austin raised his eyebrows. "You had the power to send that boy to heaven with those. Except if you had, there's no way you'd have prevented him from sharpening every blade within a two-hundred-foot radius—including your scissors."

Natalie wrinkled her nose. "That obsession sounds a little unhealthy."

"You have no idea about unhealthy. We each got our first chef's knives for our sixteenth birthday, which you can imagine made us the envy of the entire high school. We never once engaged in a sword fight in the kitchen."

Natalie's eyes widened. "Were you out of your minds?"

Austin stood away from the railing. "We were sixteen. We also never once ended up at the emergency room getting stitched up afterward." He laughed. "But he'd never slash me nowadays. Or maybe I slashed him. Did he tell you about Arson?" When Natalie shook her head, Austin said, "It's nothing to do with setting fires. If I'm the handsome twin and he's the indecent twin, then Arson was the responsible twin, as in, whenever our parents wanted to know who'd burnt popcorn in the microwave or who'd flooded the washing machine, Arson was responsible."

Natalie said, "Arson didn't pretend he couldn't use a can opener."

"Neither did Colin. Someday I'll loan you a left-handed can opener, and you can try making it work," Austin said as he flipped through the book again.

The hair raised on Natalie's arms. "You can quit doing that. I didn't damage his book."

Austin raised it toward her, cover forward. "He was reading you a memoir about the Culinary Institute of America. He wanted you to figure it out."

Natalie ran a hand through her hair. "He's just a lousy liar. He told me he worked summers in a pizza kitchen, except he forgot he'd asked me to teach him to make pizza. And then there's the fact that your website has his name and his picture beside the word, 'Owner.'"

"He's a lousy liar because he never does it." Austin's nose wrinkled. "Two kindergarteners and a guinea pig could have concocted a better ruse."

Natalie said, "Are you telling me to feel sorry for him? Because we can see where that got us."

Austin rolled his eyes. "I'm not telling you what to do. All I'm telling you is, what he did wasn't a defect of character. Just a long mistake."

"A mistake is when you forget to turn down the heat under the rice." Natalie folded her arms. "Thank you, though. I was wondering when you'd start the sales pitch."

"No sales pitch." Austin pointed to the apartment door. "He moved because you didn't want to see him again, and he promised me you wouldn't even be home for another hour. But I'm here, so I'm going to do the brotherhood thing and tell you—he's not like that."

Natalie shook her head. "In my experience, he's just like that."

"Except you've spent the last five minutes telling me what he's truly like—the geeky dreamer who uses scissors on steak and gets goggle-eyed over dish scrubbies." Austin shook his head. "In all that time, when he wasn't telling you who he was, you managed to figure it out all the same."

Austin walked into Colin's office with the package tucked under his arm, and the book he'd left at Natalie's. Austin slapped the book onto the desk, then walked out of the office, calling over his shoulder, "Congratulations on a world-class mess-up."

Reaching for the book, Colin braced himself, but Natalie hadn't soaked it in the fish tank. She'd been holding onto it.

Waiting for him?

He caught up to Austin in the function room, setting up for Family Meal. "She wasn't supposed to be there."

"A lot of things aren't supposed to happen." Austin sighed. "Also, she looks as strung-out as you do, only she's angry."

Fair enough. "What did she say?"

Austin waved a hand. "You're the story-fabricator. Use your imagination."

Colin sighed. "She's always a cut above what I can imagine."

Austin turned to him. "Do you know her? At all? Because that's where you're missing the mark. Even when we were talking, it was obvious that despite you giving her nothing but smoke and mirrors, she managed to draw a bead on your exact identity. That's what she loved. She hasn't let go of that yet. She still laughs when she mentions your quirks. You've found a woman who actually—poor soul—likes you."

Colin muttered, "That would be the first time."

"Right?" Austin rolled his eyes. "She still likes you, but not for long if you don't get back in there."

Colin lit the burners beneath the tray stands. His forearm arm still stung if he moved it the wrong way, but he wasn't taking the painkillers. He needed to know if it was getting worse. "She was entirely clear about how much she wanted me in her life."

"Listen to me." Austin's voice ticked up. "I asked her if you'd sharpened all her knives. She said you hadn't."

Colin said, "I'm not the Legendary Mad Knife Sharpener who climbs through the windows at midnight to sharpen knives without consent."

"Let me go on, although that would be an awesome

super-villain power. I told her about us having a sword fight with Grandpa's chef's knives, and she was by turns horrified and laughing. I told her about Arson, and I made fun of your fascination with kitchen gear, and she was giggling the whole time. This was all in about three minutes." Austin opened his hands. "She wasn't laughing because any of what I said was funny. She laughed because it was you."

Colin stopped and blew off a breath.

"You know how you snickered when you told me she had a whole zoo in her apartment? Or the way you rolled your eyes and smiled when you said she laid down the law on which minutes you could use for your shower? Same deal." Austin lowered his voice. "She recognizes your quirks, and she loves them. Don't let someone like that go."

Colin adjusted a tray in its frame. "Remember how I didn't sharpen her knives without consent? I'm not barging back into her life without consent either."

As he reached for the first tray lid, he said, "Although...I could try to get her consent. But how?"

Austin folded his arms. "You know her."

Did he know her? He faced Austin, but the rest of the staff were there too, watching.

Colin said, "*Amuse bouche*? *Mignardise*?"

Austin said, "You know my default answer."

Colin shook his head. "This goes beyond chocolate cake."

Danielle said, "I'm in. How do we lure her here?"

The Dish Dame interjected, "You don't bring her in here. You go to her."

Bill said, "Delivery, dude."

Danielle said, "I have a car."

Alex added, "I'll bike something over to her, especially if I'm on the clock."

Austin snickered.

Frowning, Colin paced. "Okay, let's do this. And before you ask, no, I have no idea what *this* even is."

CHAPTER THIRTY-TWO

Fighting a yawn, Natalie opened the shop door slowly enough that the bells wouldn't jingle. This morning, she craved silence.

Yesterday, Austin claimed Colin wasn't a monster. Natalie would do the same for Brooke, right? If Hal accused Brooke of being a terrible girlfriend, wouldn't Natalie defend her anyhow?

Lavender Paul had said there were different kinds of users, so what kind of user was Colin? The selfish kind, or the self-absorbed kind?

What would it take to just once have a guy in her life like that man who'd walked in thinking only of his wife's joy and knowing exactly how she'd respond, right down to the things she'd say? Someone who thought about her as well as about himself? Someone who looked at the world as someplace he could improve rather than someplace that ought to cater to him?

Lavender Paul kept creeping into Natalie's head, so Natalie went over to the register where she wrote out a "Sold" tag, along with "Hold for Lavender Paul." She pinned the tag to her shawl.

These weren't Lavender's colors at all, but who knew if it would ever get worn? Maybe Lavender would hang it on her wall to get dusty, and fifteen years from now, her heirs would throw it away with the rest of her hoard.

Like so much of Natalie's life. Use her and never notice her again. And...why?

Was that what she wanted, to be nothing more than a delivery system for services?

Colin had seemed to notice her. He'd noticed the things she said and the things she didn't say. That was why Natalie hadn't noticed the things Colin hadn't been saying —because he'd paid so much of the right kind of attention that she'd justified all the things that didn't add up.

She'd wanted to think she was helping him, so when he made progress—rapid progress—she'd embraced it and felt amazing.

A boyfriend wasn't a child to be raised. A husband should want to be with you, not need you. Each of them could survive on their own, Natalie and Colin. Since he hadn't needed the cooking lessons, and assuming Austin was right that he hadn't been mocking her, then he'd kept coming upstairs because he liked being with her. He liked talking to her, liked washing dishes with her, liked watching television with her. He'd even begun sharing his real love of cooking with her, edging it in sideways by reading her that memoir. The only thing he hadn't done was trusting her with the truth.

He'd been guarding that restaurant like treasure. He'd begun the relationship like an offended guard dog and ended it like a kicked puppy. He said men protected the things they loved, and in retrospect, Natalie had to guess that was the restaurant—or maybe cooking in general. He'd never braved up enough to risk her rejecting all that. Instead he'd shown her how important cooking was by taking care of all the details: buying the food, providing the recipes, and washing the dishes.

Contrast to Gertie. Gertie also said she was doing something important, but never important enough to do it more than halfway, and then she'd leave someone else to pick up the pieces.

Gertie had never actually said her work was important, though, had she? She'd left heavy implications of unloved, shivering seniors, and then she'd handed Natalie a round-trip ticket for a guilt trip.

Don had never demanded everyone to clean up after him. He just left his mess and expected it to be gone on his return.

Well, no more. From now on, everyone's expectations could just lie there, unnoticed, and they could rot away. "Smart stupidity," indeed. They could book her a guilt trip, but Natalie didn't have to get on the train. Lavender Paul had the right idea.

The front door clicked as it unlocked, and Natalie turned to say hello to Lilah, only at Lilah's side was a customer.

Wait, not a customer. The newcomer was wearing the black pants and white blouse plus name tag of the Fruits de Mer uniform.

"Natalie Prescott?" It was Danielle, from the Crafters Guild luncheon. She stepped forward holding a plastic container. "Delivery from Fruits de Mer."

Natalie recoiled. "I didn't order anything."

Danielle handed it off to Natalie. "*Amuse bouche*, compliments of the chef."

Natalie stared at the container in her hand. Nestled in a bed of lettuce leaves was a Japanese soup spoon with a walnut-sized creation in the bowl.

"I can't take this," she blurted out.

Danielle smiled. "Please accept it, with the chef's compliments."

A sense of worthlessness washed over Natalie—not deserving this, not deserving attention, not deserving notice. Colin had run from her when she wasn't useful, but now he was sending her a treat, and what was this leading up to? What was he softening her up to ask?

One way to find out. "What does he want?"

Danielle said, "He wants you to enjoy it."

Natalie trembled, and Lilah put a hand on her arm. "You don't have to take it if you don't want. You can send it back to the kitchen."

Natalie closed her eyes in helpless laughter. "I've never once in my life sent anything back to the kitchen."

Danielle said, "For which all your servers thank you, but I have to drive back regardless. It's all the same to me if I have this in the passenger seat."

Natalie looked at it again. Smoked salmon? Cream cheese? The nibble was seated on a circle of cucumber. Was he mocking her with the cream cheese?

Still, it looked good. It was artistic, and he knew she'd like these flavors. He'd taken time with this.

Lilah said, "That looks amazing, but now I want some too."

Danielle laughed. "Should I give *your* compliments to the chef?"

Lilah said, "Nice presentation."

Natalie said, "Fine. Please say thank you to the chef. Hang on—" and she went for her wallet.

Danielle raised a hand. "I am not allowed to accept a tip. By order of the owner. That's taken care of."

Natalie's cheeks heated up. "Oh. Well, then thank you."

As the door closed behind Danielle, Natalie looked at Lilah. "Should I eat it?"

Lilah's head pumped. "Yes! Or do you think he's intending to poison you?"

Natalie popped open the plastic lid and lifted the spoon. "It's not much of an apology."

Lilah said, "You already accepted his apology. This is reparations."

Natalie laughed, and she ate the "*amuse*" while Lilah awaited a verdict. "That was delicious," Natalie declared. "I guess that's what you can do if you're a chef who isn't pretending to be baffled by a spatula."

She set the container in the back room, wondering what should happen with the spoon and if she should recycle the plastic, and was she supposed to eat the greenery? It looked like a decoration, but it was still romaine lettuce. The guinea pigs would like it.

As soon as they opened for business, a customer arrived. She'd been at yesterday's Sit and Stitch, and Natalie's cheeks burned at the memory of losing her temper with everyone. "Don't mind me," the woman said, hurrying to the back wall. "I decided I need more fiber insurance."

Natalie said, "We have more of the same dye lot—"

"I wrote it down, no worry!" Actually, the woman had brought the entire ball band. "Perfect match! I'll just pay and be out of your hair."

Brooke entered the shop with a jangle of bells. "Pay no attention to the owner in the corner! I ended up on a live chat with a crochet group last night, and they want nine kits for their group to do a crochet-along."

Nice! Natalie's all-nighter was paying off for in spades.

Natalie rang out the fiber-insurance customer. As the woman handed over her credit card, she said, "Did you need a claw hammer to get that junk into Lavender's car yesterday?"

Natalie paused in running the card. She looked the customer right in the eye and gave a flat, "Excuse me?"

The woman sniffed. "Lavender's car is always stuffed to the gills, like it would explode if you put in one more thing."

Without any intonation, Natalie said, "I thought that's what you meant." She ran the card without looking at the woman again.

No more. None of this.

The woman added, "There should be a law against her having so much junk in her front yard."

"Lavender is a thoughtful woman who never hurt you." Natalie handed back the card. "Have a great day."

No inflection. The woman shifted uncomfortably, and Natalie turned toward the nearest shelf.

The woman said, "Her house is an eyesore."

Natalie didn't look at her. "And yet, I've never heard her

gossip."

There might as well be icicles hanging from the ceiling. The woman muttered something about the tone of the neighborhood and then fled the shop.

Brooke slipped over to her. "Whatever happened to you, it's making you effective."

"I'm sick of every last human being on earth. I'm ready to take heads off." Natalie huffed. "Well, maybe not yours. And not Lilah's. Lavender Paul may be quirky, but they tromp all over her. I'm done with it."

Brooke pointed to the display shawl. "Lavender Paul reserved your shawl?"

"She offered me two hundred, so yeah, I'll take it."

Brooke's eyebrows raised. "I've got to get a patron like that. Let me know if you meet the Doge of Venice."

The door opened, admitting a man in black pants and a black shirt with a stand-up collar. He presented a plastic container. "Lobster *accras*," he said, bowing. "Compliments of the chef."

Without debating this time, Natalie took the package from his hands, and the man bowed again before leaving.

Inside the package were three ceramic spoons, each bearing a golden, deep-fried nugget, drizzled with a dark sauce.

Lilah approached. "This may be the start of something good."

Natalie said, "I'm guessing that's one for each of us."

"Impressive." With a plastic-sounding pop, Brooke opened the package. "He's figured out that if he's going to get to you, he's got to come through us first."

Lilah said, "Or maybe it's just that he can count."

A bite, and the lobster accras exploded with flavor in Natalie's mouth. A little zest, a lot of lobster, a crunchy outer coating, and a juicy center.

Lilah said, "I approve of this development."

Just before noon, two customers entered the shop, and Natalie exclaimed, "Oh, I recognize that yarn!"

One woman unfurled a shawl. "Isn't it amazing! It

worked so well with the pattern!" She spread it out on the table. "Could you block it for me, though? It would look so much better blocked."

Natalie caught her breath just before her reflexive yes.

It would take a quarter of an hour. But that was a quarter an hour of her time—fifteen minutes that should be her business's, or her own, and—

"Actually, we have a class forming." Natalie glanced at Brooke. "Next week, right? We're doing a live blocking demonstration."

Seeming unnerved, Brooke approached. Natalie added, "It's five dollars to attend the class, or free if you buy your blocking boards or pins from us."

The woman frowned. "No, I don't think so. Just do it the way you usually do."

Natalie steeled herself. "We're not offering that service any longer. It's much better if you block it yourself, anyway. Then you'll always be able to handle your own finishing."

Brooke said, "You don't even need the boards. You can block it directly on your bed."

The woman folded her arms. "Why can't you block it?"

Her friend pulled out her phone. "What day is the demonstration? Because I've always wanted to learn to block my finished objects, and it seems so daunting."

Brooke said, "Let me grab the calendar—" because of course it wasn't already on the calendar.

The door jangled, and in walked a server from Fruits de Mer. "Natalie Prescott?" he asked. "Compliments of the chef."

Five minutes later, Natalie and Brooke and Lilah were in the back room, enjoying tiny bites of sweet potato with bacon and avocado.

Brooke said, "The longer this goes on, the more I find myself rooting for him."

Natalie sighed. "You're not helping."

Lilah said, "He's making reparations."

Brooke said, "Do you think he'll send lunch? Because

lunch seems like excellent reparations."

Natalie walked away.

Brooke followed. "If he's making you uncomfortable, tell him to stop."

Natalie said, "If I keep accepting these—aren't I telling him I'm open to letting him back into my life?"

Brooke said, "It's entirely your call, but he owes you."

Lilah approached them at the register. "So far, he isn't asking for anything. Every one of the delivery people has said it's free, and they've all refused to take a tip."

"Free comes with a price," Natalie said.

Brooke said, "Whenever you've been doing nice things for people, what was your price?"

Head lowered, Natalie clenched her hands.

Brooke said, "What was your price when you thought you were teaching Colin to cook?"

Natalie's voice was a whisper. "I just...wanted him to learn something. To enjoy himself."

"Then for now, assume that's what Colin wants." Lilah hugged Natalie from behind. "He knows he messed up, and he wants you to enjoy yourself."

CHAPTER THIRTY-THREE

Salmon tartare appetizers arrived at noon.

Cream of artichoke soup (for three) arrived at twelve-thirty.

The entree, sole meunière accompanied by a bowl of bourride, arrived at one.

An "*amuse*" of fig and walnut with a cinnamon sauce arrived at two o'clock, although the deliverer (Danielle again) called it a *mignardise*.

Standing over the stack of used crockery, silverware, and Japanese soup spoons, Brooke rubbed her hands together. "On second thought, don't forgive him. Groveling tastes stupendous."

Natalie ought to text Colin. She ought to unblock his number and tell him thank you, but this needed to stop.

At three o'clock, when nothing further arrived, Natalie hesitated before going home. "I don't want them chasing me all over Brighthead."

Lilah said, "No big deal. If they arrive with more food, we'll eat it in your honor," and Brooke gave a serious nod.

By three-thirty, though, with no servers in sight, Natalie got brave enough to drive home. The tastes of sweet potatoes and figs and asparagus lingered in her mind. That lobster accras was amazing. Even the smoked salmon and cream cheese had been perfect on the crispy cucumber.

Was this what it felt like to be noticed? Pampered?

What if she arrived home and set aside the charity projects? What if she picked up that silky fingering weight yarn she'd been saving for a special occasion and cast on something for herself? A shawl as light as a breeze and welcoming as an angel's kiss, delicate as Queen Anne's Lace but voluminous enough to enwrap her like butterfly wings.

What if she turned out the lights other than her work light, burned the scented candle she'd gotten for Christmas, and played music? She didn't have to wait for Colin or anyone to notice her in order to take care of herself. If a man who'd mocked and abandoned her knew how to treat her well, how much better could she learn to treat herself?

At home, she set up the ball winder and swift without a second glance at her stack of charity projects. She didn't even think about the almost-finished objects she'd been handed in order to weave in their ends or block them. Someday, but not now. Now she was full of amuses and soup and fish and a bite-sized dessert, and her head was spinning.

What if, just once, Natalie paid attention to what she wanted instead of what would make everyone else's life easier?

The swift kicked up a breeze, and Birdie Holly sang to her. Natalie whistled back as she cranked the ball winder. Soon she had a second skein in her hands, unwound and draped over her fingers. She snapped it to clear the tangles, then set it on the umbrella, sending it for a spin while a glossy cake grew on the winder. Natalie dug through her stash until she came up with the ergonomic rosewood hooks she'd gotten two years ago for her birthday but never used because it never seemed the right time.

Now was the right time. Henceforth, "now" would always be the right time.

She gave the guinea pigs the decorative greens from the Fruits de Mer deliveries, that way they, too, could enjoy Colin's bounty.

Colin had only been able to use Natalie because she'd loaned herself out to be used. Lavender had nailed it—Natalie jumped in to take care of everyone else's ordinary difficulties, and Colin had gone along for the ride. Whenever he'd tried confessing (by now she'd identified three certain attempts, and a possible fourth,) she'd short-circuited him because he shouldn't have to go through the trouble of being uncomfortable—not if she could guess what he needed. She'd been cutting him off to spare him discomfort, but the underlying reality was her own discomfort with seeing people unsettled. Sometimes, people needed to have uncomfortable conversations. Colin had been a coward, but in her own way, so had Natalie.

Got a problem? Natalie will solve it. Why? Because Natalie had self-identified as the solver of everyone's ordinary problems. Her discomfort counted for nothing, whereas everyone else's discomfort was unable to be borne.

Tonight, though? Tonight, Natalie would tuck in with a gorgeous yarn and a gorgeous pattern and a gorgeous hook. She'd snuggle up on the couch and enjoy her candle and her music, and maybe she'd prepare something special for dinner—although maybe not, since she was still full from lunch.

What about a bubble bath? She had a half dozen bath bombs she'd been saving for "someday." Just like "the right time," "someday" could likewise be now.

It didn't hurt anyone if Natalie used the gifts she already had, and maybe Lavender was right. Maybe treating herself like an afterthought was the reason other people treated Natalie the same way.

The rest of this afternoon and tonight would be

"Natalie-first" time. She filled the tub with hot water and tossed in a raspberry bath bomb. She luxuriated in the scent and the bubbles, reading in the tub until the water grew cold. She changed into leggings, a fleecy shirt, and fuzzy socks.

This was her. This was all for her, and now for the next question: did Colin know her? Maybe, because all that food was tailored for her. But he was just giving her food.

She'd given him cooking lessons, and he'd returned the favor by bringing groceries. Here was the difference, though: groceries weren't a meal. The meal came in the combination of ingredients and the individual touch. Now Colin was sending finished products, but they were high-end artistry. He was trying to dazzle her.

It worked: they were dazzling.

But his food hadn't been what she rejected. His food hadn't been lying to her.

That was a troubling thought. Instead of dwelling on it, Natalie set her yarn in a ceramic yarn bowl and got to work.

It was ridiculous, and at the same time, it was wonderful. Natalie sat with the pattern on her tablet and the yarn cake turning with every tug. The center of the shawl took shape, followed by the first part of the chart. She had a half-circle on her lap the size of her outstretched hand and was getting set to start the second chart when a knock came at the door.

Natalie's hair stood on end.

Nearly five o'clock. Fruits de Mer would be poised to open seating for its dinner guests.

Another knock, and Birdie Holly whistled in anticipation, setting off the guinea pigs who, despite being full of romaine and kale, doubtless hoped for carrot tops. Natalie set her yarn on the couch and braced herself.

There in the hallway stood Austin.

He extended a thermal bag. "Compliments of the chef."

Natalie sighed. "Austin, I can't."

He beamed. "Of course you can. On the house, all

comped."

"You don't understand." She stepped toward him on the landing and rested her hands on his on either side of the bag. "This isn't Colin. All this, it's dazzling, and it's romantic, and it's thoughtful. Two weeks ago, I'd have been over the moon. I have no doubt that bag contains one of the best meals I'd have had in my life, but it's not Colin."

Austin's smile faltered. "He chose the menu and prepared everything himself."

"He cooked a meal. He made a steak or a salmon or whatever—no, don't tell me—and I know he did it excellently." She steadied herself with a slow breath. "It's not him. He spent six weeks hiding himself from me, and all day he's been sending me treats—but he's still hiding himself, and I've realized I can't accept anything more from you under the circumstances. I deserve better than that."

Austin tilted his head. "What do you deserve?"

Her voice quavered. "Whatever it is he's not giving me."

With his brow furrowed, Austin was a dead ringer for his brother presented with an intractable problem. "If Colin delivered it himself, would you accept?"

"It's not the delivery agent. It's what's being delivered. But wait a minute." She grabbed a bag off the kitchen table. "I'm sorry I keep using you like the postal system, but I need to return all your spoons." Her vision was blurring. She had to end this conversation. "Give my compliments to the chef. Everything was delicious, but the meal is over."

She kept her voice steady until after she had the door shut, and then she returned to her couch. Birdie Holly squawked as she picked up her shawl, and when she tried to whistle back to him, that's when the tears broke through.

Lavender had told Natalie to put herself first. Lavender hadn't warned her it would hurt.

Colin pivoted with eagerness as Austin returned, then dread when he realized Austin still had the bag. "She wasn't home?"

Then he saw the bag of spoons, and he realized.

Austin had read the succession of expressions on Colin's face. "She wasn't making sense, but she was perfectly clear."

Colin said, "Should I go myself?"

"She was clear about that, too, because I asked. No. The refusal had *nothing to do with the delivery agent.* It's about the thing you're delivering, which 'wasn't you,' although she admitted whatever you'd sent was probably one of the best meals she'd have in her life." Austin clapped his hand on Colin's shoulder. "I'm sorry. When she accepted the first ones, I thought we had a chance."

Colin unboxed the meal and let the staff know everything was free for the taking. "Not you," he told the Dish Dame. "You get whatever you want, made hot when you ask."

He must look like garbage because the Dish Dame didn't even snarl at him.

That was the end, then. He'd never stood a chance with Natalie. If anything, pulling out the stops had made her even firmer in her conviction that their futures headed in separate directions. Making it up to her had never been an option.

The kitchen printer kicked out more tickets, and Colin got out of the way of the line cooks. He stepped in to act as relief whenever someone needed a break, but otherwise, tonight's dinner was just another night. He could keep his mind on the kitchen because he didn't have to wonder if Natalie was impressed in hers. He wouldn't have to pull someone off duty in an hour to send them across town bearing dessert.

By nine-thirty, the dining room was emptying, and the kitchen began breaking down. Everyone knew not to say anything out loud. Nothing like, "Well, I guess we can put this away because no one else will show up," lest they end up seating a table of fifteen at 9:55. By ten, the doors were closed, the last of the diners finishing.

"That wasn't you."

Colin scraped down the grill with the brick, flinching because the residual heat still stung the burn on his arm. The Dish Dame was attacking the pots while Bill mopped the floor and Austin inventoried the walk-in.

"It's not Colin."

This was him, of course. Colin Young owned a restaurant and had a high level of technical culinary skill. He'd made his best play, but he still couldn't impress her. Natalie was softening her rejection by trying to pretend she wasn't rejecting him, but what else could she possibly be rejecting when he'd put it all out there, and she even admitted as much?

She hadn't said, "It's not you—it's me." She'd said, "It's not you." Then what was it?

Front of house had the carpet vacuumed and tomorrow's silverware rolled. The closers finished with the kitchen. Ten-thirty. Colin took a final glance over the gleaming stainless steel, everything in its place and awaiting tomorrow. The big empty sinks. The fryer, off (how many times had he awakened at two a.m. wondering if he'd left it on?) and the coolers, sealed. In eight hours, he'd be back again because this was him. This was his life.

In his car, Colin turned on the engine, and he thought, *But what if it's not?*

"It's not Colin" may have meant she would have accepted if he'd given her "Colin".

Therefore, what was she saying *wasn't* Colin? Stop and think. He'd sent her every culinary tidbit he could think of that would rock her back on her heels with its presentation and taste, all of them geared toward the preferences he'd learned over six weeks of cooking together. He knew what she liked and what she avoided, and he'd struck every note over the course of the day. Anything he hadn't nailed before lunch was set up to be completed with the dinner, and the finale was a dessert that should have sealed the deal.

She claimed she wanted a man who could predict everything she wanted and everything she'd do, and per Austin, he'd succeeded—so why the demurral that none of that was him? Who did she think he was?

While the engine idled, Colin leaned against the head rest and closed his eyes.

Stopping the meal train because it wasn't him meant she'd give him another chance if it was. But not just the delivery agent—that's what she'd said to Austin. Not Colin as the delivery boy or Colin as the restaurant owner. Just Colin. Except, who was Colin?

He glanced back at the restaurant, and then he shut off the engine.

CHAPTER THIRTY-FOUR

Natalie had completed the shawl's second chart when she heard the front door open and steps approach. Colin's steps.

He probably had a *pain au chocolat* topped with truffles and ground unicorn horn, and she'd have to reject him right to his face. She set aside her project and opened the door as he reached the landing.

He didn't have a cake, but he was holding a bunch of flowers that looked suspiciously like they'd been cobbled together from the Fruits de Mer centerpieces. His cheeks were pink, and his smile abashed. "Natalie?"

At this point he lost whatever he was going to say, so Natalie said, "I'm sorry to put you to all this trouble. The food was delicious."

"But it wasn't me, and you're right. I've gone about everything all wrong." He handed her the flowers. "I did everything backward, and in all that time, we never went out on a date. So, with your permission, I am here to take you on a date."

Natalie laughed out loud. "It's eleven o'clock. And I'm in pajamas."

He gestured at himself. "And I'm in my work clothes. It's barely six hours since you shot me down, too. I did say I was doing all this backward." Looking worried, Colin met her eyes. "Please, one chance. Also, since I'm practically a stranger, it's kind of a blind date. I'm asking for a lot."

It disarmed her. His shy smile, his cloaked fear, his pure vulnerability. Natalie said, "I have plans for the rest of the evening. I took your advice, and I'm crocheting something for myself."

His eyes lit up. "Oh, bring it! Pull on a pair of boots and your coat." He reached for her hand, and she let him. "I promise, if you give me permission, I'm going to try to make everything up to you."

His touch still made her melt. "Okay. Give me five minutes."

Birdie Holly sang to her, and Colin whistled back at him, startling the poor bird. While Colin presented the bird with a carrot top, Natalie texted Brooke. "Colin wants me to go somewhere with him. I'm turning on my location, and I'm going to text you every half hour."

Brooke replied, "Acknowledged."

Natalie took her pattern and her project, pulled her coat over her flannel PJs, and followed Colin to his car.

Colin opened the door for her, and she unlocked his side before he got around to it. The life had returned to his eyes. "Tell me, did you like the lobster *accras*? I'd never made it before, but the recipe sounded amazing. That was the only piece I wasn't sure of."

"It was delicious, but you should have let me tip your staff."

"I took care of them. Don't worry." Colin snickered as he started the engine. "I hope you're hungry."

Natalie said, "Lunch was amazing. I didn't eat anything afterward."

"Good, because I have plans for that missing dinner." A smiled flashed across his face, again that mixture of fear and thrill. "Thank you for letting me take you on a date. You were right about a lot of things. You saw something I didn't see, and no matter what happens next, that's going to change."

Natalie said, "How so?"

"About me not being me." Colin turned back up Main Street toward Fruits de Mer. "About me hiding. About Austin being the whatever-twin. I was being honest about the things I thought I was cloaking, only the things I thought were honest, weren't. I made a mess, but you detangled it for me."

That didn't detangle it for Natalie, but at least he sounded confident.

They arrived at the back door of Fruits de Mer. Colin ushered her inside, flaring the lights on to bring the kitchen back to life. He escorted her to a stool at the stainless-steel prep table, and then he flipped on all the burners on the flat top griddle. "I hereby present to you, breakfast for dinner."

He laid out plates and silverware at the prep table, as well as another one of the centerpieces. Natalie laughed. "Really?"

"Really. Go ahead and crochet, and I'll get us started. First, *mise en place.*" He opened his knife roll and went to town on the knife with that honing rod, a series of metallic hums that rang through the chrome-and-tile kitchen.

He poured sparkling cider into a champagne flute. "While you deserve the best, I'm not raiding the bar for champagne. I need to be able to drive you home, and I don't want even the suspicion that I'm plying you with alcohol."

While she watched, ingredients came out of the cooler. Eggs, butter, a baguette, a slab of bacon. While slicing the baguette, he talked a mile a minute, telling her the different ways to *mise* butter and that he'd been taught to cut a pound of butter into thirds, then third it again, then chop it up, and that was best for a roux. When he did it for himself, he liked it clarified. "As soon as I get out the squirt bottle, someone's bound to say, 'The sauté chef has entered the chat.'"

Natalie said, "Is that what you are?"

Colin nodded. "Sauté is where my heart is, but I do it all. I wasn't kidding when I said that."

He pulled on an apron and rolled up his sleeves. Natalie gasped. "What happened to your arm?"

He made a rueful face. "The broiler attacked me."

"That looks painful."

"War wounds." He whipped up the French toast batter, then stepped aside from the griddle. "Behold! We have three zones on this sweetheart. I had to work breakfast one summer on a flat top the size of a postage stamp, so whenever I get to use this, I feel like I'm cruising around in a Cadillac. Right zone is 325 because I want to cook the eggs there, and I'm a lefty. If I got relief during my shift at the breakfast place, I'd always end up with complaints because it's harder for a righty to roll and pick up on that side."

Natalie texted Brooke a photo of Colin at work. Brooke texted back a thumbs-up.

Colin aimed a laser gun and shot the griddle in all three zones. "Almost." He handed the laser to her. "Isn't this awesome? It's a thermometer! Want to try?"

Natalie took the temperature of the countertop. Colin came around alongside and sat on the adjacent stool. "What kind of yarn is this? It's gorgeous."

"Pet the yarn. You have to pet it." When he stroked the cake, she said, "Next you have to tell me how soft it is."

"Very soft. I'm glad you're making something for yourself."

She showed him the pattern photo on her tablet, and he draped the small crescent over her arm. "That's going to look great on you."

She touched his arm near the bandage. "That doesn't look great on you."

Colin huffed. "Austin ordered me to go to urgent care."

Natalie's voice ticked up. "You have to take care of yourself. Wouldn't you have sent Austin to urgent care if his arm got burned?"

Colin's nose wrinkled. "Yes, I would have sent him, and I did let him shove me out the door. I wasn't going to go."

Natalie tilted her head. "So you're saying Austin is the important twin, too?"

Colin brought the temp gun back to the griddle. "This is what you helped me realize, and it's yes and no." He looked back at her. "Austin's the outgoing twin. He's the smart twin and the handsome twin and the funny twin—and for years, I've measured myself against him and come up short every time. Whenever I dated anyone, I tried to give them the best, so I'd mimic what Austin would do. Show off, make jokes, wow them, give them gifts, serve them up a great time."

Natalie lowered her eyes. "Then I came along, and you didn't bother."

Colin shook his head. "It's not about not bothering. I hadn't sold myself as the dashing restaurant owner who was going to sweep you off your feet with endless good times. I started out as the baffled downstairs tenant who ruined your shower and blew the circuit breaker, and from there I shifted to the incompetent man-child who didn't know heat would boil water. You didn't put yourself into my hands expecting signs and wonders. Not needing the showmanship was weird, but it was also terrifying."

Natalie went back to hooking a row of double crochets. "Terrifying?"

"I always got ghosted after three or four weeks, but now I'm realizing, it happened because I can't always stay in high gear like my brother." Colin sighed. "I thought my dates lost interest when they got to know me, so the real me must be uninteresting. Instead it's more like I sold them a ribeye and roasted fingerling potatoes, and delivered them a hamburger casserole."

Natalie looked up. "You are such a foodie."

He gave a timid smile."Guilty. The difference with you was that you started off by knowing me rather than seeing the façade. If you dumped me after four weeks, you were rejecting the real thing, not the image. I had to keep everything separate."

Fighting the urge to derail him, Natalie focused on yarning over and hooking through because otherwise she was going to cut him off to save him from his own awkward emotions. For once, he had to talk through all the discomfort, and she needed to listen. "You're saying you couldn't tell me because once I saw all of you, that's a vulnerable feeling."

He sighed hard, and her stomach tightened with his pain. "What you see now, this is me." Again there was fear in his smile, but also a tentative hope. "It's real food. Real breakfast. The real me. Afterward, it's up to you if you can forgive me for holding back the truth."

He zapped the griddle again with the temp gun, then gave a wicked smile. "Until then, enjoy the show."

He faced the flat top, and then he was off to the races. Bacon went onto one section of the griddle, and then he squirted butter into the middle, dunked the bread into the egg mixture and laid out the French toast. Finally, he buttered the third section and cracked open the eggs, to the right like he'd told her. The kitchen filled with the sizzles and scent of bacon. Everything was *mise en place*: the bread already cut, the utensils out. For some reason he set the plates directly on the flat top. He was a marvel in motion, keeping tabs on everything, every movement smooth and coordinated. "I haven't done breakfast for a while," he explained despite Natalie not having seen a single hesitation in his actions. "When I worked breakfast, our standard was a 'two and two,' which was two bacon and two sausage, but I'm limited to what we have on hand here. Breakfast sausage isn't a thing for us."

Natalie had to speak up over the sizzle. "And bacon is?"

"I will wrap anything in bacon. If you ever want me to make you a Thanksgiving dinner, I'm wrapping the entire brined turkey in bacon so it's the moistest bird you've enjoyed in your life." He flipped the eggs with a smoothness that defied description, then turned the bacon and then the French toast. "Set me loose in a real kitchen, and anything can happen."

Natalie grinned. "Anything?"

He met her eyes. "Well, not quite anything. But I can try."

Natalie said, "Certainly not in that super-old kitchen in your former apartment."

"The joke about chefs is that at work we plate up all these mouthwatering four-course dinners for everyone else, and at home we devour instant ramen standing over the garbage can."

Natalie said, "Or your local crochet artist makes blankets and hats for every charity on earth, but she never works up the sweet silk-merino blend for herself."

Colin looked back at her again. "I'm glad you're crocheting that, finally. You deserve something as beautiful as you are."

Her eyes stung.

Colin flipped the eggs onto the dish followed by the French toast and then the bacon. He snapped off the burners, then delivered their meals to the work bench, one for him and one for her.

Natalie set aside her crocheting. "Impressive."

"Thank you. I'm attempting to impress you the right way for once." He topped off her glass of sparkling apple cider, then raised his glass.

"To breakfast for dinner!" said Natalie.

"To a first date! I'm sorry it's a blind date." Then, again seeming unnerved, he passed her the little bowl of powdered sugar. "No maple syrup, unfortunately."

She buttered her French toast and sprinkled sugar on top. "This is all wonderful. How could you stand having me cook for you when you can do all this?" She cut a piece of the edge, then hesitated before taking a bite. "I don't know if I can get past that."

Colin's shoulders dropped.

Natalie shook her head. "I was trying to do something nice for you, and you were laughing at me."

His hand clenched hers from across the table, and she

looked up to find his eyes anguished and his face dead earnest. "I swear, Natalie, by everything, ever, that I never once laughed at you."

She squeezed her eyes shut. "I was so happy when I thought you were discovering something brand new because of me, something that was giving you joy. Instead, I never showed you anything."

"That's not how I feel." He leaned in towards the table, and his voice pitched up. "I loved listening to you explain everything. All these familiar processes—you made them new. You turned the mundane into magic. You gave me so many new ways to appreciate techniques I'd taken for granted." He shook his head. "I never want you to feel like I looked down on you. You're the most generous spirit I know. Cooking is the thing I love most in the world, and I loved sharing it with you because you introduced me to it all over again."

She lowered her gaze.

He forced a smile. "Although cream cheese in chili still seems weird."

She said, "Filling the taco shells before heating them is beyond bizarre."

"Both those things worked, right? And I did make you cookies."

"I brought most of them to the shop. I didn't want them to get stale." She cocked her head. "But you're an expert on pizza dough."

"You made that fine." He gestured to her plate. "You should eat. At the very least, even if you never want to see me again, I owed you a meal."

Natalie said, "And then it's my turn to wash the dishes afterward."

Colin recoiled. "No! The Dish Dame will have my head on a pike."

Natalie laughed. "But you're the owner!"

Colin's eyes shifted to the sink as though an astral projection of the Dish Dame would be shimmering with disapproval. "She's more necessary to the place than I am.

Any idiot can own a restaurant, but you *need* a dishwasher."

It was...odd. They were drunk with exhaustion and honesty, and at the same time everything tasted good. Tasted real. Colin had made the French toast perfectly crisp, the bacon just crunchy enough, the eggs over easy exactly how she liked them. They drank sparkling apple cider, and they talked. He told her about four culinary arts students crammed into a one-bedroom apartment. He told her about interning at a Michelin star kitchen, and on the opposite end of the spectrum, six days at a bakery where he'd walk in every morning to discover slug trails on the countertops. "I learned something at every job," he said. "I learned, for example, that the health department does, in point of fact, investigate anonymous tips."

They were holding hands across the table now, Colin reaching further up her arm. She traced his skin, careful to avoid the burn.

The phone buzzed with a text from Brooke. "Are you alive?"

Natalie replied, "Sorry, I forgot to check in. We're both still here."

Brooke sent, "Everything okay?"

Natalie looked up at Colin. "Brooke wants to know if everything is okay."

Colin's eyebrows formed an inverted V. "What are you going to tell her?"

Natalie walked around to Colin's side of the table, then stepped into his embrace. He pressed his cheek against hers, and she inhaled deeply. He smelled of smoke and steak and soap, and for a moment, that was everything. She pivoted in his arms, and with him looking over her shoulder, she texted, "We're having a first date, and it's going well."

Brooke texted back a smiley.

Natalie flipped to the camera and lifted it to get a picture of the two of them, Colin with his cheek next to hers and his arms around her shoulders.

"I don't want to be too forward," Colin said, hugging her against his chest, "but do you believe in kissing on the first date?"

For her answer, Natalie kissed him on the lips. "Yes. And on the second date, as well."

CHAPTER THIRTY-FIVE

Colin stopped in the Bright Stitches doorway, seeming flustered by the colors, the brightness, the layout. Natalie grinned at him: that was definitely the "new customer" look.

She shoved her current project back under the lip of the desk. "Welcome to Bright Stitches!"

From the Sit and Stitch table where she was working with graph paper and her laptop, Brooke called, "Have you been helped?"

Colin located Natalie at the register and aimed toward her, which Natalie assumed was his only landmark in the shop. "I believe she's been helping me."

"Helping you is kind of self-serve."

"A buffet of personal growth? I think we've *brunoised* this metaphor quite enough." He stopped in front of the register and shifted his weight, looking sheepish. "I wanted to see your home away from home. It's nice."

"Only fair. I've seen yours." She stepped out from behind the register. "Well, sir, what would you like today?"

"There's this crochet artist in my life." He folded his arms and contracted his brows. "I've been officially dating her for a month now. She tells me she has an entire yarn shop in her apartment, but after finally setting foot in one, I'm going to say she could fit in a lot more. I had this idea, but it's only half-formed and somewhat bonkers, so maybe you can team up with me."

Natalie rubbed her hands together. "I love teams."

"I've heard. The point being, this crochet artist is beautiful, and she deserves beautiful things, but I'm second guessing myself now that I see how many beautiful things she's surrounded by on a regular basis."

From the Sit and Stitch table, Brooke was making a face that clearly said, "Aww!"

Natalie tried to ignore her. "Why kind of beautiful things were you thinking of?"

"The kinds of things she describes as soft and squishy, but I don't want to create a burden for her by giving her more work." He shrugged. "Looking at all this yarn tells me I'd just be giving her an assignment if I went with my original plan, so can you maybe take me on a tour of the shop?"

Natalie shrugged. "There's not much here for a non-yarnie, but I'll try."

First stop was the gift section, and to his credit, Colin admired everything. Well, most things. "Why would anyone make that?" he asked about one set of ugly-faced wooden figurines that, to be honest, Natalie had wondered the same thing about. And yet they sold consistently, so every month, three new pieces arrived. As for the rest, he appreciated the bright colors, the wind-catchers, the tiny paintings on their little wooden easels, and the shell art.

He held up a ceramic bowl with a curly slit down the side. "Here's your stew! Well, most of it. Sorry about your lap."

"It's a yarn bowl, silly." She carried it to the table where Brook had her knitting. "Demonstrate, please."

Muttering, "You could use your own project," which of course Natalie couldn't, Brooke dutifully set her cake in the bowl and threaded the yarn through the curled opening, then started knitting stitches across the row. Every time she tugged the yarn, the cake rotated in the bowl.

Colin said, "That's brilliant!"

Natalie raised her eyebrows. "Wait until you see the yarn spindles. Same idea, except they turn like a lazy Susan."

Brooke began tinking back the stitches she'd just knit, since they weren't part of the design. "I'm not the biggest fan of those things. They never turn correctly, and half the time the yarn gets caught around the spindle. They sell because they look cool."

Colin said, "Appearance is everything. You sell the sizzle, not the steak."

"Oh, right, you can cook." Brooke waved a hand at him. "Off you pop. I'm trying to figure out the best way to line up these decreases, and you're awkwardly attempting to flirt with my cousin."

Colin followed Natalie away from the table. "I thought the knitter's cousin was flirting with me, too. Mutually consensual flirting is fun."

Natalie said, "It is, isn't it?"

Colin said, "So, since I can't buy you yarn, and you're surrounded by beauty all day long, I'm feeling outclassed."

Natalie said, "You aren't outclassed. You're just out-niched. Besides, I like yarn. That's why I'm surrounded by it."

"I had this notion that I'd buy you an armload that would transport you with joy, but that isn't going to happen." He folded his arms and leaned back on one leg. "I'd also need to give you the time to lock yourself away and make a sweater."

"You don't want me to make a sweater, anyhow." Natalie stepped forward and put her arms around his shoulders. "Sweaters are cursed."

He tensed. "This I'd never heard."

"The 'sweater curse' means that if you make someone a sweater before you get married to them, you'll invariably break up with them."

Colin rubbed her shoulders. "You're saying, if I ever want you to crochet something for me, I need to marry you first? Sounds fair."

She arched her eyebrows. "I could make you something smaller and more useful."

Colin said, "On the other hand, if you want to get rid of me, you can make me a sweater."

"If I want to get rid of you," Natalie said, stepping back, "I'll get rid of you and make myself a sweater."

"This is a conundrum indeed. I'll continue ordering sweaters from LL Bean while you figure out the best way to be rid of me." He smiled. "Would it be okay if we went for a walk?"

Brooke gave a desultory wave, so Natalie went outside with Colin. "What's so important you can't tell me in the shop?"

He put his hand in hers. "I put you through a lot when we started out, and I've been trying to make it up to you."

Natalie squeezed his hand. "And you have been."

"When you said I wasn't giving you myself, I've thought about that more than I've let on." He stopped. "What you've been giving me all along is yourself, your whole self. You haven't held back, and then I remembered something you said." He shook his head. "I'm doing this all wrong. Can I start over? I've discovered I'm good at starting over." He pulled a clear plastic bag out of his pocket. "All week I've been shucking oysters for our specials, and I wanted you to have these."

She laughed as she looked in the bag. "Pearls!"

They were tiny and misshapen and a little yellow, but indeed, in the bag were four pearls.

"You said the more you touch them, the more they become like you, so I refused to let anyone else touch these." Colin laughed. "These can be all you."

She opened the bag and touched them. "There we go. I've imprinted them. Can I do something with them, like set them in earrings?"

Colin reached into his other pocket. "I'd rather you have

something like this." He opened a jewelry box to reveal a pearl necklace.

Natalie gasped.

"You deserve better than four food-grade pearls," Colin admitted.

As he removed the necklace from the box, Natalie said, "It's not my birthday."

"It's somebody's birthday." He clasped on the necklace and stepped back to take a look. She took his hands, and he gave an embarrassed smile. "Of course, I didn't plan this very well because you don't have a mirror to see them."

She stretched up and kissed him, and he held her close to his heart. She said, "Thank you. You beat me to the punch. I'm actually weaving in the ends on a set of dish cloths for you. They're at the register."

"Thank you. That's pretty awesome, and it's probably worth more than pearls. You put your time and skill into those."

She said, "And you put thought into mine."

Colin murmured into her ear, "You did say you should wear pearls for a couple of years before getting married, that way they'll work with your wedding dress. This is a jump start. Just in case."

A wedding. A wedding with a man who would sharpen her knives and sit with her while she was crocheting. Cooking together and reading together and pulling all-nighters together—Natalie could do that. She could do an entire future of that.

"I'll keep wearing them and get them primed." Natalie kissed him again. "Just in case."

EPILOGUE: LILAH

The second meeting of the Brighthead Crafters Guild was a whirlwind of color, and Lilah adored every moment of it.

They'd booked Fruits de Mer again, but this was going to get expensive in a hurry if they kept it up—yes, even with Colin comping them quite a bit due to his auxiliary membership (and his bend-ability to Natalie's every request). They'd need someplace else they could go.

Maybe a permanent headquarters. Who knew what the future held?

Lilah moved from group to group, following up on discussions they'd held on the BCG forums. "Did that shipment of beads ever turn up?" "I was so glad to hear your customer paid that invoice. You sounded so sure you were going to court." "What did your nephew think of his first sculpture class?" Chatter filled the function room, and even the occasional spats were light-hearted.

Lilah caught sight of Natalie talking to Colin and Austin Young near the buffet table, so instinctively she looked for Brooke. Brooke hated to be alone in crowds like this. It was even odds that she'd pulled out her knitting and gone to sit at one of the tables, huddled up over a sock and hoping it would be over soon.

Instead, Lilah caught sight of her talking once again to Adrian Lim and Emerson Charles. Emerson was showing them both something on his phone. Maybe his paintings? Lilah zipped across the room to his side. "I have to see," she sing-songed. "Is it your art?"

Brooke grinned. "She's got radar for that!"

Emerson chuckled, his voice resonant in a way that sent shivers down Lilah's spine. "You should have warned me."

Lilah held out her hand for the phone, and Emerson

273

laughed when he saw her multi-colored nails. Well, she was a dye artist! Why would she put up with a boring manicure? "Remember how I told you yarn wants to be worked up into a garment? Well, paintings want to be seen. They called to me from across the room."

The paintings? Or was it Emerson's captivating smile, his deep eyes, and his gentle care for Brooke? Because all that was pretty awesome, too.

Emerson passed her the phone, and Lilah found herself regarding a painting of a sweet pea vine creeping up the downspout of an abandoned house.

"Oh," she breathed.

She spread her fingertips to zoom in on the details. The crack across one corner of the leaded windows. The wooden steps listing just a bit to the right. Brown weeds clawing at the siding. And then, among this scene of structural death, one vibrant vine, climbing the rusted downspout as its way out of squalor, all its energy channeled into one triumphant burst of floral beauty.

She trembled. "This is amazing."

Brooke said, "I liked the tire swing one, too." She leaned over and swiped twice on the photos, passing by a photo of someone Lilah didn't recognize to land on a second painting, a tire swing hanging from a frame made of metal pipe, the dirt scuffed bare beneath it, the aged rope looking so real it might leave splinters in her palm right through the screen.

Lilah handed back the phone to Emerson. "These are fantastic! The juxtaposition of hopelessness and potential—or the way you evoked the sense of coping despite struggle. They're worth more than a thousand words!"

Flustered, Emerson said, "Thank you."

Brooke said to Lilah, "You got all that from those two paintings?"

"Yes! It was all about the struggle to survive—no, to thrive—in a world that doesn't want you there." Honestly, Brooke should have seen that herself. Brooke had talked to Emerson a lot more than Lilah had. Lilah turned to

Emerson. "Right?"

Emerson forced a smile. "Based on my art classes, I'm supposed to answer you with a question. That way, you'll keep talking for hours."

Lilah opened her hands. "Thus netting your thousand words."

Emerson raised his eyebrows and nodded. "It's all a ploy to keep you thinking about my work."

Lilah snickered. "As if anyone could forget you!"

Again Emerson looked flustered. Brooke said, "Lilah, maybe dial it down a little. Not everyone is used to a geyser of emotion when they show a couple of photos."

Oh, was Brooke interested in Emerson? That would be amazing. The two of them would work well together. Emerson was already looking out for Brooke, and Brooke had been with Emerson exclusively during both BCG meetings so far.

Adrian shook his head. "Lilah, please come look at my work and tell everyone it deserves to be in a museum."

Emerson said, "Maybe I'm not ready to let her stop talking about mine, yet."

Lilah said, "I'm not ready, either. Do you remember how we were negotiating with Fruits de Mer about hosting artists in their lobby during the summertime? Guess who's number two on the list to exhibit?"

Brooke gasped. "Emerson, that's amazing! Now everyone can see your work!"

Emerson didn't know where to look first—but he ought to have been looking at Brooke. Instead he turned to Lilah. "Um, thank you. I don't know what to say." Then he pivoted to Brooke. "Surely it won't be everyone. Not even everyone in Brighthead."

Brooke frowned as though adding up the entire population of the world and then contrasting it to the traffic a popular restaurant would see in northern Maine over a two-week period. "Point granted. Slightly less than everyone."

"This is going to be a great opportunity for you." Lilah

looked at Emerson and felt the pulse of his future all around them both. "You're making friends and connections. You're going to have your first display. You may sell some art." She glanced at Brooke, then met Emerson's eyes in a gaze that felt as if it could pull her all the way inside. "You're about to find community in a way that will feed your heart—and your artwork—for the rest of your life."

THANK YOU!

Thank you so much for reading about Natalie and Colin!

I had so much fun learning about restaurants and everything that goes on in back of house, not to mention looking up fifty-five different interesting recipes. My cooking technique even improved after I learned some things from Colin. (Who, yes, is a fictional character. But once I had his personality in my head, he started making suggestions, and who am I to argue? I'm only the writer.)

To be clear, I'm "bicraftual" like Natalie. I learned to crochet first, then picked up knitting in my thirties. They're both fun, and I've gone back and forth between them because I find them useful for different things. Natalie's overnight shawl is conceptually based on the "Spring Showers" shawl, if you're interested. (You can buy the pattern on Ravelry.)   And yes, I made one in creamsicle colors.

If you join Maddie Mondays, I share tidbits like that

about twice a month, plus I'll recommend other books I think my readers will find interesting. Please consider joining us here: **https://stats.sender.net/forms/ erBXBe/view** (You'll also get a free short story that fits in with the *Last Man Standing / Always a Bridesmaid* dyad.)

If you enjoyed this story, please join us again for the next volume in the series, **Palette of the Soul**, where we delve into Lilah's colorful heart...and one very big mistake.

Palette of the Soul
By Maddie Evans

How to inspire a painter? Have him fall in love.

As an indie yarn dyer, Lilah lives to combine colors, but now there's a chance to use those skills in the real world. Her best friend, Brooke, is grieving after a bad break-up. At the same time, Lilah's favorite painter, Emerson Charles, wants to back out of his first exhibit.

Nothing will fire up a painter quite like falling in love. If matching colors is thrilling, matchmaking people must be even better. Lilah will pair these two together like one of her handpainted colorways, then enjoy the fireworks.

Emerson's sure his art is all wrong for the upcoming exhibit, but the guild president, Lilah Marcille, won't let him quit. She's loaned him space in her home to keep painting, and she also seems to be loaning him her best friend. He and Brooke... Well, she's nice. But when Emerson's with Lilah, inspiration flows fast and hot, and it's not letting up.

Turns out, people don't blend the way colors do. Lilah would rather break her own heart than Brooke's, but how can she break Emerson's?

You can buy **Palette of the Soul** in ebook and paperback.